Praise for

Trial by Fire

"Romantic suspense that has it all: a sizzling firefighter hero, a heroine you'll love, and a story that crackles and pops with sensuality and action. All I can say is keep the fire extinguisher handy or risk spontaneous combustion!"

—Linda Castillo, national bestselling author of *Sworn to Silence*

"Sizzling romantic suspense . . . so hot it singes the pages!"

—JoAnn Ross, *New York Times* bestselling author of *Shattered*

"A five-alarm read . . . riveting, sensual."

—Barbara Vey, *Publishers Weekly*

"For a poignant and steamy romance with a great dose of suspense, be sure to pick up a copy of *Trial by Fire* . . . as soon as it hits the bookstores! 5 Bookmarks!"   —Wild on Books

"Jo Davis set the trap, baited the hook, and completely reeled me in with *Trial by Fire*. Heady sexual tension, heartwarming romance, and combustible love scenes just added fuel to the fire. . . . Joyfully recommended!"

—Joyfully Reviewed

I Spy
a Wicked Sin

Jo Davis

HEAT

HEAT

Published by New American Library,
a division of Penguin Group (USA) Inc.,
375 Hudson Street, New York, New York 10014, USA
Penguin Group (Canada), 90 Eglinton Avenue East, Suite 700, Toronto,
Ontario M4P 2Y3, Canada (a division of Pearson Penguin Canada Inc.)
Penguin Books Ltd., 80 Strand, London WC2R 0RL, England
Penguin Ireland, 25 St. Stephen's Green, Dublin 2,
Ireland (a division of Penguin Books Ltd.)
Penguin Group (Australia), 250 Camberwell Road, Camberwell, Victoria 3124,
Australia (a division of Pearson Australia Group Pty. Ltd.)
Penguin Books India Pvt. Ltd., 11 Community Centre,
Panchsheel Park, New Delhi - 110 017, India
Penguin Group (NZ), 67 Apollo Drive, Rosedale, North Shore 0632,
New Zealand (a division of Pearson New Zealand Ltd.)
Penguin Books (South Africa) (Pty.) Ltd., 24 Sturdee Avenue,
Rosebank, Johannesburg 2196, South Africa

Penguin Books Ltd., Registered Offices:
80 Strand, London WC2R 0RL, England

First published by Heat, an imprint of New American Library,
a division of Penguin Group (USA) Inc.

First Printing, February 2010
1   3   5   7   9   10   8   6   4   2

HEAT is a trademark of Penguin Group (USA) Inc.

LIBRARY OF CONGRESS CATALOGING-IN-PUBLICATION DATA:

Davis, Jo.
I spy a wicked sin / Jo Davis.
p. cm.
ISBN 978-0-451-22911-3
I. Assassins—Fiction. I. Title.
PS3604.A963I4 2010
813'.6—dc22   2009033797

PRINTED IN THE UNITED STATES OF AMERICA

To Debra Stevens,
my dearest friend of thirty-seven years. My chosen sister, anchor, and coconspirator. We've had many good times, weathered our share of challenges, had fun chasing the bad boys, and come through it all unscathed.

Jude's story is for you.

Acknowledgments

My heartfelt thanks to:

My husband and children for putting up with my craziness during deadline.

My awesome agent, Roberta Brown.

My editor, Tracy Bernstein; my publicist, Elizabeth Tobin; the art department and all the wonderful folks at NAL.

The Foxes.

I couldn't survive without you.

I Spy a Wicked Sin

Prologue

"Sweet Christ."

Elbows on the ratty desk, John Sandborn dropped his face into his hands. In the wake of this terrible exercise of connect the dots, he'd be goddamned lucky if he didn't wind up at the bottom of the Atlantic. In five different oil drums.

Because a traitorous, murdering bastard was coming for him. No doubt about it.

If he had a whisper of a prayer of avoiding a grisly fate, he had to work fast.

Clicking the X in the top right corner of the laptop's screen, he closed the classified file and opened another. Fingers flying, he activated a program he'd hoped never to use, but was damned glad he'd put into place. Next he composed a simple coded message—a ten-year-old couldn't decipher it, but a trusted operative could.

"Okay . . . got it." He blew out a deep breath. It wasn't perfect, but it would have to do.

Last, he opened his e-mail and hit *Send.* He waited, every muscle tense, while the new files, along with the classified one, shot to six different destinations and burrowed into six different hard drives. A high-tech worm that would make any hacker cream in his shorts—and just might save his ass.

Action complete.

"Thank fuck." Sandborn attacked the keyboard again, clicking rapidly. His instincts screamed *Get out,* but he didn't dare leave the last two tasks undone.

Precious seconds were whittled away, scraping his nerves raw, as he accessed the script file he'd written to initiate the virus that would destroy his hard drive. The final box popped onto the screen, and he executed his CTRL+F+U command.

Sandborn gave a grim chuckle at the double entendre in his chosen three-finger salute and wiped the sweat from his brow. Time to make like a ghost.

The door to his motel room burst open, hitting the inside wall like a gunshot. Sandborn spun, the SIG from the desktop already in hand, arm leveling at the leader of the traitor's cleanup crew.

Too late. A pop split the air, and pain blossomed in his chest. He stumbled backward, managing to get off a shot, the explosion deafening in the tiny space. The leader went down with a grunt as Sandborn trained his gun on the second man, tried to squeeze the trigger—and couldn't. His arm fell limp and useless to his side.

The second man crossed the room, a smirk on his ugly pock-marked face. Cold overtook the pain, spreading from Sandborn's chest to his limbs. Numbing every muscle. Looking down, he stared in fascinated horror at the dart embedded in his left pectoral.

He swayed, speaking quickly. His life depended on it. "Tell your boss I know everything. I put safeguards in place, and he'll never find them without me," he rasped, the drug freezing his vocal cords quickly. "If I die . . . the whole world will know . . . what he's done."

Sandborn's legs buckled and he slumped to the floor, completely nerveless. Aware but paralyzed, along for the ride and at their mercy. A nightmare.

A pair of heavy-soled leather boots appeared in his line of vision as the second man paused, obviously peering at the laptop. "You smart-ass sonofabitch," Crater Face hissed.

Sandborn pictured the cartoon gopher dancing across the screen, shooting the finger at the henchman, and a hoarse laugh barked from his dry throat. The boots backed up a couple of steps.

John Sandborn's last image was a snapshot of the man's right shitkicker rocketing toward his face.

One

From the dossier saved on her laptop, Lily Vale knew without a doubt—if she'd had any to begin with—that her new target was the most beautiful man she'd ever seen.

The bastard wouldn't be quite as pretty after she sent him to hell.

Striding down the hallway of the vast mansion, she clutched her purse, comforted by the heavy weight of the weapon secreted inside. If only she could use it to take him out, clean and simple.

For his crimes against innocent Americans, men like Jude St. Laurent deserved to die. Monsters like him had murdered her father, the most brilliant, gentle soul who ever lived. Perhaps quick and easy wasn't always the best form of justice. Not that a swift end was a choice on this assignment anyway—locating the information would take time.

And while Lily worked her way into St. Laurent's confidence, he'd have no idea he was already a dead man. A bullet might be easier, but slow and painful was her specialty, reserved for the most vile of men. That alone fortified her resolve as nothing else could have.

Hearing voices, a low moan, Lily slowed her steps. Using caution, she approached the room the housekeeper had directed her to and peered inside.

Neither the photos in his extensive file nor her brief glimpses of him in the past had done the rogue justice. But the current tantalizing view certainly brought his many physical assets into complete focus.

Jude St. Laurent was sprawled on his back in a pile of pillows, eyes closed, chin-length auburn hair fanned around his head, gloriously naked. His long, athletic legs were spread to accommodate the equally naked brunette crouched between them, sucking his thick, erect cock in long, slow pulls.

"God, yes." After a few more bobs over his lap, he moaned and gently pulled her head back. "Wait. Come here, darlin'."

The woman crawled between his legs as he sat up, and brushed a kiss against his lips. "What's wrong?"

"Nothing." Giving his lover a warm half smile, he reached out, skimmed a hand up her arm, to her shoulder. He combed his fingers through her hair and then brought his other hand up as well, his palm finding her breast.

His touch was tentative, careful, as his fingers searched. Probed her feminine curves, traveled to her cheeks and lips. Her forehead. His tender exploration made the woman giggle.

"You've *seen* me a dozen times," she said.

"That was for the sake of art." He grinned, dropping his hands. "This is for fun. Lie down on my left and spread out for me."

Lily remained quiet, trying to make sense of the puzzling exchange—and of the way his dazzling smile snatched the breath from her lungs. His smooth voice, laced with a hint of the Deep

South, the New Orleans variety, was the cherry atop the sundae. She could almost forget the man didn't own a soul.

The brunette did as he asked, stretching out on the pillows like a cat, eyes glittering in anticipation. Despite everything, Lily couldn't blame her.

He laid one big palm on her thigh and moved his hand up, as though mapping new territory. Moving carefully, he straddled her torso and positioned himself on his knees, thighs spread wide. "Slide down and guide me to your mouth, sweetheart. I don't want to hurt you."

Lily's curiosity grew. How could he hurt her?

The woman scooted down and guided the broad head of St. Laurent's cock to her lips. She took him down her throat and he moaned, lean body shuddering. As he bent to her sex, Lily had the fleeting thought that a nice, decent person would excuse herself until the couple was finished.

Nobody had ever accused Lily of being either.

She had a perfect view as St. Laurent parted the woman's nether folds and lowered his head. His tongue darted out, lapped at the tender pink flesh, and his sensual, satisfied groan of male appreciation set Lily's pussy afire. She gripped the doorframe, forcing herself to remain in place no matter how badly she wanted to join them. The need to slide her hand into her panties, to relieve the ache, was barely tolerable.

St. Laurent laved and suckled his lover's little clit like a starving man feasting on his last dessert. The brunette writhed under his attentions, muffled whimpers sounding around his cock.

Thrusting his hips, he fucked the woman's mouth faster, with more fervor. The muscles of his biceps and chest, his flat stomach, bunched, playing under all that lovely, sun-kissed skin like a symphony. Graceful movement and desire, flowing rapidly toward a forceful climax.

Lily stood in the doorway to St. Laurent's studio, riveted by the scene. And yes, God help her, aroused as she hadn't been in months, years. Possibly ever, and on the worst possible assignment. In her job, to allow passion into the act of sex was to invite disaster—she merely did what must be done.

The tight fist in her gut—as well as the dampness between her thighs—hinted she was doomed from the start. Sex with this man would be anything but passionless.

Remain detached. Neutralize the threat, however necessary. Nothing you haven't done before.

Yet at the moment, she found it difficult to believe the fate of thousands depended upon her ability to deceive this unusual specimen of physical perfection, maneuver her way into his heart and bed, and then . . . She shuddered, the chilly ripple snaking all the way to her toes. A rare shard of regret lanced her breast at the reality of the situation, of her sworn duty.

St. Laurent's exultant shout jerked Lily into the present. The brunette manipulated his balls, eagerly swallowing every drop as he drove her over the edge in kind.

The woman bucked, arching her hips. Rode the waves of pleasure until she lay limp and sated on the pillows. She released his softening penis, lips curving in satisfaction. "Mmm. You taste every bit as divine as I knew you would."

Smiling, he crawled off her and lay at her side, propping himself on an elbow. "I'll bet you say that to every lusty artist who struggles in vain to capture your essence," he quipped, his tone light.

"My God, Jude. If you're that good with your tongue, I can

only imagine how talented you are with your cock—in other ways, I mean."

So they hadn't yet slept together. Lily filed away the information.

Sitting up, he laughed, obviously pleased by the compliment. "Well, I'm probably not the best judge of my own prowess. Nonbiased opinions are always welcome."

"Hmm. Is that an offer?" Giving him a hungry look, the woman stood and began to gather her clothing.

"Pardon me for being vague." Still seated on the pillows, he tilted his head toward her, burnished hair falling over his eyes. "Tamara, come back tonight. I'll have Liam make us something spectacular for dinner."

"Wine? Soft music?"

"Whatever you want."

Lily couldn't tear her gaze from him as he rose and turned a half step, groping a nearby stuffed chair for his discarded jeans.

A delectable treat worthy of making a woman forget her diet. Tonight, this woman, Tamara, would not be the only one to indulge. Lily would know every word, every deed, spoken or performed in this house.

Doing her job, of course. Nothing more.

Ducking back into the hallway, Lily paused, giving the pair a few seconds to make themselves halfway presentable and focusing on her current role. *Okay, lovebirds, time's up.* She rapped on the door and stepped inside.

"Hello, Mr. St. Laurent, I'm—" Breaking off, she pretended surprise at finding them in disarray. The woman closed her blouse over bare breasts. He was shirtless, wearing nothing but faded jeans, the fly unzipped.

Lily let her gaze drift over both of them, her tone and body language making it clear she was not the least bit averse to what she saw. St. Laurent was no longer the only one in this house skilled in seduction.

"I'm so sorry," Lily continued, sounding anything but. "A housekeeper greeted me at the front door and said I should come on back."

"Miss . . . Vale. Is that right?" He shrugged on his shirt and began to button it, casual as anything. He didn't quite meet her gaze, which she found odd. Tamara, however, had no such compunction, giving Lily an assessing look as she put her clothing to rights.

"Yes, I'm Lily Vale," she answered honestly. No point in using a second alias in this case. He wouldn't remember her name from the agency, and if that ever changed, it still would make no difference in the outcome.

"You're early."

"I'm on time. Always."

His full lips curved upward. "I stand corrected. When will I learn that women are always right?"

Tamara patted his chest. "The sooner the better, if you're a smart guy. Your new personal assistant doesn't appear the type to take crap off of anybody, even from a master bullshit artist like you," she said, gathering her purse.

St. Laurent looked relaxed, not offended at all. "I beg to differ—I use oil and watercolor on my canvases, not manure. And I don't know whether she'll agree to be my PA until after she and I meet in person."

Lily suppressed a scowl. She wasn't used to people speaking around her. "I'm ready to talk whenever you are."

"Seven o'clock?" Tamara said, and gave him a lingering kiss.

"I'll send the car for you."

"Sounds good. Nice to meet you, Lily."

"Same here." Lily watched as Tamara disappeared from the studio, and wondered whether the two knew she'd seen them playing. She turned her attention to St. Laurent again, to find he hadn't moved.

He stood in the center of the room facing her, sunlight streaming in from the glass windows and catching his long hair, setting it ablaze. The muscles of his chest and arms filled out his shirt wonderfully, and she grew wet thinking of what those muscles had been doing a short while ago. His thumbs were hooked in the waistband of his jeans and he sort of stared past her, his eyes a sparkling, beautiful green. And strangely blank.

Lily had never felt quite so . . . ignored? No, that wasn't quite right. "Where would you like to meet?"

"In my study. Hand me that, if you don't mind."

Squelching the urge to deliver a sharp retort that would jeopardize her mission, she turned to see what item he was gesturing for. A PA's job entailed seeing to her boss's every need, and she had to play the part. For now.

Glancing toward his padded stool, she hesitated, her jaw dropping in shock. The earlier interaction between the couple clicked into place. To be taken completely unaware by this sort of revelation wasn't a familiar—or comfortable—feeling. There, propped against the stool, was a cane. A white one.

"You're—"

"Legally blind, yes." The warmth bled from his voice like blood from an open wound. "You have a problem with working for a boss who can't see?"

"No. Only one with an attitude or a chip on his shoulder."

Slowly, his smile returned. "Fair enough. I'm still learning to cope, but I'm far from helpless. Should you accept the position, I won't expect you to wipe my ass. I'm a grown man, not an infant."

Oh, yes, sweetie pie. That's apparent.

"Good to know." Walking to the stool, she retrieved the cane and went to him, taking his hand. She guided the handle to his palm, and he grasped it. "Here. Lead the way."

"Thank you. Point me toward the door, and I'll be glad to."

She did, letting him exit the studio first, and then walked beside him down the long, tiled corridor.

"Lily of the valley," he said suddenly.

A shiver trailed down her spine. "Excuse me?"

"Your name, and the perfume you're wearing." He grinned. "They say, whoever *they* are, when one of the senses is lost, the others make up tenfold for its absence."

His acute perception shook her to the core, and she was damned thankful he couldn't read her expression. "So I've heard. Is there any real truth to the claim?"

"I think so, though it's a bit too soon for me to be certain. It's only been twelve weeks since my accident, and with the migraines—no, never mind. We have more important things to discuss."

His "accident." *God, if you only knew.* And he was in pain? Guilt speared her, fierce and intense, regardless of the fact that she hadn't been a part of the number done on his brain. Dammit to hell, she empathized with him.

Despite his being a killer.

Like herself.

Free to scrutinize his face, she noted the two-inch scar above his left eyebrow. She could well imagine how he'd gotten it, and the unaccountable anger it inspired filled her with confusion.

Especially since, according to Robert's intelligence and the fat file in her possession, he deserved much, much worse.

Why the hell hadn't Robert informed her St. Laurent had been rendered blind by the procedure? The answer was simple. Robert Dietz, the son of a bitch, enjoyed playing mind games, tossing zingers at his agents to see them react. Sometimes fail. And with Michael Ross, SHADO's leader, in seclusion, Robert stirred the pot more and more often.

"Do you often enjoy playing the voyeur, Miss Vale?" He tapped the cane on the floor, sweeping it from side to side as they strolled. He didn't appear angry or even annoyed by her indiscretion.

Taken by surprise, again, just when she'd decided he hadn't been aware. Not pleasant. "I see everything because that's my duty," she answered honestly. "But I rarely enjoy the things I learn."

"Such as your new boss's penchant for naughty trysts in unexpected places?"

Ahead of them, a bucket and mop had been left unattended, by his housekeeper, she presumed. The bucket sat directly in his path, and she resisted the impulse to grab his arm, to steer him around the hazard.

His cane missed the obstacle and as his toe kicked it, he almost lost his balance. "Shit!" Recovering quickly, he took a step backward and tapped the object, sniffing. "What is it? Cleaner?"

"Yes, in a bucket. Move around it and you're all clear ahead."

"Thanks." He cocked his head as they continued down the corridor. "Would you have let me fall, Miss Vale?"

"Falling is how we learn to get up, Mr. St. Laurent," she said softly.

"True," he replied with a throaty chuckle. "And I did imply I prefer not to be coddled, didn't I?"

"You did. Lucky for you, because my nurturing gene is defective."

"You never answered my question," he said, redirecting their banter.

"Which was?"

"I'm not accustomed to hiding my sexuality, especially not in my own home. Will this be a problem?"

"As you said, this is your place. What you do here or anywhere else is your business. But to answer you, no. I suppose you could say I'm . . . freethinking when it comes to sex."

"A kindred spirit, then."

"Pardon?"

"You're like me, it would seem. I like to think my friends and I are sexually enlightened. Doing what feels good, with whoever it feels good, as long as everyone is happy and safe. I do enjoy indulging." He shook his head. "You're probably wondering what you've gotten yourself into here. If you want to bolt, I won't blame you."

The picture he'd painted plucked her nipples, made the heat in her pussy torturous. "Not at all. Your lifestyle sounds . . . wonderfully tempting." God! What would it be like to really let go, to explore her desires without the albatross of her assignment always hanging around her neck? Without subterfuge?

Reaching a door, he felt for the knob and pushed it open. "Good, because I'd hate to get slapped with a sexual harassment suit from my new PA on top of everything else."

Once again, guilt reared its ugly head and she tamped it down. "Not going to happen." She allowed her voice to warm with suggestion as she trailed him into his study. "I was quite captivated watching you and your girlfriend."

He gave a quiet, good-natured laugh as he eased around his desk to lower himself into his chair. "Tamara is one of my favorite models, not a girlfriend. My subjects know I love to play, and sometimes they're willing to indulge. No strings, no harm."

"Models? If I can ask without sounding rude, how do you *see* your models in order to paint?"

He appeared amused. "How did Ray Charles *see* to create beautiful music on his piano? With his hands and his soul."

Of course. She'd observed him "looking" at Tamara by using his hands. But the idea of St. Laurent possessing a soul capable of creating beauty disturbed her. A great deal.

"Well, my question seems foolish in light of your answer." She settled into a chair across from his desk, blinking at his openness. So unorthodox, unlike anyone she'd ever met. "Back to the point—does your circle of bedmates ever extend outside your stable of models? Just so I'll know what visitors to expect."

"Don't worry, I'll make sure you know who to allow inside, whatever their business. As for lovers, I take those who arouse and intrigue me, Miss Vale," he said, his voice deep and husky. "Whenever I'm lucky enough to find them, in every type of social setting. I don't have a line formed at the front door, but I won't shy from doing what pleases me. I've found life is much too short, so I live it like there's no tomorrow."

A truer statement was never made.

Staring at this vibrant, enigmatic man, her throat closed to the size of a pinhole. "Then you're light-years ahead of most people, Mr. St. Laurent. It's a policy many adopt much too late."

He sat back in his chair, falling silent for a moment. Eerie how he appeared to be studying her with those beautiful, sightless eyes. He'd been a goddamned good agent, one of the best. If he was faking the blindness, not to mention the gaping blanks in his memory, she was in deep shit.

Because that would mean he'd made her from a thousand miles away, and he knew why she was really here.

She'd played this game many times, but never with her equal. Never with one of Ross's deadliest assassins.

"Why do you want to work for me, Miss Vale?"

The question threw her, though she'd prepared for it. Had seasoned her answer with half-truths. Mentally, she fumbled the punt, but was careful to keep her expression placid. Just in case he *was* acting, or could see more than he let on. Besides, any deviation from normalcy would reflect in her voice and mannerisms.

"Besides the fact that you're delicious naked?"

This gained her a brilliant smile, breaking the serious tension that had been about to descend. "Thank you, and yes. Aside from your flattering observation, what else?"

"I need a change of pace. Working as an assistant to the governor of California, nice as he may be, was the most stressful job I've ever done," she said. This much was the truth, though she'd been on an undercover assignment to assist the governor at the time. Since she'd foiled an assassination plot on his life, he'd graciously agreed to back her reference, no questions asked.

"I can imagine." He drummed his fingers on the desk. "The governor returned my inquiry in person. He tells me you were invaluable."

"I'm not afraid of long hours, and I don't intimidate easily. I'm no pushover, but I do get along well with others. If that's the sort of PA you're looking for, I'm ready."

"People don't just *leave* a lofty position in the governor's mansion," he mused. Obviously, this troubled him.

A sticking point she'd anticipated. Fortunately, the governor had agreed to allow her this small tidbit for the sake of her new cover. "All right, I'll admit there's more to my vacating the position than simply abandoning the frantic pace." She paused for emphasis. "What I have to tell you cannot leave this room."

"Goes without saying."

"Recently, there was an attempt on the governor's life. The authorities kept it very hush-hush and the men involved were taken into custody." And dispatched. "The whole thing was frightening."

St. Laurent frowned. "I'll bet it was. I'm sorry to hear this, but I'm glad the criminals were caught. So, this is why you're seeking greener pastures?"

"Yes. I hope you don't think less of me for wanting to work in a safer environment," she said, letting a tiny tremble into her voice. Even the strongest of normal women would have been afraid.

"Everyone deserves to feel comfortable in their job," he assured her. "While I can't promise the excitement of politics, I don't believe you'll be bored living here, working for me."

"Does this mean I have the position?"

He grinned. "It's yours if you want it."

She smiled back, even if he couldn't see. "I accept. And please, call me Lily."

"Jude," he returned in kind. "*Mr. St. Laurent* is a mouthful and makes me feel ancient."

"Which you certainly are not." She eyed him in appreciation. "You're, what? Thirty-five?" She knew the answer from his file, but wanted to hear it from him.

"Close. Thirty-seven. Feels double that sometimes, especially these days."

"Because of your accident?" She studied his reaction care-fully.

"Yeah," he said on a sigh. "Car crash, or so they tell me. I sustained a head injury and lost my sight as a result. You should know I have headaches, at times so bad they lay me out for an entire day. I have medication, but the pain can get so intense I might need you to get it for me and help me take it. Liam lives on the estate as well, so you can work out taking turns with him if you want. It's not fun for anyone. I have nightmares, too, though not as frequent as the headaches, so I'll apologize in advance for waking you."

For a few seconds, he looked so sad her heart went out to him.

"No need for apologies," she said softly. "You have no control over what's happening to you."

A knock at the door interrupted their talk. Lily turned in her seat to see a man stride into the office. He appeared a few years younger than Jude and moved with a confidence that belied his youthful appearance. He was of medium build, lean, and had a small, tight ass, a very *fine* ass, to go with the rest of him. He parked his rear on the corner of Jude's desk and glanced between them. His black hair was cut shorter in the back and longer in the front, falling attractively over gray eyes.

"Hi, I'm Liam O'Neil," he said, his tone friendly as he reached for her hand. Curious. "Jude told me to give you guys a few minutes, then come and introduce myself."

"Lily Vale." She shook it and liked his grip. Firm, warm. "I'm Jude's new PA. I assume you're the chef, since he was bragging about you making something fabulous for dinner."

He took his hand back and smiled, pleased by the compliment.

"That's me. I make sure his appetite is satisfied, and believe me, it's huge."

Immediately, his face reddened, and he shot Jude a pained look. Oh, Liam was too cute. Lily couldn't help but tease him.

"Really? Just how voracious is his hunger, Liam? Or is it 'Don't ask, don't tell' around here?"

Liam launched himself off the desk. "Um, I'd better get to work. Any special requests for tonight, Jude?"

His boss's lips quirked with humor. "Whatever you want to make is fine. Just prepare enough for Lily from now on. Oh, and tonight, I'm having a guest, so you can bring the cart to my suite."

"Sure thing. See you later, Lily." With that, Liam fled.

The door shut behind the young chef and Jude grinned, propping his chin in one hand. "Oh, you're evil, Lily dear. I do believe we'll get along just fine."

"I'm beginning to think you're right. I'm going to like it here."

And for the first time ever, Lily hated her job with a passion. For once, she longed to be one of the general population, able to forget the sacrifices that must be made in the name of national security. That the innocent must be protected at any cost.

That the gorgeous ray of sunshine sitting across from her was a very real threat to said security . . . even if he no longer remembered his own treachery.

She couldn't fall for this man. Had to hold on to her reason for being here. To do what she did best.

Locate the information. Assess and neutralize the threat.

And eliminate the source.

Two

Sitting across from Lily, Jude stared at her shadowy form and mourned the loss of his sight, as he did every waking moment. He wasn't quite so casual and accepting of his situation as he'd led her to believe. Not by a long shot.

The pain never ceased. Relentless, the agony and the confusing images battered him physically and emotionally until he wanted to scream. Most days, he wished he'd been born a different man, one who wouldn't hesitate to down every last one of the pretty capsules his doctor had prescribed for the migraines and just drift away. Separate himself from the mockery his life had become.

What was my life before? Gallery showings, plentiful sex, one endless party after another filled with beautiful people, the world his for the taking?

Yes, sometimes. But those good memories had yawning, ragged holes in them. In those dark recesses, something terrible lurked.

And he was too fucking stubborn to give up without learning what.

Score one for Liam for encouraging Jude to hire an assistant.

The younger man, who'd become his best friend over the past few years, had been after him for weeks to take on some extra help, someone to oversee the details of his day-to-day existence. Maintain his schedule, run errands, coordinate the business end of his showings, serve as his escort at various society functions.

Then, once she proved herself trustworthy, perhaps he'd take her into his confidence. Enlist her aid in his search for answers.

"Jude?"

Lily's soft smoke-and-whiskey voice jerked him from his musings, sent tiny little fingers down his spine. In a pleasant way. "I'm sorry. Where were we?"

"I said I'm going to like it here." Her tone held a trace of amusement.

"Right." He smiled, hoping his expression didn't look as tight as it felt. The dull pressure in his head usually signaled the onset of a side trip into hell, and he prayed for a break this once. "Wait until you see how hard I'm going to crack the whip before you decide."

"Whips? Ooh, now I'm convinced this is where I belong."

He laughed. Damn, he wanted to see her. *Really* see her, without relying on his hands or Liam's description. "Why don't I give you a tour of the grounds while we discuss your duties?"

"Good idea."

He rose and grappled for his cane, wishing he were the man he used to be. That he were whole and trouble free instead of feeling as though he were teetering on the edge of a cliff with someone's hand at his back.

Knock it off, St. Laurent. Self-pity and paranoia will make you an old, bitter man before your time.

He led Lily out of his study, aware of her at his side. Pushing away his unpleasant thoughts, he focused on her light scent, the dainty click of her heels on the tile, her light step. A small woman, then? Was she as attractive as her smoky voice?

Dammit, he hated not knowing for sure. Again, he squashed the useless anger and frustration, forced himself to concentrate on familiarizing her with their routine. On getting to know each other. Moving through the foyer past the staircase, he turned left, stopping when his shoes touched carpet.

"This is the formal living area, though not much living goes on in here, except for the occasional party. I've always found it to be on the stuffy side, like I'm a guest in my own home."

"But it's gorgeous," Lily protested. "All those windows letting in the sunshine, antique furnishings, and that big wet bar! What's not to love?"

"It's okay, but Liam and I prefer to hang out in the media room upstairs. It's more comfortable and has dozens of amenities."

"I'm guessing a wide screen and surround sound are among those?"

"And a fridge full of beer." He grinned, smothering another pang of loss. That room in particular was stuffed with gadgets he could no longer fully enjoy. "You'll see. Anyway, the formal dining is through here, then the kitchen. Shall we?"

This part was trickier, navigating around the furniture. Not to mention the vertigo that still assaulted his senses on occasion. But the contrast in his vision between light and dark helped him discern the shapes, and he made it without mishap, running his free hand along the back of the sofa for a point of reference and bringing them into the dining room without falling on his face. God knew he savored each small victory, because he had no other alternative.

"I take it you don't use this room much, either," she noted. "It looks like it was cut straight out of a home magazine and the table doesn't have a single scratch."

"You're right. I take most of my meals in my studio or the media room, and the rest of the time I simply eat in the kitchen with Liam. There's something too depressing about eating alone at a table that can seat twenty."

"You have a point there," she said softly, with a tinge of sympathy.

What the hell had made him say that? The last thing he wanted was Lily, or anyone, feeling sorry for him. "Not that it matters since I can't see the damned room anyhow. Let's go bug Liam."

He continued walking, aware he'd been abrupt and not proud of the fact. His charm deserted him more often these days, his moods less predictable and more difficult to control. Granted, he had a good reason, but that didn't assuage his confusion and dismay. His sense of self had taken a beating and the loss of his sight was only a modest part of that.

However, none of this was Lily's fault, something he'd best remember. He had a feeling she wouldn't put up with his shit like Liam did, employee or not.

He paused inside the kitchen door, sniffing. "Something smells terrific."

"Caramel crème brûlée for after dinner," Liam said, sounding happy. In his element. Jude could hear the younger man shuffling around, banging metal lids and stirring something at the stove.

Lily groaned. "I can already tell living here is going to pork me up like a Macy's float."

Liam snorted. "You? Don't believe her, boss. She's five-foot-nothing and a good strong wind will blow her all the way to Times Square. A few naughty carbs will fix what ails her, though."

"Sounds like it might take more than a few, but we're all about naughty around here, so she's doomed."

"Totally."

"Are we still talking about food?" Lily asked with a laugh.

Jude turned slightly in her direction. "After your eye-opening introduction, do you honestly wonder?"

"Hmm, I suppose not. But since two of us actually have work to do, unbridled sin will have to wait." Her tone reverted to crisp and businesslike, yet remained friendly. "How much will my job overlap with Liam's? I assume he's been running your errands and such?"

"In truth, he's been overloaded, cooking and doing much of what a PA's job would entail, without complaint." Jude regretted not realizing sooner all he'd been asking of the man. "He can help with errands when he's not busy in the kitchen, but I'll let you two work out the details. As I've said, we're not formal around here, so whatever works best for you both is fine."

"All right," she said. Liam chimed in with agreement.

Jude nodded and went on. "Liam decides the menu each day, so if you have special dietary requests, dislikes or favorites, you'll have to let him know."

"Is the kitchen off-limits? What if I sneak in here for a midnight snack?"

"Sneak all you want, but if you kill it, let me know so I can fill it," Liam said. "Nothing more aggravating than starting a meal, only to discover that someone—ahem—has gobbled the last of an ingredient I needed."

Jude lifted a brow in mock annoyance. "Excuse me? Whose kitchen is it, anyway?"

"Mine, and don't you forget it."

Jude chuckled. The man was right. "That's why you've been working for me for how many years now?"

"Four. I'm surprised I've put up with you that long," the younger man commented good-naturedly, needling him.

"Why? Don't I take excellent care of you?" Jude asked, putting a hint of suggestion in his tone.

"When you're not disappearing for weeks at a time with no word, letting me wonder if . . ."

You're dead somewhere. The thought hung unspoken in the air between them, dispelling the companionable atmosphere, and the silence grew charged.

The younger man stilled. "Shit. I'm sorry, Jude. It just slipped out."

"Hell," he muttered, curbing the impulse to snap out a reprimand. Despite Liam's gregarious nature and the lapse just now, he could always be trusted to keep a confidence. Dammit, Jude hadn't wanted to get into this so soon, but Liam had made an honest mistake, one that must be dealt with.

Lily broke into the tension, curious and concerned. "You make it a habit to vanish without informing your employees of your whereabouts? Why?"

"I can't answer that," Jude said curtly. The pressure in his head increased, along with a vague sense of anxiety. "I don't have any idea where I used to go or what I did there. And if there are any clues in the house that might help answer those questions, Liam and I haven't been able to find them."

"Jude always let me know when he was leaving," Liam clarified, taking his cue to be able to speak on the matter. "But I never knew when he planned to return until he called me from his cell phone on the way home. He always said what I didn't know couldn't hurt me, whatever that means."

"So, you have memory gaps? Because of your accident?"

A sliver of guilt crept in. "Yes. Perhaps I should've told you up front, before you accepted the job, but I don't see why my few limitations should affect our working relationship."

"No, no, it's fine," she said. "You did tell me about the headaches and the nightmares. After what you've been through, it stands to reason for there to be physical consequences. It is very strange, though, that only specific periods of time are a blank for you."

"Head injuries can do weird things to the human brain," he agreed. "Anyway, my intention was to eventually tell you about the gaps, maybe use you as my eyes to help me investigate where I went three or four times a year and why."

Her stillness was almost tangible, her voice soft, but with a hint of warning. "Going by what you'd told Liam, you might not like the answer."

"I think he has a hot babe stashed in a warm climate some-where," Liam joked in an obvious attempt to lighten the mood again. "He flies off, gets himself a little jungle lovin', flies home a new man."

Despite the quiet laughter the three of them shared, he and Liam strongly suspected the truth wasn't nearly so fun.

"Nice thought," Jude said with a wistful smile. "But if my visits with this imaginary woman caused me to come home wound tighter than an iron coil and seclude myself in my bedroom for days afterward, then I'd obviously need a new mistress."

Lily's tone became sharp. "You know for a fact that you acted this way each time you returned? Or are you just repeating what Liam told you?"

Jude paused. Why would she care either way? Still, he saw no harm in answering. "Repeating, mostly. It's hard for me to separate what's just a result of stress since the accident, and what might be real memories."

Liam fell quiet and continued moving around, going about his tasks, his actions more telling than words. The younger man was fretting, his normally cheerful mood dampened. Lily, however, seemed undaunted. A woman used to tackling problems head-on.

"Well, if there's anything to these mysterious trips of yours, I'm sure we'll uncover the reason. In the meantime, I'll settle in and get my bearings."

"Thank you, Lily." The vise on his brain eased a little. "Why don't we continue our tour and let Liam finish his masterpiece?"

"After you."

"Lunch in an hour," the younger man called after them. "Grilled chicken salad with toasted almonds and balsamic dressing. Oh, and I already put your bags in the suite connecting to Jude's."

"The salad sounds yummy," Lily called back as they walked out together. "And thanks."

Jude shook his head. "I don't know what I'd do without him. That man is amazing."

"Sexy as hell, too. Is he one of those people who 'arouse and intrigue' you?"

It took him a moment to recall what he'd told her, and when he did, his lips curved upward. "Frequently. Does that bother you?"

"Yes. But not in a bad way," she said, her husky tone wrapping around his balls and squeezing. "Many women feel that two men together are beyond hot, same as some men feel about two women."

Sweet Jesus, he'd hit the lottery. Any illusions he might've harbored about maintaining a strictly professional relationship with Lily were swiftly withering on the vine. Their views on sexual freedom seemed to be a perfect match. He'd be an idiot not to explore the possibilities.

After she has a chance to catch her breath. Christ, give her a break!

Though *she* was the one who'd brought up the subject again, making her interest plain. God, his jeans were going to strangle his cock.

As he struggled for a suitable reply, she went on as though she hadn't struck him speechless. "Have you ever been in love?"

"What?"

"Love. You know—cupid, hearts and flowers, prenuptial agreements."

"No," he said, smiling. "I had a couple of close calls when I was younger, but I'm pretty sure I can safely say that I'm a poor candidate for the status quo."

"You crave too much swirl in your personal vanilla?"

He laughed. "Something like that."

"You're an interesting man, Jude."

The way she said it made him think she was dissecting a curious bug rather than paying him a compliment. "Not really, but who am I to spoil your delusions so soon?"

"Oh, this is stunning!"

Halting his steps, he realized they must've come to the sunroom, a glorious space bathed with sunlight and brimming with plants. Considering he hadn't been paying attention, he'd either improved on negotiating his way around the mansion or just been lucky.

"Like it?"

"I love it. Do you spend much time in here?"

"I used to. It was one of my favorite spots to relax because it overlooks the pool and the gardens beyond." The accident had stolen even that simple pleasure from him. To simply chill out and *be*, to soak in the beauty of his private oasis.

"Can we eat lunch in here?"

She was so enthusiastic, he was loath to refuse. "Of course we can. I'll do just about anything to prolong the company of a beautiful woman."

"You don't know that." The smile in her voice was evident. "I might be a hideous little troll."

"Impossible. Your self-confidence shines through—and that, to me, is beautiful."

After a pause, she murmured softly, "That's the nicest thing anyone has ever said to me. Thank you."

"You're welcome, but don't believe I'm some wonderful guy. I'm ashamed to admit that isn't something I would have bothered to say four months ago, even if the thought crossed my mind. Inner beauty wasn't a concept I ruminated on much."

"That doesn't make you a terrible person. A bit self-absorbed in the past, maybe, but not awful."

The bald truth made him wince. "Until I got a huge God-smack upside the head. Literally."

"Not to sound insensitive or cliché, but it's funny how those seem to come along right when they're needed."

"Hmm. Are we talking about my experience or yours now?

Because I have to tell you, if there's some cosmic reason a higher power decided I needed to be aimed down the path to becoming a better person, it eludes me."

"Just making an observation," she said. "I've never been on the receiving end of a major smackdown, at least none that was my fault—my conscience is clear."

Jude wondered at the edge in her tone, her declaration almost defensive. However, his sixth sense warned him it would be prudent to let the curious statement pass, for the time being.

"Then consider yourself very fortunate. Want to see the rest?"

"Yes, please."

Easy companionship was restored as he showed her the work-out room, the media room with its many forms of entertainment, and Liam's quarters on the lower floor just down from the studio. A half hour later, he stopped outside the door to her suite, gesturing inside.

"I'll leave you to get settled in while I buzz Liam and let him know to serve lunch in the sunroom. When you're ready, knock on our connecting door and we'll go down together."

"Will do. And thanks for the welcome," she said in the husky tone that made him shiver.

"My pleasure."

He left Lily to her own devices and shuffled toward his suite, tired but more optimistic about the future than he'd been in weeks. He had a feeling Lily would be an asset, in more ways than one.

Oh, yes. Hiring her was the smartest move he'd ever made.

·   ·   ·

Lily watched Jude go, carefully guarded emotions tossing on a restless sea.

By all appearances, SHADO's doctors had effectively erased every trace of the horrible man St. Laurent had been.

But one couldn't erase evil. Right? Mask it perhaps, but not completely obliterate it.

Which did nothing to resolve the lingering doubts in her mind. A man couldn't hide his true nature forever. Way down deep, people were who they were, good or bad. A procedure such as the one performed on St. Laurent would not change that fact. Eventually, his true colors would show.

And yet . . .

He'd requested her assistance in mending the ripped fabric of his life, the greatest of ironies. He was astute enough to realize something truly alarming lurked in his past.

"If you only knew," she said under her breath. As he disappeared into his suite, she did the same, pushing inside and letting out a low, appreciative whistle.

"Sweet."

Even for a SHADO agent—*former* agent, she reminded herself—the estate reeked of money. A lot more green than even the best assassin could afford on the agency's pay. Espionage must be really fucking profitable.

Or perhaps the bulk of it was old money, inherited from his deceased parents. Not to mention the padding from his side career creating erotic paintings that sold for exorbitant sums. The pieces he'd done before his blindness had likely skyrocketed in value, if she had her guess.

Once he was dead, they'd be worth even more.

The thought made her stomach lurch and she shoved it aside,

busying herself with emptying her suitcases. Nicer outfits she hung in the spacious walk-in closet. Casual wear, nighties, and underwear were tucked into the dresser drawers.

One drawer was reserved for her collection of naughty toys—dildos, plugs, clamps, anal beads, and more. These were tools for a successful mission; they were weapons, the same as her guns, poisons, and array of frightening devices designed to deliver death to the unwary.

At the moment, however, Lily wasn't thinking like a professional sent to do a job. Thanks to the sexual tension in this place—which was thick enough to cut with a knife—the ache in her nipples and the insistent burn between her legs was about to drive her mad. If she had to endure another second without relief, she'd scream.

Eyeing the big purple dildo resting innocently among the other toys, Lily cocked a brow. A woman must do what she must to get through the day.

Hefting the phallus, she tested its flexibility and girth. Not as grand as Jude's cock by any means, but it would suffice. Kicking off her heels, she crawled onto the king-sized bed with her prize, hiked her short linen skirt to her waist, and lay on her back.

Spreading her legs, she ran a palm over her bare abdomen to the tiny, neat triangle at the apex of her thighs. She loved the sensual feel of naked skin and springy curls under her fingers, her pussy exposed and ready—underwear being a confining irritant she avoided unless absolutely necessary. Sporting a bare bottom was also her private acknowledgment of the needs she held in ruthless check. Her brand of rebellion, her secret kick.

Moving her hand lower, she skimmed the slick, naked folds,

her blood singing with passion she rarely allowed past her barriers except when alone. Here, she could indulge in her fantasies and leave the coldhearted bitch behind.

Dipping a finger into her hot channel, she moaned, working the digit in and out, then spreading the cream all over her pussy. All around her clit, teasing as much as she dared, until her sex dripped and her body ached for release.

Fully prepared, she gripped the base of the dildo in her right hand and nudged the bulbous head between the swollen lips. Pushed inside, bit by bit, until the fake cock was buried in her needy cunt.

"Oh, yes," she hissed. As she pumped it slowly, a face formed in her mind. A gorgeous face taut with ecstasy and surrounded by long auburn hair, muscles flexing as he drove into her depths, unable to get enough of her. "Jude . . . God, yes, fuck me."

And in her fantasy, he did, cock shiny and thick, owning every part of her. Then her lusty daydream shifted and she imagined him doing the same to Tamara tonight, perhaps while Lily watched. Or even joined in the fun . . .

Helpless against the onslaught of sizzling images, she hurtled over the edge, hips bucking as she cried out. Orgasm slammed her with a series of jolts that fried her nerve endings, spun her out of control.

Gradually, they tapered off and she lay boneless, satisfaction sinking her into the bed. Damn, she'd needed that, and it was good.

But the real thing would far surpass the experience.

With a contented sigh, she removed the dildo and slid off the bed, heading for the bathroom to freshen up. As she stepped inside, it occurred to her that she hadn't exactly been quiet. Jude might've heard, and the idea caused her to flush with rare embarrassment. And longing.

If he had heard, would he comment? Would he even care?

Shaking her head ruefully, she caught sight of herself in the mirror and paused, taking in her appearance. Her small, fine-boned face was pink from exertion, brown eyes large and surrounded by a fringe of dark lashes. Disheveled black hair tumbled in a glossy mess almost to her waist.

She was cynical and practical about her looks—she knew men found her attractive, and her appearance served a purpose. It had always been the best weapon in her possession.

Except for now, when it counted the most.

Why wasn't she sorry about that?

Because for once, I want to be a woman, not a weapon. I want to forget why I'm here. I want a man to see beneath the surface, and like what he finds.

Then she thought of her father, cold in the ground, never again to know joy or sorrow.

Because of a traitor like Jude St. Laurent.

"Suck it up," she told her reflection. "That destiny was never meant to be yours."

Armor firmly in place, she reached for a washcloth and set about wiping away the traces of her weakness.

If only cleansing her soul were so simple.

Three

Jude stood frozen near his bed, listening to the husky cries drifting from the adjoining room.

"Jesus Christ," he muttered. His cock lifted in appreciation of the extracurricular activity taking place next door, a scant few yards away.

Apparently, Lily was quite affected by her introduction to his household.

With a grunt of frustration, he adjusted his crotch. Hell, he wasn't twenty-one anymore; if he were, he might be able to coax his semiawake cock to revive. But he'd come such a short time ago, he'd need longer to recover.

The chirping of the cell phone in the front pocket of his jeans stopped his morbid thoughts on aging before they could run rampant. Digging the slim device from his jeans, he found his bed and sat on the edge before answering.

"Hello?"

"Jude, how the hell are you?"

"Dev! It's good to hear your voice, man." He smiled. Nobody could sustain an irritable mood around Devon Sinclair or his pistol of a wife. "I'm fine, just bored as shit. Or I was until my new PA started today."

"Yeah? Do tell, my friend." He could picture Dev waggling his blond brows.

"I don't know much about her yet," he said, hedging some.

"How much *do* you know? Come on, don't leave me hanging!"

"Well, her name is Lily Vale. She's petite and has a killer whiskey voice. Smarter than me, according to her references."

"Like that would be a stretch," he joked. "And?"

"She's . . . sexually open. By her admission."

Dev spluttered. "How the fuck did you manage to learn that so fast when she just got there?"

"She walked in on me and one of my models practicing the big six-nine. To say she didn't take offense to my lifestyle is an understatement."

His friend burst out laughing. "Jesus, you're a piece of work. You know Geneva and I simply *must* meet her, right?"

"Oh, I figured it wouldn't take you long to get around to that suggestion, considering," he said, lips curving wickedly.

"How well you know me." In the background, Jude heard Dev flipping pages. "Crap, we're booked solid until next Friday. Dinner, followed by giving Lily a quick tour of the gallery, then a nightcap at our place? What do you say?"

"Dinner in public? I don't know, Dev. . . ." But he wasn't as adamant about avoiding going out as he'd been in the previous weeks, and Dev seized the opportunity to push the matter.

"You can't stay indoors forever, shut away like a bat in a belfry. Time to start living again, Jude."

"I . . . all right. Yes, let's do it." His stomach flopped just from imagining the ordeal.

"Great! You know we'll be there for you every step of the way. This is going to be fun!"

Jude chuckled, his friend's enthusiasm overshadowing his nerves. "It will, but I won't push Lily into a scene she's not ready for. If she's the least bit apprehensive—"

"You wound me, buddy. We've never forced anyone to play and we won't start with your Lily. You know me better than that."

"I do. Sorry."

"No problem," he said, good cheer unfazed. "Next Friday, then. Eight o'clock?"

"Perfect. We'll swing by and pick you two up."

"Geneva and I will look forward to it." His friend hesitated a moment. "So . . . how is Liam these days?"

His friend's odd tone gave him pause. Liam played with Dev and Geneva occasionally, same as himself. The couple adored him. They'd even commissioned a nude painting of Liam for their gallery last year, which hung on proud display. But what was this concern? Where was it coming from?

"He's fine. Same old happy Liam, you know?"

But was he?

"Oh. Well, that's good." Dev cleared his throat. "Just wanted to ask after him. Geneva thinks the boy is all that and a bag of chips, so she told me to ask. Give him our best, will you? See you next Friday, then."

They said good-bye and disconnected. As Jude tucked away his phone, he put the last part of their exchange out of his mind and realized his mood had lightened considerably. Lily's arrival had helped, and the plans with Devon and Geneva had put him over the top. He looked forward to next Friday—it had been far too long since he'd enjoyed his friends' company.

He had a sneaking suspicion Lily could show the voracious couple a trick or two.

A knock on the common door between his and Lily's suites interrupted his musings.

"Are you ready for lunch?" she asked, the door squeaking on its hinges.

"Starving," he said, getting to his feet. He grabbed his cane, squelching the pang of discomfort at having to eat in front of someone he'd just met. Wasn't that a laugh?

Sex with and in front of strangers? He wasn't uncomfortable in the least. Enduring the mechanics of feeding himself in front of those same people? There was a load of stress he could damned well do without.

But Dev was right—he couldn't hide indefinitely.

He'd consider the next few days as rehearsals for next Friday night. No need to panic. He'd survived far worse.

On the heels of that thought several images assaulted him.

Sitting at a ratty desk in a shitty motel room. Anxious, flicking the lid on his antique Zippo lighter. Fear like acid on his tongue.

"Jude, is something wrong?"

Belatedly, he became aware that he'd come to a dead stop in his route to the door. His skin felt cold. Clammy. "What? No, I just got distracted thinking about something I have to do later. Shall we?"

If she heard the lie, she didn't comment. As they walked together, Jude's mind wandered back to his prized lighter, a sentimental item he'd rescued from his grandfather's effects after the old man's passing. Jude wasn't sure what unsettled him more—forgetting about the beloved object or his own steady smoking habit.

How could I not remember an item associated with Pop, a man who was everything to me? And how could I forget a two-pack-a-day vice?

Even weirder, the memory did not bring on a craving for a cigarette. But he was suddenly anxious to know the fate of Pop's lighter. Where could it be?

Jude did his best to put the question temporarily out of his mind as he and Lily made themselves at home at the glass table in the sunroom. He'd search later. The thing had to be lying around somewhere.

"You're awfully quiet," Lily remarked. "Are you sure everything is fine?"

"Perfectly." He propped his arms on the table, leaning forward. "I should ask you that question. Was everything all right in your room? I could have sworn you were in pain."

She swatted his arm lightly. "Oh! You know very well what was wrong with me, and I lay the blame solely at your sizable feet. A gentleman wouldn't have brought it up."

"Honey, I'm no gentleman. There's no fun in it."

"And I'm not your honey."

He didn't miss the edge behind her teasing. "Sorry. It's a leftover Southern habit. No disrespect intended."

"None taken." She paused. "Where in the South are you from, if you don't mind my asking? I can hear a hint of . . . Cajun?"

"Not bad, though I'm not Cajun. I grew up in New Orleans, though living in New York has taken care of most of my accent. I haven't lived there in over twenty years, but it's true what they say—you can take the boy out of the South . . ."

"But not the South out of the boy. How did you wind up in New York?"

"I left home at seventeen, eventually made my way here for my work." There. The incessant pressure, the vague anxiety that accompanied a hole where part of his life should be. "I guess I believed New York was where a starving artist belonged. I took odd jobs to keep myself in paints and canvas, keep a roof over my head. Some of those jobs weren't exactly legal. It's a miracle I didn't land in prison."

And he almost had, hadn't he? How had he avoided such a dismal fate? Dev wasn't the one who'd saved him; he was positive.

"But you didn't, and now you're a huge success. I suppose one could say crime pays."

Jude frowned. "I never hurt anyone, and I certainly didn't get rich fencing hubcaps."

"I'm sorry," she said, contrite. "I didn't mean to imply you did. I was kidding."

"Forget it." Puzzled, he tried to catch the subtle undercurrents. He could swear he detected the slightest thread of anger in her tone, and he couldn't fathom why. Unless she held his humble beginnings against him. A woman like Lily could not possibly understand what it took to survive on the streets.

"How did you get your break?" Nothing but warmth now.

"I met a man by the name of Devon Sinclair—"

"*The* Devon Sinclair? Of Très Geneva gallery?"

"The same," he said, impressed. "You keep up with society news. Good. One of us has to, because I hate the limelight. Dev rags me unmercifully about going out of my way to avoid the press while he and his wife, Geneva—the gallery's namesake—lap the publicity up like cream."

"Don't you need to put in an appearance once in a while? Making sure you attend some functions is part of my job, after all."

"Let me confess something—I loathed going to society events before, but I occasionally took one for the team. Since the accident, however, the idea positively terrifies me. I have to get over my fear somehow because I owe Devon. He launched my career, and sells my paintings for unreal sums."

"We'll get you out of the house, then," she said firmly. "Baby steps. Lunch here, a party there. A vacation, perhaps."

"I don't recall the last time I took a real vacation," he mused, surprised by how much he liked the suggestion. "Start working on a list of destinations and we'll take it from there. Somewhere warm where clothing is optional."

"Super."

"In the meantime, I let Dev talk me into going out for dinner next Friday night. You'll be my date, of course. He and Geneva will love you."

He considered warning Lily about his friends' naughty appetites, but decided to let her find out as the evening progressed. More tantalizing for everyone if things developed naturally.

"Where are we going? Do I need to take care of the reservations?"

"I'm not sure where we'll eat, but no. Dev will take care of the plans and you'll be my escort. We'll take the limo and pick them up. After dinner, Dev wants to show you the gallery—unless you've already visited."

"I never have, but I've seen the outside. It's a gorgeous building."

"Oh, just wait. I promise you'll be blown away. After the gallery, we're invited to their place for a nightcap."

"Sounds like a lovely evening. I can't wait."

"It will be. And the Sinclairs are . . . interesting people."

"Tell me about them."

Ah, he had her curiosity piqued. He suppressed a grin. "I think I'll let you find out for yourself. Dev and Geneva must be experienced to be fully appreciated."

"Not fair—"

"Lunch, guys?" Liam called, rolling in his squeaky cart. He quickly set out their salads, silverware, and glasses. "Jude, your salad bowl is in front of you, fork on the right, napkin underneath. Iced tea at one o'clock, rolls in the middle of the table."

"Got it."

"Liam, this looks delicious," Lily said. "But where's yours?"

"I'm eating in the kitchen, giving you two a chance to get acquainted. Plus, I've got a ton to do. Chow down, and let me know if you need anything else." Wheels squeaked again. "I'm leaving this cart parked against the wall over here for when I come back to clean up, but it shouldn't be in your way."

Jude nodded. "Thanks," he said, throat tight. In his lap, his hands knotted into fists.

After Liam's steps receded, Lily spoke with concern. "I assume dining is part of the fear you mentioned regarding going out in public."

"How did you guess?" His attempt at humor was heavy with bitterness.

"Do you want me to—"

"No. I'll manage." Damn, he hadn't meant to snap.

"Fine," she fired back. "Then wipe that lost-puppy expression off your face and do it."

Lost puppy? Okay, that fucking pissed him off. She had no clue what this goddamned hell was like, day in and day out. Suddenly her take-no-shit attitude wasn't quite so charming. Being pitied was bad enough, but to be accused of trying to elicit sympathy?

His hand shot out to snatch a roll, nearly knocking over his iced tea in the process. Acting on pure reflex, he saved the liquid from spilling too much, then placed the roll to the left side of his salad bowl. Hands shaking, he lifted his fork, laid his napkin in his lap, and found the edge of the bowl with his left hand as a guide. Finally, he speared some salad and popped the leafy greens and savory chicken into his mouth.

"You're doing well," Lily observed. "I don't know why you're so afraid."

He swallowed his bite. "I'm dealing."

"Bullshit, you're hiding."

"Fuck you."

"Only if you're lucky."

"I don't need luck, sweetheart."

"I'm not your sweetheart any more than I'm your honey."

"You think? We'll see about that, won't we?"

Silence descended. One heartbeat, two, three.

Lily burst out laughing. Real, honest laughter. So infectious that Jude's mouth started to quirk. Dammit, he couldn't hold on to his foul temper if he wanted. He gave up and joined in, shaking his head.

"I must have looked like a jerk, huh?"

"Nah, you're cute when you're in a snit," she said.

"Good God, I haven't been called *cute* since I was ten."

"Really? Because you're pretty good at *acting* ten."

"Lily dear, the only thing about me that comes close to ten is in inches."

She choked on something, recovering quickly. "You *wish!*"

"Dirty-minded woman, I was talking about my bicep."

"Uh-huh."

They ate in comfortable silence for a few minutes, until Jude realized something. "How did you do that?"

"What?"

"Manage to put me at ease, make me forget about how much I'd been dreading sharing a meal with someone other than Liam?"

"No trick. There's really only two ways to distract a man that a girl needs to know—tick him off or make him horny."

"Or feed him. That's three."

"True. But under the circumstances, that one didn't count."

Laughing softly, he resumed his meal. "Tell me about yourself," he said between bites. "Are you close to your family?"

"I have none," she said shortly. And didn't volunteer more.

If anyone could understand the reticence to discuss the folks, he could. Since he'd opened the subject, he offered a bit of himself. "Me, either. At least none who care to claim me. I'm the son of a whore and her john, and the red-light district was my playground. The one bright spot was my pop, Mother's dad. He lived with us because he had nowhere else to go and wouldn't have left me anyway, and I was glad. As I grew older and Pop died, my mother's hovel—no, the entire city—became a prison I couldn't wait to escape."

Gentle fingers stroked his arm. "And you succeeded."

"One would think so." A sudden surge of emotion almost blocked his windpipe. "But you know what I've learned? All prisons look the same in the dark."

"Jude," she whispered. "I'm so sorry."

God, what had made him admit the one depressing truth he

hadn't even been able to share with Liam in his blackest moments?

Her hand traveled down his arm to his denim-clad thigh and rested there. Her sweet scent, her nearness, drove the wayward spurt of self-pity back into its lonely corner. Her palm burned him right through his jeans as she slid it to the inside of his thigh, very near the telling bulge.

Was she being bold? Or coy? Secretly smirking at his predicament? Lily was a blank page, and his hands itched to find out.

"May I look at you?" Putting his fork aside, he skimmed the back of her hand resting on his leg, up her arm, gratified to feel her tremble slightly at his touch.

"Yes, by all means."

Encouraged, he moved his chair to face her direction. Reaching for her legs, he was surprised to encounter dainty bare knees. "Spread your legs and scoot closer." As she complied, the insides of her thighs resting on the outsides of his, he was tantalized with the unmistakable musk of her arousal. It chipped at his control as he began his exploration.

He ran his palms up her thighs slowly, pleased by the feel of toned skin over solid muscle. This woman, however petite, was no weakling. She pushed her body and he found that sort of discipline damned attractive.

Above midthigh, his fingers reached the edge of a skirt and he was tempted to stray underneath. But not yet. He continued his journey to her middle instead, finding a lightweight blouse untucked and riding high, and he couldn't resist spanning her tiny waist with his hands. Moving upward to her ribs.

"Your skin," he prompted softly, so as not to dispel the sensuality developing between them. "Are you pale, or tan?"

"A healthy golden tone. I tan easily, though I prefer not to. When I lay out, I wear sunscreen."

"I'm glad. You will be as well, years from now."

Her breathing quickened as he brushed his thumbs just underneath the curve of her breasts. He longed to touch them, but held back again. He wanted her straining for his hands, her body begging even if she wouldn't.

Next, he found her slim shoulders and explored the column of her neck, the curve of her jaw. Carefully, he probed her cheekbones and forehead, discovering the sharp structure of her small face. Stronger and bolder than he'd expected.

Her brows were thin and smooth, her lashes long and feathery. "What color are your eyes?"

"Brown and large. My father always said I had doe eyes." Affection and a smidge of sadness bled into her voice.

He chose to pursue the past-tense reference to her father later. Much later.

She remained perfectly still while he brushed her full lips. Her mouth was a little wide, generous, and he wondered what those lips would feel like wrapped around his cock. With any luck, he'd find out soon enough.

He found the shell of her ears, so delicate. Then he forked his fingers through her hair, delighted to find the tresses long and silky.

"My hair is jet-black," she offered, anticipating his question. "Do you like what you see?"

"Oh, yes. Very much. But there's still a couple of pieces missing from the picture," he said, fingers trailing to her collarbone. Dipping to the vee of her blouse.

"Then why don't you complete it?"

Taking the husky command at face value, he freed the buttons of her blouse one by one. Parting the material, he slid it off her shoulders and gently cupped her breasts. They just fit his palms, small, the pert nipples stabbing him insistently. With a half smile, he plucked them, loving her throaty groan. The way she scooted forward, arching into him.

"Do you always go braless, pretty Lily?"

"Most of the time," she said, breathless. "I have little to put in one."

"Mmm. I think you're just right, and I like the idea of you bare underneath your clothing."

"Then you'll love the fact that I despise underwear."

"Fuck, yes."

"Please . . ."

He knew what she craved. Had known since he heard her cry out in her room, driven to self-pleasure. His fully revived cock throbbed in his jeans, begging to be loosed from its confines and buried deep in her pussy. Preferably from behind, with her long hair wrapped around his wrist, clutched in his hands.

Soon. For now, he wanted to satisfy her just enough to leave her writhing for more.

"Sit on the edge of your chair, sweetheart." She did, and this time voiced no protest at the endearment. He figured it prudent not to point that out.

One hand continued to tease a tight nipple while the other sought the mound at the apex of her thighs. As she claimed, he found her absent of panties, and her sex . . .

"Christ, yeah," he murmured, rubbing the tender folds, already slick and hot for him. "I'm a fan of naked skin, especially here. Triples the sensations."

"*Jude.*"

Lily clung to his shoulder, moaning, her body vibrating under his attentions. So responsive. He swirled her clit, picturing her spread for him, pink pussy glistening, black hair cascading all around her. It was nearly enough to make him come without touching himself.

"I'd love to paint a portrait of you, posed just like this," he said seductively.

She stiffened, grip on him tightening. "Oh, yes," she panted. "Yes!"

He worked the nub relentlessly, tempted to penetrate her with his fingers. But a bit of patience would make the wait worthwhile for both of them.

"Oh, God!" She bucked, exploding, riding out her orgasm as a warm rush coated his hand.

"That's it, honey. Take what you need." When she went still, he lifted his hand and licked her essence from his fingers. "Delicious. Taste yourself."

Lily took the initiative, much to his satisfaction, cupping the side of his face and pressing her lips to his. Her tongue darted into his mouth, tasting their combined flavors.

Incredibly erotic. Heaven.

Her slight frame felt so good against him, a heady combination of softness and strength. She dominated the kiss and for a few seconds he let her, intrigued by this tiny woman who would play the aggressor. Then his nature took over and he met her with fervor, the two of them coming together with such force he had to stop while he was able.

With reluctance, he broke the kiss and extricated himself gently. "Thank you, sweet Lily."

"Thank *me*? All I did was enjoy. I could return the favor, though," she suggested playfully.

"I'd love nothing more, but that was for you. Rain check?"

"Well . . . sure."

She sounded so puzzled, he couldn't help smiling. "I'll look forward to it." Rising, he abandoned the rest of his lunch and reached for his cane. "I'm going to spend some time in the studio this afternoon, then rest before tonight. Make yourself at home. Feel free to set up at the extra desk in the corner of my office."

"Is the computer on that desk mine to use?"

"Yes, as well as everything on or inside it, including the BlackBerry for my appointments and such. Don't worry about doing any real work today—just get your bearings and then relax, visit with Liam, maybe take advantage of the pool."

"That sounds wonderful." She paused, then said thoughtfully, "You were wrong about something."

"What's that?"

"You *are* a gentleman."

He laughed. "Not hardly, dear Lily, as you'll soon discover. By the way . . . the door connecting our rooms?"

"Yes?"

"It's never locked," he said, pitching his tone to make his meaning clear.

"Except when you're entertaining a lover, like tonight?"

"*Never.*" Grinning, he turned and started for the door. "Like I said, I'm no gentleman."

"Jude?"

He paused his steps. "Hmm?"

"I'm no lady."

"Then I believe we understand each other very well, sweetheart."

Shuffling out, he left her to chew on that for the rest of the day.

And to take care of the painful jackhammer in his jeans.

Four

ily tidied the desk that was to serve as her work space for
the next few weeks, arranging pens and Post-its, and
playing with the snazzy little BlackBerry. Nice.

Next, she logged into her PA's e-mail account Jude had set up
for her and was dismayed to discover fifty-six messages in her in-
box already. "Well, shit. Efficient bastard."

Jude must have taken for granted that she'd accept the job,
because it seemed everyone in the area had e-mailed her about
something or other they wanted Jude to attend, a painting they
were salivating to purchase, or a charitable contribution they
coveted from his wallet.

Scowling, she was tempted to delete the whole list. But her
"boss" might get his tighty-whities in a bunch if his new PA ignored
all his correspondence. She was about to log out when her eye was
caught by a familiar name in the *From* column—Devon Sinclair.

Curious, she opened the e-mail and read the brief message:
*Lily, Geneva and I look forward to the pleasure of your company next Friday
evening. We also thank you for enticing Jude out of his lonely cave—the man
needs a night out with friends. Best, Dev.*

So, his buddy and benefactor was feeling her out. Fine. If he'd really been worried about Jude for the past few weeks, she couldn't blame him.

Lily pondered the missive for several minutes before coming up with a suitable reply: *Devon, how nice to hear from you. I understand I'm in for quite a dazzling evening. I can't wait to meet you both, and to visit your lovely gallery. Until then, Lily.*

There. Polite but not gushing. Logging out, she sat staring at the screen, thinking over Sinclair's words, reflective of something Jude said at lunch.

Was Jude lonely? Did he honestly feel imprisoned, or had the heart-wrenching statement been designed by a shrewd man to play on her sympathy? Somehow, she didn't think so. He seemed to truly hate the idea of being pitied.

The story of his upbringing had gotten to her, too. More than she cared to admit. Nowhere in his file was there a single word printed about his past, and she'd be willing to bet Michael, being the head honcho, was the sole person at SHADO who knew the tidbits Jude had shared with her today. Which wasn't so unusual. Many of the agents' backgrounds were classified "need to know" only.

Lily's thoughts turned to their lunch . . . or, rather, the dessert. So to speak.

Over and over, she relived his rapt expression as he'd mapped her body with those big hands. Like he'd discovered some sort of priceless treasure as he explored her face, skimmed her thighs, pinched her nipples. The way his brow furrowed as he concentrated on bringing her pleasure while denying his own.

No man could fake the joy she'd seen on his striking face. He was a study in contradictions, thwarting her analytic brain and negating the damaging information from Dietz.

"Come on, Lily," she admonished herself. "Just because he doesn't remember he's the twenty-first century's answer to Lex Luthor doesn't mean that man isn't hiding under the surface, waiting to pounce."

If he remembered, she shuddered to think what might happen.

Honey, I'm no gentleman.

Then again, perhaps some corner of his tattered mind recalled more than anyone knew. Including Jude.

Whether he was reformed or not, she had a job to do. He was still guilty of a horrible crime. Historically, even the most heinous of killers tended to possess magnetic personalities. The moth-to-the-flame effect.

She'd have to be damned careful not to get zapped. Pushing from her chair, she walked to the office door and scanned the hallway. Empty. No voices or noise of any kind, which meant Jude and Liam were off doing their own thing. She had the office to herself.

Time to begin. Turning, she perused the walls, running the layout of this wing through her head. Every SHADO agent she knew, at least the mobile ones who went into the field to handle the dangerous stuff, had a secret "war room." A reinforced space that held weapons, computers, disguises, passports, and all sorts of fake IDs. Jude had such a room. But where was it hidden?

Not here. This large space was a corner office with only one inside wall, the workout room on the other side. She hadn't expected it to be that simple, finding it on the first go. She had a hunch it would be located closer to his private quarters upstairs where it was more defensible, rather than on the ground floor.

Just to be sure, she ran her hands over the panels, checked the seams. Knocked quietly, testing for hollow places. He probably kept a small hidey-hole for emergencies as well, and if so, she'd find it.

But she wouldn't find it here. The walls were solid. Her attention strayed to his desk and she lowered herself into his chair, examining the excellent craftsmanship. The piece was an antique, an expensive one if she had her guess, ornate and loaded with drawers. Exactly the sort of old relic that might contain a hidden compartment.

But if it did, she couldn't locate a mechanism to spring it. Blowing out a frustrated breath, she began opening drawers.

Every one empty except for the usual drawer crap. "Goddammit!"

"What are you looking for?"

Jerking upright, heart pounding, she met Liam's cool, appraising gaze. "Jude's appointment book," she replied, meeting his stare evenly. "He told me to make myself at home in here and set up to start working."

"Oh." His expression cleared and he slouched against the doorframe, posture relaxing. "I've got his planner. I'm the one who's been helping him until someone else could take over, remember? I'll get it for you."

"Thanks. I can't do much without all of the information I need. I already have more than fifty messages in my in-box, and a third of those are dates I need to confirm with Jude."

"And you can't take care of those until you cross-reference what he's already got on the agenda." He gave her a sheepish grin. "Sorry, I should've left it in here for you before you arrived."

She waved a hand, vacating Jude's chair. Her runaway pulse began to calm. "No sweat. Just leave it on my desk when you get a second. I doubt I'll get much work done today anyway."

"In that case . . . would you be tempted to lounge by the pool with me?"

Her gaze swept appreciatively from his sleepy gray eyes fringed with black lace, down his lean body to slim hips and long legs. *Gee, let me think.*

"Very. Would Jude be interested in joining us?"

He shrugged. "Maybe later. He gets lost in another world when he's working in his studio and doesn't typically like to be bothered."

"He certainly didn't seem to mind my walking in earlier," she remarked, thinking of his tryst with Tamara.

"Was the door open?"

"Yes."

"Then all's fair game. Jude's rule."

"No matter what he's doing?"

A dimple appeared at the corner of his sexy mouth. "Or who."

"From the mischievous expression on your face, I wonder exactly how many times you've found the door open."

"At least as many times as I've been the one behind it." He ran a hand through his black hair, causing it to fall around his face in attractive disarray. "Why don't we continue this conversation by the pool with something cool and potent to drink?"

"Give me ten minutes to find my suit and change," she said, giving him a smile. "Then I have lots of questions for you."

"Well, I have lots of alcohol, so we're good."

Lily hurried to her room and located one of her best bikinis, her mind filled with stuff she might be able to pry from Liam—especially if his refreshment loosened his tongue. The younger man seemed to be pretty open, but she'd take every advantage she could.

The file hidden in her closet contained valuable information about Jude as an agent, but was almost useless concerning his daily life at the estate. An omission she found troubling and intriguing. Who better than the resident boy toy to get the lowdown from?

Once she'd changed into a suit that was made of nothing more than three microscopic red triangles, she searched for sunscreen among her belongings and couldn't find it. Giving up, she grabbed a thick towel and headed to the pool.

Liam wasn't there yet, so she took the opportunity to appreciate the view. A momentary punch hit her swift and hard when she reminded herself Jude could no longer see all this. The huge, sparkling pool edged by elaborate stonework and a waterfall, the gardens overflowing with colorful flowers, the outdoor kitchen and bar area. Such a waste.

But then, he deserved what he'd gotten, not to mention what he had coming. Didn't he?

Yes, he did. He'd betrayed the citizens of the United States and put several allies in grave danger. She'd best not forget that.

Liam arrived with two glasses, a pitcher, and a big smile. She did a double take at his scrumptious body clad in only swim trunks with a towel slung over one bare shoulder—the man might be lean, but he was nicely muscled, tanned, and toned. Had a smooth chest graced by two perfect, bronzed male nipples and an abdomen cut by a master sculptor. Mouthwatering.

"Pink lemonade?" she asked, hoping he didn't hear the croak in her voice.

He set the glasses and pitcher on a small table between two padded loungers. "Yep. With an extra kick. Make yourself comfy."

She settled in the lounger, squinting up at him. "Do you have sunscreen? I couldn't find mine."

"Sure do." He spread the towel on his chair, nodding toward a nearby building. "Got some in the pool house. Be right back."

He trotted off, giving her the opportunity to view his fine ass in action before he disappeared into the building. A minute later, he returned with a blue tube in hand. "Here you go."

"Thank you." She took the sunscreen from him and laid it on the table for the time being, turning her attention to the drink. She picked up the slightly fizzy pink concoction and brought the straw to her lips, taking a tentative sip. "Oh, that's good! So, what's the kick?"

His dimple deepened. "Beer and vodka."

She coughed. "What? You're not serious! Those two words in the same phrase sound completely disgusting."

"Totally." He laughed at her pinched expression. "My friends and I dubbed it Fuck-Me Punch. 'Cause a couple of glasses of that and you'll wake up trying to figure out where your clothes are."

She took another sip. "It *is* good. You can't even taste the alcohol. Weird."

"Which is why that recipe can sneak up on you. I'll have to watch your intake or you might rip my shorts off."

"You are incorrigible. I have a strong feeling you and Jude are dangerous when mixed."

"You'd be right."

She eyed him as he took a few swallows of punch. "Indulge me on something?"

"If I can. Shoot."

"Give me some insight on Jude. Tell me who this man is to you, to those around him."

The happy mood surrounding Liam faded along with the spark in his pretty eyes. "Which Jude would that be? The powerful force of nature who first hired me? The cold, distant stranger he became last year? Or the lost, vulnerable soul I brought home from the hospital? I'd hardly know where to begin."

His palpable anguish tore at her heart. "Any of them. All of them."

He looked away from her, staring out over the gardens. "I wish you could have known him in the beginning," he said quietly. "Jude was always so sure of himself. On top of the world and confident of his place in it. Then those mysterious trips become more and more frequent. He'd come home exhausted and strung out. Depressed. He'd shut himself in his studio for days after he returned, and his paintings became angry. Violent."

"Can I take a look at those particular works?"

He glanced at her in surprise. "I can't imagine why you'd want to, but you can if you go to Très Geneva gallery. Jude completed five of those hideous things before the accident and his *buddy* Devon Sinclair sold three of them for more than a million each. Dev displayed the other two and refuses to part with them. Says they're important works from Jude's 'transitional period,' whatever the hell that means."

Do I detect a hint of animosity toward Sinclair? Interesting.

"And his work since the accident?"

"He's still struggling," Liam said sadly. "It's early yet. His raw talent survived and anyone with a practiced eye can recognize the one he's managed to finish is a St. Laurent, but . . ."

Lily reached across the table, laid a hand on his arm. "I understand."

"Really? I'm not sure anyone can. No one except me was here

when I brought him home. He shut himself in his bedroom and hid for days. Wouldn't let me in, refused to eat. He was so alone, broken, and confused, and I didn't know what to do, how to help him. Those were the most difficult few weeks either of us had ever endured."

"But you both made it," she pointed out, wanting to comfort him. "Based on what you've told me, he's come a long way."

"He's got a long road still, but yeah. I'm starting to see a glimmer of the man I first knew, the man who let nothing stand in his way, and it's a damned fine thing to witness."

Retracting her hand, Lily considered her next words for a long moment. She decided to probe a bit, gauge Liam's reaction. "Do you love him?"

Liam gaped at her, eyes wide. "Jude? No. I mean, *yes*. But as my best friend, not in the romantic sense."

She gave him a soft, encouraging smile. "You two play together, though, and I can see how close you are. Doesn't that blur the lines of friendship?"

He flopped back in the lounger, a smile curving his lips, good humor restored. "Not for us. We're great friends, with benefits. I'd do anything for him and I know for a fact he would for me, too. It's just . . ." He waved a hand idly. "You can't put two highly sexed guys like us together on a daily basis and not have a nuclear reaction on occasion."

Yum. "Tell me more."

Liam turned his head to squint at her, expression amused. "As you might have guessed, he's dominant, which appeals to my inner slut. He fucks like a dream, especially when he's primed to play a little rough."

The image of those two beautiful men playing together seared itself into her brain. And the image made her squirm—in a good way.

"Do you share lovers?"

"Sometimes. I have a few friends in the city who hang here once in a while, and then there's Jude's models. It's never dull, for sure."

"You're lucky," she said, almost to herself.

"How so?"

Her gesture encompassed their surroundings. "You have all of this, a hot best friend who shares your open lifestyle, your freedom. You have everything."

He slanted her an odd look. "But so do you. All of this is yours now, too."

Again, the burden of why she was really here weighed more heavily than any assignment to date.

In truth? She had nothing and no one to call her own.

You need information, however you have to obtain it, she reminded herself sternly. *No matter how sweet he is, this man is not your friend. He'd hate you if he knew who and what you are.*

"Thanks. That's awfully nice of you to say."

"Call it like I see it," he said, shrugging. Sitting up, he flashed a sunny smile. "Want me to help you with the sunscreen? You're turning pink."

"Go for it, sweetie," she said, flipping onto her stomach.

She felt his weight settle on the lounger, one knee between her legs, the other foot braced on the ground. Leaning over, he squirted the cool lotion on her back and began to work it in, his touch light and efficient. His palms smoothed over the crease in her spine, her sides. Under the string of her top, to her shoulders, rubbing with more pressure.

"Wow, you've got some serious knots," he said in concern. "Want me to work them out for you?"

"That's okay—oh," she moaned in bliss. He ignored her weak protest and began to massage the tense muscles, thumbs kneading the sore knots she hadn't realized were there.

"There you go. Just relax and let me make it better. Are you under a lot of stress?"

Who, me? Oh, no, I'm just going to kill your boss—you know, your best friend? And I didn't expect to like him, either. No conflict at all.

"Just the usual. Moving, taking a new position, learning the ropes."

"You'll have it down in no time; don't worry."

"Mmm. Your hands are heaven. Do you treat Jude to this magical brand of stress relief?"

"Are you kidding? Every chance I get. Besides, the knots in his muscles are always bad. Painting for hours without a break wears him down."

Through the pleasant haze, Lily became aware of Liam's erection. It rode the back of her thigh, high and hard, his heat branding her through his trunks.

"Um, Liam? Is the pistol in your shorts for me, or *him*?"

Laughing, he pressed against her back, his breath tickling her ear. "I'm sprawled across the hottest woman I've ever met. She's practically naked and I haven't had sex in days. Answer your question?"

In spite of how great he felt against her, she couldn't resist teasing. "So I'm convenient?"

"You're not convenient—you're smart and attractive." He kissed the shell of her ear, nibbled a tender spot on her neck. "We're young, we're consenting adults, and I'm dying to know if you taste as sweet as you smell."

She wiggled onto her back and cupped his face, brushed a lock of black hair from his eyes. "We can't have you expiring on top of me, can we?"

God, his weight felt so good, his scent clean and male. The encounter with Jude at lunch had merely whetted her appetite, left her aching for a man's thick cock filling her.

Lily pulled his head down and he took her mouth, delving his tongue inside for a thorough exploration. He moaned, grinding his length into her mound, creating wonderful friction as they sampled each other. His kiss was so different from Jude's—slow and passionate, where Jude's was like a tornado tearing at her well-constructed walls, shaking her foundations.

Liam kissed like a lover skilled in gentle seduction, the sort that sneaks up on his partner by degrees until he or she is consumed without quite recalling how it happened.

Two different men, each devastating in his own way.

Pulling back, he kissed a path down her throat, moved lower, and grazed her nipples with his teeth through the fabric of her swimsuit top. Tiny little shocks curled her toes in pleasure and she wanted more.

Arching, she untied the string at the nape of her neck. Taking his cue from her, Liam untied the one at her back and pulled the top away, dropping it to the ground.

"Pretty," he said reverently, dipping his head.

He flicked one rosy tip, coaxing it to attention with his clever tongue. Then he suckled, laving it, every rasp sending sparks of delight to her nerve endings. She loved how his hair fell around his face, brushed against her ribs. How his long, graceful fingers caressed her skin as though she was priceless.

Shifting, he heaped equal attention to the other breast,

scraping and teasing until she writhed under him, eager. "Less clothes, more skin," she said, voice quavering.

Releasing the nub with a pop, he gave her a grin. "Gladly."

He pushed up to stand next to the lounger and she watched hungrily as he shoved the trunks past his hips and off.

His long cock jutted from a light nest of ebony curls and curved toward his stomach, perfectly proportioned to his body. The mushroom-shaped head leaked pre-cum, the entire length flushed dark with arousal. A yummy, blue-veined treat she couldn't wait to devour.

Liam started to join her on the lounger again, but she sat up and grabbed his hips. "Stay where you are and spread your legs. I want some of this."

"Take all you need, baby."

Widening his stance, he waited for her to make her move. She wasted no time, gripping the base of his erection and licking the salty tip. His balls hung heavy below the shaft and she reached out, manipulated the velvety orbs as she swallowed him down her throat.

"Christ," he hissed, thrusting forward in reflex. His hands fisted in her hair, guiding her deep.

She loved sucking cock. Always had, ever since she'd discovered the joys of reducing a boy to a puddle of mush. The thrill of power. As she'd grown older, she'd learned a man would do anything, promise the moon, for the decadence of a woman's lips caressing his cock.

Liam didn't promise anything, however. Probably because he couldn't speak.

His dark head was thrown back, eyes closed, lips parted. He looked like a man who'd found heaven by slamming into the pearly gates. Headfirst.

Lily indulged them both, drawing him so deep the hair at his groin tickled her nose, slurping him in slow, noisy rhythm. She pulled out until only the head remained in her mouth, then in again. Out and in, feasting on his rod and glancing up occasionally to watch the bliss grow on his sexy face.

"Lily, stop." He pulled back. "Jesus, stop or I'm going to lose it any second."

She withdrew with a slow lick and slanted a look at him. "Thought that was the whole point."

"Not like this." He reached for his trunks, fished in one pocket, and yanked out a foil packet. In short order, he tore it open and covered himself. His jaw clenched as he fisted himself, eyes blazing with fire. "I want you to ride me."

His words sounded like an order, albeit a quiet one, and cleared up a question in her mind. Although sweet-natured, Liam was no pushover when it came to sex. He'd give as good as he got, and he'd allow her only so much power over him before he reined her in. An attractive quality in a lover, and a huge turn-on for her.

She stood and shimmied out of her bikini bottoms while Liam took her place in the lounger. He sprawled on his back, feet flat on the concrete on either side of the chair, lips curved into a fetching smile.

"Come up here before my balls turn blue."

"Poor man."

She crawled on top of him, straddling his hips, and positioned the blunt head against her opening. He hadn't even played with her pussy, yet she was wet with arousal, burning to have him inside. Slowly, she sank onto his cock, moaning as he stretched and filled her. Lower, until his balls were nestled against her ass and they were connected as intimately as two people could be.

"Oh, yes," he muttered, thrusting upward. His fingers dug into her thighs. "God, fuck me, baby."

Hands splayed on his taut stomach, she began to move, up to the tip, then down again. Drawing every sensation out like pulling a wire tight, heightening the pleasure. Over and over she impaled herself on him, drinking in the ecstasy on his beautiful face, her own desire building. Spiraling from her womb outward, making her shake.

"Faster. Fuck me harder." He began to pump forcefully to her downstrokes, leading them in perfect rhythm.

"Yes! Give me your cock. . . . Give it to me hard!"

She bounced on his lap in wild abandon, Liam slamming into her, driving them closer, higher. . . .

Her orgasm exploded into a million shards of brilliant light. "Oh, God! Yes!"

As she rode the waves, he thrust once, twice, and stiffened with a shout. He jerked inside her for several moments, whispering things like "baby" and "fuck, yeah," until he lay still, the only movement his chest, his breath sawing in and out of his lungs.

"Holy shit, you drained me. I don't think I'll be able to come again until sometime next week." His eyes fluttered open and he peered at her from under those killer lashes. "Was I too rough?"

Sprawling on his chest, she brushed his lips with a brief kiss. "You were awesome."

"Good enough to warrant a repeat performance?"

Suddenly he seemed unsure, and she found his hesitance touching. "I'd say the chances are better than good."

The furrow between his brows disappeared and he smiled. "I

really like you, Lily. I don't play with a person if I don't feel a connection. I thought you should know that."

A lump formed in her throat. "I really like you, too." That made having to deceive this man even more difficult.

"Is something wrong?"

"Not at all. I was just wondering if you'd take a swim with me."

"It's a plan. Let's go!"

She climbed off him and he discarded the condom, hiding it on his chair under the edge of his towel to toss out later. Grabbing her hand, he tugged her toward the pool.

"No suits?" she asked.

"Who needs them? We have total privacy and even if someone dropped by . . . well, our crowd isn't exactly on the prude side."

"Good point."

He took off at a dead run for the deep end, not letting go of her hand. She squealed as they jumped together, hitting the water in a noisy cannonball, and thought, *I could get used to this.*

Not good, Lily.

Not good at all.

. . .

Jude froze half in and half out of the patio door, the sounds of fucking, the cries of pleasure, ringing in his ears long after they faded. His heart clenched, a wave of loneliness sweeping over him despite his efforts to stave it off.

But not because his closest friend and his sexy new PA were doing what came naturally. No, his views on sex were liberal and would never change. What got to him, for some strange reason, was the joyful noise of the couple splashing and shouting in the pool.

Ridiculous to let that, of all things, bother him. Especially when he knew without a single doubt they'd welcome him with the same enthusiasm should he join them.

What the fuck is wrong with me?

He had no clue. He should strip off his clothing and head out there, have some fun.

But the longer he remained in place, unnoticed, the more like an outsider he felt. Confused by the turmoil inside him, he retreated and carefully made his way back in the direction from which he'd come.

At least he had tonight to look forward to.

Even if the prospect of his liaison with Tamara no longer seemed quite as exciting as before.

Five

Lily stepped out of the shower and toweled off her hair, humming. The afternoon delight with a certain hot chef had done wonders for her mood. It had been liberating to ditch her cold, calculating alter ego, if only for a while.

Maybe she didn't have to be "on" every single second. What would it hurt to loosen up some, see things from a different perspective? What if Jude wasn't—

The soft tune vibrating her cell phone dispersed the thought before it could form, and she crossed to the dresser and flipped it open. She didn't need three guesses as to who would be on the other end.

"You don't waste much time," she said by way of greeting SHADO's interim boss.

"We don't have any to piss away, Agent Vale," Dietz answered with deceptive calm. "Stay focused and locate those remaining two missing files before they wind up in the wrong hands. The last thing we need is the press getting a whiff of one of our best men going bad, stealing a weapon of mass destruction, and selling it to our enemy. SHADO will be roasted in the news and the government will go up our asses and around the corner."

She frowned and sat on the edge of the bed. "I still don't understand why St. Laurent would send out six worms containing damaging evidence of his own guilt. I mean, he had to know we'd eventually be able to trace the route back to him as the source."

"He *did* know," Dietz reminded her. "He'd already completed his dirty deal and the weapon is gone. Terrorists love to grandstand, Vale, and publicity is as great a weapon as the weapon itself. The majority of them don't care about capture, death, or anything but their cause. They don't do it for the money. Tell me I'm wrong."

She couldn't. St. Laurent certainly didn't need the extra millions in the bank. But something kept nagging her. "Then what is the root of his motivation? What would turn a man so completely against his country?"

"Lily," he sighed, dropping the formalities. His voice became sad, as though the world rested on his shoulders. "When your upbringing is as pathetic and hardscrabble as St. Laurent's, it can damage a man. Sometimes to the point of no return. I can only imagine that his resentment simmered and grew year by year as he clawed his way to the top, obsessed with someday being in the position to do exactly what he did."

"Stick it to everyone who failed him, in the most spectacular way," she said, drawing the conclusion. "I know he refused to cooperate, even under torture, so why did you bother with the mind sweep instead of just putting him down?"

This was the longest conversation they'd ever had, and she took the opportunity to continue asking him the questions that had been bothering her. Usually, he simply relayed the information and barked the next orders. Today, he seemed uncharacteristically patient, as though making a concentrated effort to be more like Michael.

Perhaps Dietz was taking some heat for his methods, which were cold even by Lily's standards.

"I was attempting to buy SHADO time to unravel what St. Laurent had done, discover his contacts, and find the files he planted. On the off chance we'd need him, I didn't want him eliminated just yet."

"And now? I've found four of the six files." Encrypted files she'd been ordered to hand right over to Dietz with no time or way to decipher them.

"Depends. Is the sweep holding?"

She knew what was coming, and a part of her dreaded telling him. Even considering what Jude had done. "Honestly? I think it's starting to break down. He says he's having migraines and nightmares."

"All right. That's it, then." He paused, let the truth fall into the space between them. "If he's allowed to remember, his vengeance against SHADO—against both of us in particular—will be swift and merciless. You understand what must be done."

Bile rose in her throat. "Yes. Quick and clean?"

"No, he's a society figure and too many questions will be raised if we make it an obvious hit. Use the poison in four evenly spaced doses, no more than a week apart. His health will decline steadily, and once he's dead, our sources will plant in the newspapers that Jude St. Laurent, renowned artist, never recovered from his accident. No one will question his death."

Except Liam. She kept her lips sealed. The younger man had done nothing to deserve to die.

"Consider it done."

"I'll be in touch."

Lily disconnected, sick to her stomach. She was doing the right thing for the best of reasons—eliminating a traitor before he could regain his memory and do any more damage to the United States. But why did it feel wrong?

Something about her talk with Dietz tugged at her brain, but the significance escaped her.

She put it out of her mind. If it was important, it would come to her later.

• • •

Robert Dietz leaned back in his chair and gazed into the pock-marked face of his right-hand man. "Finally, the end of the so-called indestructible St. Laurent."

"She's found all the files?" Tio asked, crossing his beefy arms over his chest.

"We're still missing the same two, but if they haven't been discovered by now, I'm willing to bet they never will. And he could've been lying about how many he sent."

The other man scowled. "Maybe. But the asshole said himself he's the only one who knows where they're hidden. The whole reason you were keeping him alive was insurance against his death triggering the fucking things."

"Be that as it may, we'll have to take the risk. We can't wait any longer." He stood, went to the wet bar, and poured himself two fingers of scotch. "Our overseas friends are becoming anxious for their delivery and I want my goddamned money."

He didn't say that if he failed, his life wouldn't be worth the ink on his birth certificate.

"Unlike real terrorists, who just want glory." Tio smirked, showing the gap in his front teeth. "Nice spin, by the way."

Dietz raised his glass in a toast. "Wasn't it? I should win a frigging Oscar." He drained the amber liquid, relishing the fire that burned all the way to his gut.

The other man regarded him thoughtfully. "All these months wasted babysitting St. Laurent when we could've moved by now. We're damned lucky Ross is still grieving and hasn't returned to the helm yet. He comes within a mile of this and he'll smell it in an instant."

"First of all, luck has nothing to do with my success. I don't wait for breaks; I make them. Second, our next project will be to ensure our poor, distraught widower *doesn't* return."

Tio popped his big, scarred knuckles. "A plan I can get behind."

"Good." He slapped his highball glass onto the counter. "I'm already running this place, so we'll make certain it becomes official."

"Death to taxes and the weak."

"I'll drink to that, my butt-ugly friend."

"We're not friends."

"You learn fast." He pinned Tio with a steely glare until the other man flinched first. "Keep it up and you might live to spend your share."

But I wouldn't count on it.

. . .

After a nap and a shower, Jude felt much more together. Less off-balance. His odd melancholy had abated along with the pressure in his head, much to his relief. No migraine tonight and, with any luck, no nightmares. His mood lightened.

By the time Tamara arrived, more than his spirits had taken flight. No reason why he shouldn't enjoy his evening. His libido had been on a slow boil all day and now he trembled in anticipation like a racehorse at the starting gate.

A knock from the hallway sounded and the door to his suite opened. "Jude? Tamara's here," Liam announced.

"In the flesh," she said, swishing toward him.

Liam moved past them. "I'll leave the champagne and glasses on the table by the window, along with a small tray of chocolate-covered strawberries to start."

"Perfect, thanks."

"When do you want dinner served?"

"Give us half an hour?"

"You got it."

Jude considered inviting Liam to play later. His friend sometimes joined him for a ménage, and thoroughly enjoyed himself when he did. But Jude knew Liam preferred one threesome in particular. And that trio didn't involve Jude.

Liam gave no indication he'd like to hang around, so Jude took his cue and let it go.

When the door clicked shut, Tamara ran her palms down the front of his dress shirt. "You seem different tonight."

"Really? How so?"

"I'm not sure. More upbeat, maybe."

"I suppose I am." A wet tongue grazed his ear. "I'm not as tense as I've been. But then, you have that effect on me."

"Glad to hear it," she said in a low voice. She pressed into him, full breasts squashing against his chest. "You look scrumptious, all *GQ* in your white shirt and gray dress pants."

"I clean up okay. What about you? What are you wearing?"

Moving back a shade, he touched her hair, pleased to find it loose.

"Little red dress, clingy, way above midthigh. Plunging neckline. Matching high heels."

His groin tingled, and he traced the swell of one breast. His other hand crept under the hem of the dress, up her smooth thigh to a bare ass cheek. "No underwear?"

"Thong."

Groaning, he released her. "How am I supposed to get through our appetizer, much less dinner?"

She giggled. "There's something to be said for willpower. The wait makes the fruit sweeter."

"We'll test the theory and draw out the anticipation, then. Want to sit?" He gestured in the general direction of the table.

"Yes. And what a lovely table it is, with the bubbly and the strawberries. Thank you, Jude."

"Thank Liam. I just ask him to make it fabulous, and he does."

"My compliments to him, in that case. I'll tell him myself, later."

Tamara poured the champagne and placed strawberries on little plates Liam provided. Jude sipped his drink and smiled in his date's direction as she exclaimed over every small thing. She complimented his paintings as well, not mincing words that it would take some time to find his groove in developing his new style.

She was a refreshing, genuine woman, a charming companion, and he found himself having a good time. No matter how much he was looking forward to another taste of her lush body, he wouldn't have tolerated her presence if he didn't like her as a person. He wasn't someone who could completely disassociate and just have sex without clicking with a lover. Even with a stranger, he had to find the other person interesting.

Liam outdid himself on dinner, and they ate, making small talk, the sexual tension stretching like a laser beam between them. When Jude finished his crème brûlée, he'd about reached his breaking point.

"God, that was heaven," he said, pushing his chair from the table. "Are you finished?"

"Only with the food," she replied huskily.

He rose, holding out a hand. "Come here."

She clasped his fingers and stood, and he pulled her close. Nuzzled her neck, her musky perfume arousing him. His dick tented his trousers, fully hard and begging to be freed. He ignored it for a moment, cupping her breasts through the sheer dress, grazing the nipples with his thumbs.

They sprang to attention and he investigated the neckline, glad to find it cut so low all he had to do was part the material to reveal naked flesh. The mounds were weighty in his hands and he bent, laved the areola. Sucked each one greedily, rolled them with his tongue.

He liked the little noises of pleasure she made as her fingers strayed to his pants. In seconds, she unbuckled and unzipped him, releasing his cock.

"Oh, yeah," she breathed. "No underwear. I love a man who doesn't waste time."

Before he could reply, she sank to her knees and grasped the base of his erection. Then his world spun as her mouth surrounded him, pulled him deep. He spread his legs for her, gave her full access to fondle his balls. She squeezed them with gentle pressure, her lips sliding along his cock, tongue exploring every ridge. Tight, hot suction.

He could come like this, but he didn't want to go too soon. "On the bed, sweetheart."

"Oh, yes."

It was then he heard it. A soft bump that came from the direction of Lily's room. A rustle of, what? Fabric? So faint he barely discerned the sound—but it wasn't his imagination. He knew for sure when he heard an almost inaudible intake of breath.

Lily was watching.

She'd taken his hint about their connecting door being unlocked, and given in to curiosity. To her lust. At that realization, what had merely been a mutually satisfying encounter became something altogether wicked. His entire body lit as though by a torch, excitement singing in his blood.

She'd watched them before, but this was different. This time he knew she was there, and could give her a show she'd not forget. One that would have her creaming, her entire body flushed and hot. Perhaps she'd wish she were in Tamara's place.

Jude tugged Tamara onto the bed. "Know what I'm going to do to you? I'm going to remove that dress from your gorgeous body, like this."

Grasping the hem, he pulled it up and off over her head, careful not to tear the fabric. "Next you're going to lie back and spread your legs for me, and keep on the thong and those fuck-me shoes."

The bed wiggled as she complied. "All right. Now what?"

He removed his shirt and tossed it aside, shucked his shoes, socks, and pants, taking a condom from one pocket. He knelt on the bed and laid the condom aside, hyperaware that Lily had a great view of everything he planned to do to the other woman. His cock had never been so hard, or hurt so much.

"I'm going to kiss my way from your nipples down that pretty body, like this."

He did, licking and nibbling each puckered tip, down her flat belly to the top edge of the little scrap of material. Crouching between her thighs, he hooked a finger under the thin strap and pushed it aside, revealing her sex. God, he missed his sight so badly. For once, however, knowing Lily was watching made up for the loss.

"Now I'm going to tease your sweet pussy until you're begging for my mouth." He began to finger the lips of her sex, parting them, making certain her cunt was on display. He massaged her clit, dipped a finger into her moist channel to capture a bit of cream, spread it around.

"Oh . . . Jude," she rasped.

"What, gorgeous?" Two fingers now, fucking her slowly. Another few circles around the clit, sensitizing the nub, driving her crazy by degrees.

"Please!" She grabbed a handful of hair, making her wishes clear.

He gave a quiet laugh and found the waist of the thong, worked it down her legs and off. "This is where I eat you until you scream, coming all over my face and begging me to pound my cock into your pussy. Do I have the story right?"

"Yes! Hurry!"

"I thought so. Now relax and give yourself over to me," he said seductively. "Trust me and I'll make you fly."

On his knees, he scooped his hands under her ass, lifted her off the bed, and brought her sex to his mouth. He had an image of feasting on a juicy watermelon in the summertime, and figured that to be a good analogy.

Pink, succulent flesh yielding to his will. Spilling its sweetness onto his taste buds, making him lap it up, loath to waste a drop. He stabbed his tongue deep into her sheath, fucking her that way, swirling, and out again, licking up to her clit. He repeated this several times and she began to thrash, harsh sounds breaking in her throat.

Not good enough. He wanted her mindless, all her control lost. So he fastened his mouth to her sex and began to suckle, ate her like a five-star banquet, relentless.

She began to vibrate in his hands, writhing. "Oh, shit! Jude, yes!"

He didn't let up and she bucked wildly, screamed so loud his ears rang. Salty-sweet cum splashed over his tongue and he devoured all she had to give.

"Fuck me!" she cried. "Please, fuck me!"

Lowering her once more, he groped for the foil packet, tore it open, and covered himself. Then he hooked her legs over his shoulders and impaled her in a single smooth glide.

Tamara was beyond coherent speech at this point, just what turned Jude on the most—a lover who was totally under his control, his to play with, fuck without mercy. Whatever he desired.

And Lily was still there. Riveted. He couldn't say how he knew, he just did. Her presence was palpable, the air supercharged. He could almost smell her arousal, and it brought out the feral male animal in him. Mastering one lover while another observed, hidden in the shadows.

He pumped his slick length into her with steady strokes,

holding back his orgasm as long as possible. His cock was on fire, balls tight and on the verge of detonation.

"Fuck," he muttered. "Goddamn! Can't hold back . . ."

Giving in, he hammered into her, plunging deep. The storm built, the familiar buzz starting at the base of his spine. His balls drew up and he exploded with a shout, filled her with his cum. He held himself seated to the balls until the spasms receded, leaving him empty. Satisfied.

And boneless, too. Smiling, he lowered her to the bed again, leaned over, and ran a hand up her arm, to her shoulder. When he found her face, he gave her a kiss on the cheek.

"Thank you, Tamara. You are amazing."

"Me? No way. You fucked me stupid." A yawn punctuated the statement.

"Stay for a while longer? Take a nap?"

"Then go for round two?"

"Give me a bit to recuperate, and you're on."

He sat up and removed the condom, tied it off, and tossed it in the direction of his clothes. He'd take care of it, and any others, later.

Much later. Spooning to Tamara's back, he realized he no longer sensed Lily's presence. Irrationally, he felt a little disappointed that she hadn't stayed. Maybe even joined them.

Good grief, give the woman a break! Her first day here and she walks into a lion's den.

He ought to consider himself fortunate that Lily was sexually open and hadn't already packed and run for the hills.

She wouldn't, either. He knew she was intrigued and would stay to build her place here.

And one day soon, she wouldn't be on the outside looking in.

. . .

Lily stood riveted, entranced by the sight of Jude's big body quivering over Tamara's. His thick cock buried in her pussy, the woman's long legs dangling over his muscled back.

He pulled out of his lover and Lily retreated into her room, hand over her pounding heart. She'd never witnessed anything so . . . so *raw*. Untamed.

And completely unrepentant. He'd known Lily was there. She'd made a noise and he'd turned his head slightly to the side, lips curving into a wicked smile. He hadn't faltered. Instead, he'd ravished the other woman like a starving man, with double the fervor.

Over and over, Lily's mind replayed Jude undressing her. Sucking her nipples. When Tamara had gone down on him, Lily longed to be the one taking his cock into her mouth, deep-throating him, pushing him to the edge. She could practically taste his earthy flavor, the salt and musk of him.

And when he'd spread the other woman wide and feasted on her . . . Lily shivered. In all her travels, all her dealings, she'd never played the voyeur before today. Spied on people who were breaking the law, yes. Not on people having sex. Never cared to because, to be honest, most of the men she ran across during her assignments just weren't that compelling. They were rich, lazy, spoiled. Crooked as hell, with few redeeming qualities.

Jude blew all her preconceptions out of the water.

The man was powerful. Exciting.

And her job entailed dousing that fire forever.

For once in her career, she couldn't reconcile the damning evidence and the task ahead of her with the man. The loss of self-assuredness scared her. She couldn't breathe.

Slipping on a short silk robe, she left her room, intent on taking a walk and regaining her equilibrium. But the film reel of Jude's glorious ass flexing as he drove into Tamara wouldn't leave her alone. He was everything Lily desired in a sexual partner and nothing she could have long-term.

She wandered aimlessly, locked in turmoil. To try to resist the lure of becoming part of Jude's lifestyle, his world, would be fruitless. She craved the pleasures he could give her like an addict craved another hit.

So she'd take all she could, for the time they had. Because he was a killer, she could justify and compartmentalize her actions. To survive, she had no choice.

With new resolve, she padded downstairs, feeling somewhat more settled. Not great, but less conflicted. In moments, she found herself in the sunroom, darkened now save for the light reflecting from the pool outside and bouncing around inside, where she stood. All was peaceful. Maybe she'd sit out there, or go for a skinny-dip.

The instant the idea formed, she caught a silhouette seated on the pool's lip. Liam's profile. The younger man's legs dangled into the water, arms braced on either side of him. He stared across the wide expanse before him, unmoving. A beautiful, naked statue carved of marble.

She was about to go outside when he slumped and hung his head. His long bangs hid his expression, but she didn't need to see it to read the emotions when he rested his elbows on his thighs and buried his face in his hands. Pain rolled off him like blood from a mortal wound. Backing away, she respected his privacy, though she wondered.

What was Liam's story? Why was he so upset?

Earlier, he'd given no indication anything was wrong. Seemed as though she wasn't the only one around who had learned to compartmentalize—or was trying, and miserably failing.

Little did Liam know how she empathized.

She made herself scarce, wishing she could force Liam's silent agony from her mind. *Oh, sweetie. The pain you feel now? That's nothing.*

In less than four weeks, you'll learn your first real lesson in loss. Disillusionment. And you'll never forgive me.

But he'd survive.

Like Lily, he'd have no choice.

Six

The man's head was centered in his crosshairs.

The hot desert sun scorched his skin right through his shirt, but he was cold inside. Dead.

Almost as dead as the man in his sights.

He was exhausted and ready to catch his flight for home.

Concentrate. Business first. Always.

Anger filled the void in his soul and he tightened his finger on the trigger. Assholes like these were cockroaches. For every one he killed, there were thousands to take his place.

But he'd take out this one, let God sort the rest.

The man's skull exploded and he folded like a puppet with its strings cut, bright blood splattered on the sand like droplets of rain. Pooling around his head.

Mouth open, eyes accusing—

Jude gasped and bolted upright, confused by the dark veil over his vision where there had been death moments before. A horrible scene in living color, vanished in an instant. Where was the dead man? *Where am I?*

Gradually, he came to his senses. He was sitting up in bed, clutching a sheet to his sweaty chest. And he was still blind.

"Another fucking nightmare," he muttered to himself, swiping a shaking hand down his face.

Pain throbbed at his temples, squeezed his brain in a vise. Dammit, he needed his medicine if he hoped to stave off a full-blown migraine. He swung his legs over the side of the bed and stood, only to be broadsided by a wave of dizziness that knocked him on his ass.

He flopped onto his back, legs dangling over the side, and breathed through the sickness roiling in his belly. Too late. No way could he make it to the bathroom to get his capsule. Clutching his head, he curled onto his side in the fetal position, determined to ride it out.

Dimly, he became aware of the mattress dipping with someone's weight. A hand smoothing his hair.

"Are you all right?" Liam asked quietly. "Do you need a pill?"

"God, yes. Please."

"Hang tight, man."

Jude almost groaned at the loss of the soothing touch as the other man retreated. In the bathroom, the medicine bottle rattled and the faucet ran briefly. Then Liam returned, helped him sit up, and pressed a glass into his hand.

"Thanks," he said, voice raspy.

"No problem."

Liam placed the capsule in his open palm and Jude downed the thing, hating the inevitable stupor to come. But it was either oblivion or puking for hours until he passed out anyway. Some choice.

Liam took the glass from him and set it on the nightstand. "Lie down again and be still."

"Like I have another option?"

"I wish you did, my friend."

"Me, too."

Jude settled on his pillow and closed his eyes, giving a sigh as his friend continued stroking his hair. "Your fingers are magic."

"You know better than anyone."

In spite of the drill bit boring into his skull, Jude smiled. "Maybe not better than Lily."

Liam froze. "You know?"

"I'm blind, kid, not deaf." Damn, that had come out awfully short.

"Jude, I'm sorry. I—I—"

"What's this?" Reaching for the other man, he found his knee and gave a reassuring squeeze. "We've never apologized to each other for indulging our appetites and there's no reason to start now."

"Yeah? Well, don't growl at me next time." His tone reminded Jude of a sulky boy.

"What? I did not."

"Afraid so."

Despite the sledgehammer pounding behind his eyes, he thought back. "Okay, maybe I did. It's this damned headache."

He had snarled, a little, not just because of the migraine. For some reason, knowing his friend and sometime lover had taken Lily first, four days ago, annoyed the hell out of him. No, it sort of pissed him off, truth be told. Which wasn't fair to Liam.

"It's all right," Liam said, sounding mollified.

"No, I make the rules. I ought to be able to live by them. I'm the one who owes you an apology, and I'm sorry."

"Forget it." The hand resumed stroking his hair. "You're in no shape to get worked up."

"I don't like arguing with you."

"Shh, we didn't argue," Liam soothed. "Sleep."

"Don't know if I can." Even as he made the claim, his body sank into the bed, the medicinal fuzz taking the edge off the pain and making his friend seem miles away. "That goddamned nightmare . . ."

"They're getting worse." A statement, not a question.

"I can't escape them," he said hoarsely. "They're brutal, frightening, and they make no sense."

"What was it this time?"

"I killed a man." His big frame shuddered. "In cold blood. I was perched atop a building in some small desert town with a rifle and scope. Blew his brains out and the worst part was . . . I was glad to exterminate him."

Liam's voice cracked. "God, Jude."

"The dreams aren't always that bad." No, sometimes they were worse. What his sweet, sensitive friend didn't know was for the best.

"If you say so."

He didn't sound convinced, and Jude didn't have the heart to lie. Instead, he drifted off to the comforting lull of Liam's fingers raking through the strands of his hair, as he wondered what type of man dreamed of murdering other people without remorse.

And whether they were nightmares at all.

· · ·

Lily glanced up from her computer to see Liam hovering in the office doorway.

He gave her a wan smile. "Emerging from e-mail hell yet?"

"Getting caught up. What's the matter?"

"Nothing, I . . . shit," he sighed, unhappy. "Jude won't be working today. He had a nightmare and now he's down with one of those bastard migraines."

She pushed back from the screen, straightening. "Oh, no. What can I do for him?"

"Not much except to help me check on him, if you don't mind. I've got to run to the store later and get groceries."

"Of course. I'll keep an eye on him." She was afraid to ask the next question, but she had to know for her report to Dietz. "Have any idea what the nightmare was about?"

He nodded, mouth in a grim line. "He killed a man, in his dream. Shot him in cold blood. That's what a lot of them are about," he whispered, shaking his head. "Death. Killing. Sometimes at his hands, other times at someone else's. Almost as soon as I got him home from the hospital, it started. Though they're getting worse, and it's harder for him to recover after each episode. It's as though he's being torn apart."

She stared at Liam, stomach flipping. If she'd needed more proof, she had it—Jude's memories were trying to return. Despite her reluctance to administer the first dose, she couldn't delay much longer. Either Jude would remember or Dietz would call her on the carpet for neglecting her orders.

Either way, she'd be a dead woman.

She met Liam's worried gaze. "Has he seen anyone for counseling?"

He made a face. "Jude? You're talking about the same guy who used to vanish for weeks and reappear without an explanation. He's not exactly the type to share secrets."

"Right." And thank God for that. She hated to think of some poor, unsuspecting psychiatrist being silenced by Dietz. Never mind doctor-patient confidentiality.

She'd be damned lucky if Dietz didn't focus on Liam as a potential threat to security.

"Anyway, I'd better run," he said, glancing away. "You need anything from the store?"

"More of that wonderful Malbec you served with dinner the other night?"

"Done."

"Liam . . . are you all right? Other than being worried about Jude." Standing, she went to him, laid a hand on his chest. His heart thrummed a mad tempo under her palm.

"I'm not sure what you mean." His body language said something else.

"You've barely made eye contact with me since our fun by the pool. Was it so terrible?"

"What? No!" He pulled her into a hard hug, then drew back and looked into her eyes, appearing genuinely shocked. "I loved being with you, and I'd do it again. I've just had a lot on my mind."

"It's nothing I've done?"

He shook his head, kissed the corner of her mouth. "I swear. Sorry I haven't been myself, but I'm doing my best to shake off this weird mood."

"Anything I can do to speed things along?" she asked suggestively. One male nipple hardened, poking her palm through his T-shirt.

"Later?" His smile softened the rejection. "I guess I'm not in the right head space lately."

"I won't push. But if you need a friend—"

"I know. Thanks." He gave her another hug and extricated himself gently. "Gotta go."

Watching him retreat, she sighed. What would happen to him after Jude was gone? She'd suggest bringing him into SHADO's main compound, but what use would they have for a chef? Perhaps Michael could think of something. All she knew was the idea of leaving Liam alone, grieving, and out of a job did not sit well.

Yet coming up with a solution might not matter when Liam hated her guts.

She squashed the pang of regret and returned to her e-mail, still amazed at the amount of correspondence Jude received. She scheduled a couple of charity events and dinner with an acquaintance, rescheduled a meeting with an architect regarding renovation of a building Jude had purchased, and answered several pleas for donations. Seemed her "boss" was a generous man to those less fortunate.

What an irony.

Two hours passed with record speed and Lily blinked at the clock. She'd promised to check on Jude and she had no idea how long the other man had been gone.

She hurried out, heels clicking on the tiles, then digging into the carpet as she ascended the stairs. Too bad she couldn't go barefoot, but she couldn't dress down when anyone might stop by to see Jude.

What wasn't underneath the clothing didn't count.

She reached Jude's bedroom to find the door cracked a bit, so she pushed it open and tiptoed inside. His big body lay sprawled on his stomach, sheets tangled around long legs, a slice of tanned, bare ass making her mouth water and fantasies run rampant.

Too bad the man was out of commission or she might be tempted to caress that delectable rump, see whether she could entice him to finish what he'd started between them the other day.

Considering her mission, however, perhaps it was better that he remain distracted by Liam and Tamara.

The thought depressed her and she shook it off, walking over silently to check and make certain he wasn't in distress. He slept soundly, auburn hair spilling over his face, lips parted slightly. He looked so young and vulnerable, though she knew he was anything but.

"Why couldn't you have been one of the good guys?" she whispered, aching at the sight of him.

But he wasn't, and with Liam gone, his boss unconscious, she had a prime opportunity to extend her search beyond the previous boundaries.

Where . . . ? Her eyes fell upon his walk-in closet, the door ajar. A tingle went up her spine and she crossed toward it. Was it possible?

The master closet didn't share a wall with Lily's room. Instead, it was situated across his room, on the outer corner of the house, on the wall with the window overlooking the pool. His office on the first floor was directly below.

The familiar thrill of the hunt warmed her blood. She was on to something. Easing inside, she flipped on the light, careful not to make too much noise. The space was so huge it could've served as a pro football team's locker room.

Suits, jeans, slacks, and shirts—both dressy and casual—

lined the walls on rods. Shoes of all types were parked on several rows of shelving, four pairs wide. Doing a double take at the clothing, she realized the outfits were organized by color and style, pants and the appropriate shirts hanging together. Liam had likely done this so Jude wouldn't have to worry about trying to match his things.

The care and consideration that had gone into his gift brought unexpected tears to her eyes. With a quiet sniff, she began checking cubbies and boxes, what few there were. The closet was pristine, free of the typical clutter one might expect to find.

Next she pushed hangers aside, disturbing the clothing as little as possible. As she'd done in Jude's office, she checked the walls of the space for seams, hollow places. What was unusual about the closet was the detailed molding work. People normally put effort into such decor in a living or dining room, not a place guests wouldn't really see.

The molding formed long, vertical panels more than six feet tall and three feet wide, which, in itself, aroused her suspicion. She pressed on each one with no luck, and was about to quit when one panel gave under her palm.

Pay dirt! Suddenly nervous, she went and peeked at Jude to find he hadn't budged an inch. His soft snore reassured her and she returned to her task.

The panel was located in the perfect spot should it conceal a small hidden room—at the corner of the house where no one would notice the discrepancy in the scant number of feet between the panel and the outside of the house. Not in a million years.

Her excitement grew as she gave a quiet knock. Definitely not solid. But if it opened, where was the spring? "Come on," she muttered, pushing all around the inside edge of the panel. No luck. In frustration, she leaned against the right-hand strip of molding.

And the whole piece popped inward. In surprise, she jerked away and it popped out again, spring-loaded. The entire panel slid neatly and almost soundlessly to the left, revealing a metal ladder facing her, affixed to the brick.

"Holy shit," she breathed. "Robin, I think we found the Bat Cave."

She peered over the edge. The ladder descended into darkness and, she bet, to Jude's "war room" underground. There, she was likely to find one or both of the missing encrypted files.

A groan from the bedroom kicked her pulse into overdrive. Cursing her bad luck, she pushed the strip again and the panel slid into place once more. She'd have to return when the coast was clear, but at least she'd made progress.

Glancing around to be sure all was as she'd found it, she turned off the light and moved stealthily out into the bedroom. Jude was sitting up on the side of his bed, back to her, stretching and obviously trying to wake up.

She was halfway to escape when he stiffened. "Who's there?"

God, he must have the supersonic hearing of an owl. She cleared her throat. "It's me, Lily."

He turned his head toward her, a slight frown on his handsome face. "What are you doing?"

"I came to check on you like I'd promised Liam."

His expression cleared and he made no attempt to cover himself. "Oh. Well, that was sweet. I hope my being naked doesn't bother you."

"Not in the way you mean, which I believe we've established," she said, smiling. "How do you feel?"

"Surprisingly, much better. I'm usually out for the day when it hits, but the nap and the meds seem to have done the trick."

Lily closed the distance between them. The proof of how much better he felt jutted from between his thighs. Licking her lips, she wondered if he always got morning wood.

"I—I'm glad. No more nightmares?"

"None that I recall." But his posture tensed, shoulders hunched as though to weather a blow.

Seemed she'd touched a nerve. Was he telling the truth? She thought so, but it was hard to say.

She brushed a stray lock of fiery hair from his face. "Liam told me about it earlier. Are you sure you're all right?"

"I am now. No problem."

She had her doubts. He fell quiet for a few moments, clutching the bedcovers. "Right. That's the same load of bull I'm getting from Liam."

"Well, then, that should tell you I'm fine. He knows me better than anyone."

"I'm not talking about *you*. I'm talking about Liam."

He frowned. "What do you mean?"

"Are you completely oblivious to anyone but yourself? No matter what he claims, *he's* not fine at all. Haven't you sensed something's not as it should be with him?"

After a moment's hesitation, he nodded. "I suppose so," he said slowly. "Now that you mention it. Has he confided in you?"

"No. I asked him, but he doesn't know me well enough to feel comfortable sharing whatever's bothering him."

"Yet he's plenty comfortable enough to share other parts of himself with you," he said shortly.

Warmth spread in her tummy. "And that bothers you?"

"Yes, and no." He gave a soft laugh. "I don't know why it should confuse me. It's not as though Liam and I haven't shared lovers before."

"I'm not your lover," she pointed out.

"Yet." Then he lay back on the bed, propping himself up on his elbows. Slowly and deliberately, he let his legs fall open, treating her to a delicious pose. "But that can be remedied."

A mischievous half smile curved his lips, green eyes visible through the fiery hair falling all around his face. The corded muscles of his chest, stomach, and biceps stood out in relief, bunched under golden skin. His long, thick cock rested on his belly, heavy balls nestled underneath.

"Are you trying to memorize me, honey?"

He knew she was ogling, damn him. "You have no idea."

"Really? Why don't you come here? I'll give you something to remember me by."

Oh, God.

"My memory is excellent."

"Tactile experience will sharpen it even more," he said, playful.

He looked positively wicked. And so sure of himself, confident in his sexuality. He seemed certain she'd cave, give them what they both wanted.

And the son of a bitch was right.

Lily stepped out of her heels, unbuttoned her blouse, and shrugged it off. Next, she unzipped her skirt, let it fall to the floor, and went to stand between his spread knees, ran her hands up his strong thighs.

"If you're not as naked as I am, you're overdressed," he said, holding out a hand to her.

She took it, crawling up with him. "No worries. I've wanted

to be with you like this for days." That much was the absolute truth. "You enjoy anticipation, don't you?"

"Guilty. I believe good sex, like fine wine, was meant to be savored. Held on the palate and sipped until you become intoxicated with the richness of it."

A vivid picture of him eating Tamara, fucking her, rose in her mind and she had to agree he was fantastic at savoring and sipping. "I've never heard anyone put it quite like that. I'd like to savor *you*."

"I'm at your mercy," he said in a low voice. "Don't let me stop you."

Taking advantage, she stretched out next to him and raked her fingers through his silky hair as she'd been itching to do, enjoying its weight and texture. The other palm she skimmed across his chest, pleased at how his nipples tightened under her touch.

She bent and tasted them, pulled and nipped each one. Jude sucked in a breath but didn't move, simply allowed her to explore at will. Moving south, she admired his flat stomach that, like the rest of him, evidenced time in the workout room. But the real prize was the package between his legs, and she crawled between them for better access.

Lord, he was big. He'd probably brought ecstasy to many lovers with that huge cock. God knew he'd made Tamara scream. For the first time, she imagined him impaling Liam's pretty ass, sliding deep, making the sexy younger man cry out. . . .

Lily's body ignited. Fire flared in her pussy and she grasped Jude's organ, pumping the base in a firm grip. He moaned, arched his back, seeking more. Pre-cum leaked from the bulbous head, the shaft flushed a purplish red.

"Want to know what I'm thinking?" she asked.

"Y-yes, honey. Tell me."

"I'm picturing you fucking Liam." A hearty groan punctuated her statement as she continued to stroke. "You've fucked him, haven't you?"

"Yes, I have."

"Do you love bending him over, splitting his ass with this huge cock? Being buried deep inside him?"

"God, yes," he rasped. "He's an incredible lover, as you well know."

She laughed softly. "That I do. Tell me something. . . . Could I watch, the next time you fuck him?" She'd show Jude anticipation. She was going to drive him crazy. Bending, she licked the head of his cock, tasting the salty drops.

He hissed, making a visible effort to control the thrust of his hips. "I'll go one better. You can join us."

A thrill went through her at the idea, but she hesitated, thinking of Liam and whatever was troubling him. "Will he mind?"

"I have a feeling he'll welcome the suggestion with open arms. He's already becoming quite fond of you, in case you weren't aware."

"I feel the same about him. You'll ask him?"

"Just try to stop me now that you've put the delicious thought in my head."

"Good."

Putting aside the talk for now, she licked his shaft from base to tip. Then she suckled his testicles, rolling them between her fingers to heighten his pleasure. From his writhing and the increasing throaty noises, she was succeeding.

When she slid his cock between her lips, sucking him down, he bucked, called out her name. His girth filled her mouth, stretched her so wide she couldn't possibly take him all the way down her throat, but she took all she was able.

It was enough. After several pulls, he gently pushed her back. "You're going to make me go too soon, baby. Want to last." Sitting up, he said, "I want you on your hands and knees."

Lily shivered. She was no stranger to sex, but rarely did she allow a man to take such a dominant position. And this man was nothing if not in command. But the quiver she felt was one of excitement, not dread. He wanted this, and she couldn't wait to give it to him.

She assumed the position, poking her ass out and spreading her knees. Her pussy was wet, burning at the knowledge that she'd willingly made herself vulnerable to whatever he wanted. She wanted this powerful man for herself, splitting *her* pussy, *her* ass.

Whatever he desired.

Jude fumbled in the bedside table for a moment, taking out a condom and small bottle of lube. Items in hand, he carefully moved around behind her, touching her side to guide him.

Fingers skimmed down her spine to the crease in her rear. A cap snicked open and she gasped as cool gel squirted onto the puckered entrance of her ass.

"I'm only going to give you my fingers here, this time," he reassured her. "I'm not sure you're ready to take me this way."

"I've been fucked like that before, but not in a while." And never by anyone as big as Jude.

"Relax and let me savor, hmm? Just feel."

A lubed finger worked into her hole, past the tight ring of muscle. The strange pinch was accompanied by the peculiar warmth that quickly became pleasure, spreading tendrils of heat to her clit. The bud throbbed as a second finger joined the first, stretching her bit by bit.

He shifted and his tongue laved her slit, soft and warm.

"Oh!"

Lily couldn't help but arch into him, swept away by the naughty act—a man finger-fucking her ass while eating her from behind. Her body hummed, the sensations almost too much.

"You have such a sweet cunt, baby," he whispered against the bare lips of her sex. "Juicy like a ripe peach. Want me to eat your peach, baby?"

"Yes! Please, yes!"

The rasp of his tongue against her skin fanned the flames higher. Then it dipped between her folds, licking at her cream, fucking her channel in tempo with the fingers tunneling in her ass. Angling his head, he found her clit and fastened his mouth to the nub, suckling, shorting out her nerve endings.

"Jude," she gasped. "Oh, God, I'm going to come!"

"You'll come on my cock, honey. Wait for me." His fingers left her ass, and the condom wrapper crinkled.

Grasping her hips, he positioned the head of his cock between her soaked pussy lips and began to push into her channel. His rod was scorching hot, stretching her impossibly wide, filling her as she'd never been filled before.

"Goddamn, you're tight and you're so small," he groaned. "Am I hurting you?"

"No, don't stop."

"Thank God."

He continued in a slow, sensuous glide, until they were locked together, groin to ass. His balls were snuggled against her sex, fingers digging into her flesh. His cock was a torch inside her, setting them both aflame.

"Fuck me, Jude. Oh, please . . ." Was that her voice, begging?

"Shit, yeah. But I'm not going to last long."

"Just do it!"

He pulled out to the head, pushed in again, slow, torturing them both. Out, slow, then in. She backed into him, impaling herself, urging him to go faster, give them what they needed.

His strokes became harder, deeper. They panted together, bodies slapping as he fucked her fast and hard now, driving her mindless. Nothing mattered but his cock hammering into her, claiming her as his.

Her clit began to pulse and her orgasm exploded. "Oh, yes! Jude!"

With a guttural cry, he buried his cock deep and held there, heat spilling into her. Her sex convulsed around him, milking every last drop as his big body shuddered again and again.

At last, he pulled out with a sigh of regret. Wrung-out, she flopped onto her back and watched him remove the condom, tie it off, and pitch it over the side of the bed.

When he lay beside her and opened his arms, it seemed like the most natural thing in the world to cuddle against his side and pillow her head in the crook of his shoulder.

"Being with you was even more awesome that I imagined it would be," he said quietly, kissing the top of her head. "Thank you."

"Same here, and no thanks necessary. I don't plan on it being the last time."

He chuckled. "Woman after my own heart."

For some reason, Lily's throat tightened and something hitched in the region of *her* heart. Sex had never made her so emotional before.

It couldn't be because he was the most extraordinary man—not to mention lover—she'd ever met.

Or because he was nothing she'd been told to expect.

And certainly not because he'd put her comfort above his own lust.

"Jude?"

"Mmm?"

"When you asked me if you were hurting me . . . if I'd said yes, would you have stopped?"

"What?" He sounded surprised by the question. "Of course I would have. Contrary to what you might believe, I *do* think of others besides myself. I take care of the people close to me."

She swallowed hard. "I apologize. I suppose I'm not used to a man like you."

"Whatever that means." He snorted, hugging her close. "And I *will* find out what's wrong with Liam, now that I'm fully aware something's up."

"I shouldn't have implied otherwise," she said.

"No worries. Let's take a nap before we face the rest of the day, shall we?"

"Okay."

Listening to Jude's heart thump under her ear, Lily realized she'd never felt so safe in her entire life. So complete.

Or so hopelessly confused.

This man was a good man, one worthy of respect. Love. This man deserved to have a life, based on who he was *now*.

But what about the monster he was before?

Lily drifted off with visions of blood, death, and heartbreak tormenting her mind.

Seven

Jude leaned forward on his stool, arm sweeping bold, angry strokes across the canvas.

"Jude, are you attacking that thing or painting?" Somewhere in front of him, Tamara wiggled on her mound of pillows. He felt her curious stare, heard the concern hidden behind the humor in her voice.

"Damned if I know." Frustrated, he set aside his brush. "This isn't working."

"Can I help?"

"I don't think so." He hung his head, blowing out a frustrated breath. Today, she couldn't hope to touch the darkness inside him, threatening to swallow him whole. Making love with Lily yesterday had earned him a brief and much-welcome reprieve. Last night, however, had brought horror to his dreams again.

Hold up—is that what Lily and I did? Made love?

As he tried to wrap his mind around that idea, slender arms snaked around his neck. Tamara pushed close, maneuvering to stand between his knees, pressed her breasts to his chest.

"Are you sure? I bet I can find a cure for that sad face," she said, almost purring.

"I'm sure you could, but . . ."

Clever fingers unsnapped his cargo shorts, burrowed inside to grasp his cock. She kissed his jaw, rubbed against him like a cat, skillfully played with him. A nice buzz began in his groin and he became half-hard.

And then nothing. He couldn't dredge up the desire to give her what she sought, and it wasn't fair to drag her into the pit with his black mood. Gently, he disentangled himself and removed her questing hand from his shorts.

"Sorry, beautiful, I'm not good company and I'm sure not getting anything accomplished. Rain check?"

"If that's what you want," she said with a tinge of disappointment. "Call me?"

"Sure."

Neither of them believed he would.

As soon as she dressed and left, he tossed aside the almost-completed nude she'd been posing for, grabbed a blank canvas, and let his demons loose.

He ditched the soft flesh and earth tones for tints of red and orange, shades of black. What he couldn't see with his eyes, his mind saw clearly enough: rivers of blood, broken bodies, brain matter, vacant eyes.

The weight of a ghost rifle replaced the brush to fill his hands, familiar and terrible. As awful as the knowledge that he was capable of taking out his target from a mile away and vanishing before anyone was the wiser.

Is this what I am?

A killer? A monster?

Why is this happening to me?

Pressure built in his chest, constricting his lungs as he slashed at the canvas, too massive to contain. Pushing outward, crushing him, until the rage exploded.

"*Why?*" he bellowed.

Grabbing the wooden frame, he smashed the canvas over the easel and kicked it, sending the whole structure flying. He whirled, subjecting his table full of paints, brushes, palettes, and thinners to the same treatment. They hit the floor with a resounding crash, which served only to fuel the madness rather than abating it.

Yelling his despair, he lunged toward the models' stage area, searching for something else to destroy. Just as his life had been destroyed. His entire world.

He tripped over a chair, righted himself, picked the fucking thing up, and hurled it as hard as he could. Glass shattered in a huge, satisfying crash, but it still wasn't enough.

He stalked toward the tinkling sound of falling glass, hardly aware of the sting on the soles of his feet. Intent only on finding something else to obliterate.

His foot snagged on something—a cord?—upsetting his balance. With his forward momentum, he couldn't stop his fall. On reflex, he thrust his arms out in front of him as his body hurtled through jagged teeth that tore at his shirt, his skin. The air rushed from his lungs as he hit the ground hard and lay prone on the grass.

He was on his lawn? Which meant he'd taken out a section of the wall-to-ceiling glass in his studio. And plunged through the opening.

"My God, Jude!" Liam shouted. "What the fuck?"

He didn't answer. Couldn't think past the whirling cacophony in his head. The rage, the pain, that had nowhere to go.

Liam was crouched at his side in an instant, helping him to sit up. Strong arms encircled him from behind, hugging his chest. "Jesus Christ, what are you doing?"

"I don't know." He tried to breathe through the insanity, regain his balance. "There's death all around me, *because* of me, and I can't get away from it—"

"Easy, boss," his friend whispered. "I've got you. They're just nightmares, and you're letting them get to you."

He shook his head, clasped his trembling hands. "No. I think . . . maybe they're real. I have a rifle in my hands, and I know how to kill. I'm good at it, damned good."

Liam hugged him tighter. "Doesn't necessarily mean anything. You've been through a terrible ordeal, and—"

"I'm a monster," he said, almost too low to hear.

"What? No," Liam countered fiercely. "You're my best friend, the finest man I know."

His voice broke. "There's something wrong with me. I've done terrible things, maybe on those trips when I didn't tell you where I was going."

"I refuse to believe that."

"Why didn't I just die?" The plaintive question was out before he could stop it, but what did it matter? It was how he felt.

Liam scooted to face him, taking Jude's cheeks in his hands. "Don't ever say that again, do you hear me?"

The younger man's lips moved against his, warm and pliant. Jude melted, a helpless sound escaping his throat. The turmoil inside eased as his friend swept his tongue into his mouth, deepening the kiss. This was what he needed right now, not some fling with a lover like Tamara, nice as she might be.

He needed someone to assuage the hurt in his soul, someone

he really cared about, who cared for him in return. Liam was a lifeline, had been there for him these past four years.

Their tongues tangled, the other man's stroking the roof of his mouth, behind his teeth. Jude drank him in, reveling in his taste. A hint of a sweet treat he'd been making for dessert, perhaps. His erection hardened, no longer uncooperative, but eager to penetrate. To own the body pressed to his.

Liam broke the kiss first, trailing his fingers down Jude's cheek. "We need to get you cleaned up. You're bleeding."

"Where?"

"Your neck and right arm got a couple of scratches." He moved down Jude's torso to his legs, checking every inch. "Small ones on the bottoms of your feet, too."

"Damn. Yeah, they're starting to sting some."

"Come on." Grasping Jude's hand, Liam pulled him up. "Take my arm. Considering the mess you made, it'll be faster than finding your cane."

"God, I'm sorry," he muttered, ashamed. "No telling how long it will take the housekeeper to clean up, and I can't even be of help."

"Forget about that—just leave it to us. I'll call a window and glass company after I get you patched, and they'll have it fixed in no time."

"You're too good to me, buddy."

"I know."

Liam's quiet laugh made him feel marginally better, even though Jude had no clue how long the demons would be held at bay. He had a feeling the break wouldn't last, but he'd take what comfort he could find.

"Can't go in through the smashed window because of your

bare feet. We'll have to enter through the kitchen so you don't track blood on the carpet."

Liam led him carefully around the side of the house to the kitchen's entrance. Wonderful aromas scented the air and Jude began to ask about dinner, but was distracted by another thought.

"Where's Lily? I can't believe she didn't hear the commotion."

"She's not here. She borrowed the Mercedes and drove into the city to run a couple of errands. It *is* okay that I let her take your car, isn't it?" Worry colored his friend's voice.

"Yes, of course." He was beyond grateful she hadn't been around to witness his meltdown.

"Good. I should've asked first, though, or let her borrow mine."

"Why? The Mercedes is more yours now than it is mine. I'm not likely to jump in the damned thing and take off."

"Jude . . ."

He grimaced. "I know. Sorry."

Liam hated his bitter sarcasm. God knew Jude did his best to stay positive, but on days like this one, it wasn't easy.

Holding on to Liam's arm, he let the man lead him out of the kitchen and down the tiled hallway. Instead of taking the stairs, however, they continued past.

"My room is closer," his friend explained. "And it's not far across the carpet from the door to the bathroom, so there will be less to scrub."

Finally, they made it into Liam's bathroom without mishap. "How do you want me?"

"Naked."

Jude grinned. "A plan I can get behind."

"Literally, I can tell," Liam said in appreciation, squeezing

Jude's erection through his shorts. "First we have to take care of those scratches. Back up and park your butt on the counter."

Releasing his crotch, Liam guided him backward. Jude braced his palms on the edge of the counter and hopped up, scooting into a comfortable position. Or as comfortable as he could be with his cock aching to be freed.

"Take off your T-shirt," Liam ordered. A cabinet opened near Jude's head and the other man rummaged through the contents.

Jude did as he was told, laying the shirt aside. He waited, listening to items being placed on the counter. The faucet came on and was quickly turned off, the water squeezed from a cloth, he imagined.

"These aren't bad." Liam dabbed at the side of his neck. "The skin here is barely broken. The one on your arm is worse."

The other man turned his attention to that wound, gently wiping his forearm, then moving on to his feet. With a soft whistle, he picked up something metallic and began to probe the bottom of Jude's left foot, admonishing him to be still.

"What is it?"

"Piece of glass in here, about the size of a nickel."

"No wonder it hurts." Jude hissed as his friend probed with the tweezers.

"Man, you ought to let me take you in to get this checked. It might need stitches."

"Forget it," he said tersely. "I've had far worse."

Silence. It grew heavy as they both mulled over what he'd said without even thinking.

Liam's voice was taut with concern. "When?"

"I—I'm not sure. I don't even know why I said that."

As his friend continued working to remove the shard, Jude

was assailed by confusion and doubt. The words had spilled forth from his subconscious, and the implication combined with his visions scared the hell out of him.

"There, it's out. I'm going to clean these with alcohol, bandage that foot and your arm—then you'll be ready to run laps."

So, the younger man wasn't going to make an issue of either the wound or his comment, thank Christ. Just as well, since Jude didn't know what to say.

Liam was quick and efficient, taking care of him, fingers gentle, the heat of his body so near. After he'd finished and washed his hands, he came to stand between Jude's spread knees, placing his palms on Jude's chest.

Jude slid off the counter and cupped Liam's ass, bringing their erections together, rubbing. The delicious friction had them both moaning, straining to get as close as possible. Liam claimed his mouth again, treating him to a long, passionate kiss, then broke away and dropped to his knees.

"I want to taste your cock," he said hoarsely.

"Like I'm going to stop you?"

His shorts were undone and pulled down his legs, and he stepped out of them, widening his stance, making certain the younger man had complete access.

"You beautiful son of a bitch," Liam whispered.

And swallowed Jude's cock down his throat. His hot mouth bathed Jude's length, electrifying him, sending sparks of delight to every limb. Jude fisted his hands in Liam's hair, fucking the sweet cavern slowly, imagining how great it would be to watch those sensual lips gliding along his dick. Feasting on his shaft, making his blood boil in his veins.

The younger man manipulated Jude's balls as he sucked, driving him too close to the edge, and he yanked on Liam's hair. "Lube," he rasped. "I want in you *now*."

"Fuck, yes."

Liam rummaged a bit more. "Got it."

"Make me ready."

Liam's excited breaths, the snap of the tube, were the only sounds as he squirted gel onto Jude's cock. A fist encircled his shaft, slicking it. God, he was so ready he wanted to throw Liam against the wall and rut like an animal.

"Enough. Now prepare yourself for me," Jude commanded, low and rough.

Liam let go of him and, from the noisy sucking sounds, did as he was told. Spread his own ass, stretched the tight channel, making ready for his lover.

"Done."

Jude reached out, found the other man's hip. "Brace your hands on the counter, legs spread wide." Liam complied, taking hold of Jude's wrist to guide him into place. "Good. Now just relax and give yourself to me."

"I always have," he said softly.

Yes, he had. Without fail, his loyal friend had been there for him, had helped him weather every storm.

Jude parted Liam's firm ass and brought the head of his cock to the tight opening. Grasping Liam's hips, he pushed into his lover's body. All the way in, burying himself deep.

"Ahh, fuck, yes!" He leaned over, kissed the younger man's shoulder. Ground his balls into that delectable ass. "God, you feel so good. You hug my cock so fine."

"Move, please," Liam begged, arching into him. "Take my ass."

"Yes."

"It's yours."

"Mine."

"God, yes! Fuck me!"

Moments like this, Jude was goddamned glad that he didn't have to worry about taking Liam bareback. For convenience, since Liam lived on the estate and sex between them was spontaneous, they got tested regularly and used protection with their other playmates, without exception.

He began to shaft his lover's ass, savored each long thrust, not able to get enough of the scorching vise driving him insane. He pumped into that velvet glove, sure and hard, losing his mind a little. Hammered home, thrusting furiously.

Reaching around, he fisted Liam's cock, stroking in tempo to their movements. He wanted the other man to get off, wanted to feel him lose control.

"Come with me," Jude ordered. "Let me feel you."

"Oh! I—please, please!" He began to shake. "Harder!"

Jude slammed deep several more times, and then his balls drew up tight, the hum gathering in the base of his spine.

"Gonna come inside you . . . so deep."

"Ah, God!"

Jude exploded, jetting his release inside the hot channel as Liam cried out, ass fluttering, milking his cock. They shuddered together for endless moments, floating down gradually, the sound of their harsh breathing echoing in the bathroom. Neither of them cared to part.

Jude kissed his lover between the shoulder blades, liking the earthy, male essence of salt on his lips. The other man tilted his head back, nuzzled Jude's neck.

"I needed that, thanks," Liam said.

"Me, too."

"I'm glad I can be here for you when you need . . . you know." His tone sounded wistful. A bit sad.

Jude nipped his shoulder. "No, I don't know."

"Well, s-sometimes a guy just needs a warm body."

"Is that all you believe you are to me? A good fuck?" he asked, frowning.

Liam didn't answer. Reluctantly, Jude pulled out and turned his friend to face him, hoping he could see the sincerity there. "Listen to me. It's easy to use a carnal word such as *fuck* in the heat of passion, but make no mistake—I don't fuck you. I make love to you. Always have."

His friend sniffed, sounded choked up. "If so, you're the only one."

"That's crazy." Jude brushed that plump mouth with a soft kiss, then pulled the other man close. "Suppose you tell me what this is all about?"

"Wh-what do you mean?"

"Come on, my friend. This is me, remember? I know when you aren't yourself."

Liam tried unsuccessfully to push away. "I'm all right."

"No, you aren't."

He tensed, then relaxed with a heavy sigh. "I don't guess you'd have any advice for a guy who's in the throes of unrequited love?"

"Someone has hurt you?" He'd snap the neck of the un-fortunate asshole who screwed with Liam's head.

"Relax, man. They don't know how I feel," he replied softly.

"They? As in an established couple?"

"Yeah."

"Damn." He laid his hands on Liam's shoulders. "Must you do everything the hard way, kid?"

"Like you can talk."

"This isn't about me. I—"

"Oh, it sort of is," he said, bitterness coloring his voice. Just as quickly, his tone changed to apologetic. "I'm sorry. Forget I said that. The crappy state of my love life isn't your fault."

"I'm confused. How am I involved? Tell me what's going on!"

"Forget it. Things will either work out or they won't, okay?" His tone begged Jude to drop the subject.

"Just tell me one thing—am I involved because you're in love with me?" he asked gently. "Because, Liam, I—"

"No," he interrupted, placing his fingers over Jude's lips. "There are all types of love, and what we have is special, but it's not romantic love. Not what I feel for . . ."

"I understand that part at least. When you're ready to talk about the rest, I'm here to listen." It was all he could do, and he felt rather helpless.

"Thanks." Liam pushed away, and this time Jude let him. When Liam spoke again, his voice was quiet. Thoughtful. "Speaking of relationships, have you fu—made love to Lily?"

The distinction in terms didn't escape him. "Yes. Does that upset you?"

"Of course not."

Jude smiled. "Seems our Lily was being straight about sharing our kinks. She—oh, crap."

"What?"

"I sort of promised her that she could join us the next time you and I were together. Would you like that, all of us making love?"

"Yeah, man. That'll be freaking hot!" Liam poked his chest, good cheer restored. "Except we didn't wait for her."

"A situation that can easily be remedied tonight. Are you sure you're okay with this?"

"I'm cool, trust me. I like Lily. There's something special about her. She fits in here."

Warmth spread through Jude's middle. "She does."

"Jude, I—I . . ."

He waited.

"I'd better get back to the kitchen before I ruin dinner."

Jude squashed his disappointment that, in the end, his friend opted not to share what was bothering him. "Nothing fancy. You'll need lots of energy for later."

"Hey, you didn't hire me to cook you boring food."

"No, I hired you because you were the kindest, most beautiful young man I'd ever met," he said, letting the emotion in his words carry his message. "You had the soul of an angel and you steadied me, made this empty house a home. Don't ever doubt your place as my dearest friend."

Liam grabbed Jude, gave him a brief, hard hug. "That's all I need to hear," he said, slapping him on the back.

"You've got me, my friend, and I'm not going anywhere."

Liam turned loose of him and stepped back. "You need help getting dressed?"

"No, but I do need my cane. It's still in the studio." Which he'd trashed. Not his brightest moment.

"Wait here and I'll find it."

Liam yanked on his clothes and left to fetch the cane, while Jude pulled on his shorts. More like fled. Too much honesty between two guys, he supposed.

Despite his concern for Liam being put through hell by his mysterious lovers, Jude felt better than he had in days. Maybe it was selfish, but having his best friend and an intriguing woman to fill his home with light was just what he needed. Perhaps it would be enough to pull him back from the precipice, keep him from falling into whatever pit of doom awaited in his dreams.

Maybe the horror would vanish altogether and he'd never worry again about what he might have forgotten in his past.

Those secrets would simply vanish into the mists of time as though they'd never been.

Whoever you were, you're not that man anymore.

No matter that his nightmares insisted differently.

· · ·

Lily pulled into a space near the park and glanced around furtively. Pretty sure nobody was paying attention, she flipped open her cell phone and speed-dialed her boss's number—her *real* boss, not the arrogant shithead who'd taken over and made the protocol at SHADO nearly unrecognizable.

"Ross residence," a very British man said in greeting.

"Simon? This is Lily Vale. Don't hang up on me—I *have* to talk to Michael," she said, more than a little desperate. "This is regarding one of his agents and he needs to know—"

"Miss Vale, I'll impart to you what I've said at least twice before. Michael has given me strict orders that he is not to be disturbed under any circumstances."

"But—"

"That includes fire, flood, the next apocalypse, and wayward agents."

"He has to hear—"

"The man is grieving and he has a full staff of educated personnel quite capable of handling whatever conundrum they've muddled their way into," he said politely. But firmly. "I promise to have him phone you at his earliest convenience. Good-bye, love."

Click.

"Fuck! Fuckity-fuck-fuck!"

A knock on her window nearly sent her into cardiac arrest. Jumping in her seat, she whipped her head around to find Robert Dietz smiling at her in amusement. Jackass.

Shouldering her purse, she shoved the cell phone and keys inside, got out, and punched the lock. Dietz stood back, waiting, and gestured toward her purse.

"I think you beat your poor phone to death."

She shot the tall, sandy-haired man an annoyed look. "Crappy service. What can you do?"

"I can relate," he said, nodding. "Let's walk."

They headed into the park, two nice professional-looking people out for a stroll. No one paid them any mind. "When you called, I told you I don't have much."

She braced herself for his question.

"Have you administered the first dose?"

"I have it planned for tonight," she answered truthfully. Her stomach rebelled.

His piercing blue eyes pinned her with a searching look; then he seemed to relax. "Not as soon as I'd hoped, but it will do. What else do you have?"

"What makes you think I have squat?"

"Because you're one of my best agents, that's why." He smirked.

One of Michael's *best, needle dick.*

"As a matter of fact, I do. I've found St. Laurent's war room."

The instant the words left her mouth, she felt as though she'd betrayed Jude. She hated the crawling, oily sensation on her skin. "Or at least I believe so."

"I don't pay you to tell me what you believe. I want results." He said it as calmly as if he'd remarked on the Yankees' current stats.

She restrained the sudden urge to break his nose. "The access is in his master closet. Behind a hidden panel there's a ladder descending to what is, in my opinion, an underground room. I think it's likely we'll find one or both of the files secreted there."

"And were you planning on receiving an engraved invitation to visit it? Why the hell haven't you been down there?"

"I'm not exactly alone in the house," she snapped. "The housekeeper only comes once a week, but his chef lives there full-time. . . ."

In horror, she trailed off, hoping to keep the bald emotion from her expression. Sweet Mother of God, she'd just thrown Liam to the wolves. Her pulse beat a mad tattoo in her chest. If Dietz suspected she had an ounce of feeling for her new friend, he wouldn't hesitate to use it to his advantage.

"Make an opportunity, slip St. Laurent and the chef both something if you have to, but get down there and see exactly what he's got. I'll expect a full report tomorrow."

She stopped walking and gaped at him. "You want me to go down there tonight?"

"What better time? You're giving our rogue agent the first dose, putting the chef out of commission. Hell, poison him, too. Who will know?"

Lily felt the blood drain from her face. "No. Both sick at the same time? If *they* didn't suspect foul play, someone else would, eventually. It's too risky."

"Fine. I don't give two shits how you corral the O'Neil kid, just do it."

Oh, God. "You know his name?"

"Vale, I know everything." Dietz gave her a wolfish grin. "I know, for example, when sweet Liam makes his trips into the city, and who he meets for a torrid tryst when he's supposedly out buying groceries. I know he likes to jog along that isolated road out there in the mornings. Alone. Unprotected. Do I make myself clear?"

"Crystal," she said, choking down her rage.

"Good. Don't fail in your mission to kill St. Laurent, and pretty Liam lives to fuck you by the pool another day." Reaching out, he touched her cheek. "Talk to you tomorrow, Miss Vale."

He left her there, rooted to the spot, staring at his retreating back. In the space of ten minutes, the motherfucker had redefined the meaning of hell.

Dietz was everywhere, eyes and ears watching her every move. He knew things, personal stuff, he wasn't supposed to—

Like a cog clicking into place, she recalled what Dietz had said during their last phone conversation. The pesky detail that had escaped her.

When your upbringing is as pathetic and hardscrabble as St. Laurent's, it can damage a man.

Dietz was referring to Jude's past. His upbringing in the red-light district of New Orleans, son of a whore and her john.

A past that was *not* noted anywhere in Jude's file.

How had Dietz learned that information? What the fuck was going on? No answers, and night would fall too soon.

Then she'd have to begin killing Jude.

One wicked sin at a time.

Eight

Lily's nerves were frayed by the time she returned to the estate. Just so she didn't show up empty-handed and risk arousing suspicion, she'd stopped at a trendy boutique and bought a blouse, hardly noticing what she'd chosen. She couldn't bring herself to care.

Shopping bag in hand, she parked in the massive garage and entered through the kitchen, halting in her tracks at the sight of Liam stirring something on the stove and singing. Happy as the proverbial clam, handsome face shining.

Glancing over at her, his gray eyes lit up. "Hey! I see you found something. What did you buy?" His smile died. "Jesus, what's wrong? You look like someone boiled your bunny."

She shook herself mentally and rolled her eyes. "Traffic. It's not quite as bad here as in California, but I'd forgotten how insane the drivers are in Westchester. I think I need a Valium now."

"Hmm. How about a glass of Merlot instead? It'll taste better, too."

"Sounds lovely."

Liam took a bottle from the wine rack in the corner of the

kitchen and uncorked it. He fetched two glasses and poured the wine, then handed her one.

"Thanks. You're a lifesaver."

"I get that a lot. Cheers."

They clinked glasses and Lily took a sip, moaning in bliss. "Oh, this is good."

"Yeah." He stared out the window over the sink with a dreamy expression, a half smile curving those yummy lips.

"What are you . . . ?" She giggled. "He nailed you, didn't he?"

"So crude! I'm shocked, Miss Vale."

"Oh, you'd be surprised. Somehow, though, I doubt anything could shock you where Jude is concerned." She studied him, wondering if there was more information she could pump from Liam, stuff he wasn't even aware of.

Liam sighed. "He's an incredible man, unlike anyone I've ever known. Except maybe you. Being incredible, and *so* not a man."

"I hear a *but* in there. Is this where you fess up as to what's got you turned inside out? Or who?"

Belatedly, she recalled Dietz hinting at Liam's secret liaisons with someone and cursed herself for not questioning it at the time. Though if she'd shown interest, the bastard probably wouldn't have told her.

"And ruin a perfectly nice afternoon? Of course not."

"All right. I can take a hint. Just remember, you're pretty incredible yourself and nobody has the right to make you feel otherwise."

Sadness flashed in his eyes, there and gone. "Nah. I'm just the short-order cook, dishwasher, and onetime window repairman as of today."

She arched a brow, ignoring his self-deprecating joke. "Window repair?"

"Correction. *I'm* not going to fix it. The glass people are. Tomorrow." He took a healthy drink of his wine. "You missed the fireworks. Jude had sort of an episode earlier. The nightmares, his situation, all of it exploded and he trashed his studio. Hurled a chair through the big picture window and cut himself."

"Good Lord," she breathed. "Is he all right?"

"On the outside, a few cuts, the worst ones on his arm and the bottom of his foot. On the inside? He's falling apart, Lily." Setting down his glass, he pushed a hand through his dark bangs.

"He's become convinced he's killed people. Called himself a monster. H-he asked me why he didn't just die in the accident. God, he was so down it broke my heart."

Lily's broke, too. Clean in half.

Jude knows he's a murderer. The pieces are falling into place and when he remembers what he's done, it will tear him in two.

The only humane thing to do was to put him down. Out of his misery, before he recalled the atrocities he'd committed against his country.

Before he turned and went back to the dark side.

"I don't understand what's happening to him," Liam went on.

"Maybe he's never really recovered from the accident," she offered quietly. "What he's suffering could be a health issue he might never get over."

There. She'd planted the seed. She hated herself.

He nodded. "I've thought of that, but I refuse to believe it. There has to be another explanation."

Oh, baby. There is, but you don't want to know.

"Brain injury, coupled with stress, can have serious consequences on a person's well-being. If he won't see anyone, there's not much you can do except be there for him."

"I suppose." He turned to stir one of his pots.

"Tell me, how did you and Jude meet?" The change of subject did the trick, the happy light returning to his expression.

"I ran over him." He snorted. "On my moped."

This time she laughed. The picture was too absurd not to react. "A *moped*? People still drive those?"

"Struggling chefs who can't afford a car drive them. It got me where I needed to go—until I wrecked it while making Jude into a pancake."

"And it was friendship at first sight?"

"Right. He was so mad, he threatened to sue me." Liam chuckled at the memory. "I had twelve dollars and fifty-six cents in the bank, another fifteen in my pocket. I offered to make him dinner at my shitty apartment instead to make up for flattening him, and when he found out I was fresh out of chef's school, he accepted."

"Then you became friends?"

"By the time we finished eating, we'd hit it off. Anyway, when he demanded to know how I was going to fix my bike, he forced me to admit I'd spent every last dime I had to my name just to make him dinner. He was looking for a live-in chef, and the rest is history."

The actions of a kind, considerate man who hadn't stayed angry with someone who'd run him over. Who knew a gem when he saw one, and pulled the younger man out of dire straits. And that was long before Jude's brain had been swept.

Lily was more uncertain than ever.

"Let me guess—you don't drive a moped anymore?"

He shot her a sly sideways look from under his long lashes. "The Porsche in the garage is mine."

"A gift from Jude?"

"He's a generous man. Stick around and he'll spoil you, too."

Rather than forcing a lie, she hid behind her wine. Not for long, though. Liam's enthusiasm for life was an addictive drug. She could listen to his chatter for hours and not grow tired of his company.

By the time they'd consumed two glasses of wine, Liam had finished dinner while telling her about growing up in Chattanooga as part of an average, blue-collar family. When he'd come out to his parents as bisexual, they'd kicked him out and told him never to darken their door again. He'd hitchhiked to New York with only the clothes on his back.

When she asked how he'd gotten the money for chef school, his beautiful eyes flashed with sorrow. He told her she didn't want to know.

Fortunately, Liam's melancholy was brief. Jude walked into the kitchen and leaned on his cane, breathing in the spicy aroma. "What smells so good? Christ, is that seafood gumbo?"

"Yep, and corn bread." Liam winked at her. "Our boss has to have his New Orleans fix every now and then."

"Minus the filth and the stink of the river," Jude added.

Lily eyed the enormous pot. "Is it spicy-hot?"

"My gumbo could strip the paint off the side of a house," the younger man boasted. "But don't worry—we've got plenty of wine."

"Oh, boy. I hope you keep a bottle of antacids around here."

Both men laughed, and she waved at the pot. "What are you going to do with all of that? There's no way we'll be able to eat that much."

"One of Jude's employees from the shelter is coming to pick it up, along with two extra pans of cornbread and dessert. They have their own cook, but I treat them a couple of days a week to give Mrs. Morgan time off."

What? "A shelter? What shelter?" She glanced between the two men, noting how Jude straightened, lifting his chin.

"It's a shelter in town for abused spouses and children who are desperate to start their lives over. I renovated a big, older home and opened it several years ago. We started with five families and two runaway teens, and now we have double that."

"We realize it's just a drop in the bucket, but Jude's expanding this year, opening two more locations," Liam said, pride in his boss unmistakable. "He has a waiting list longer than your arm."

Lily stared at them, stunned. "That's incredibly generous of both of you. These people are very lucky to have you behind them."

Jude shrugged. "Someone helped me once, when I was at my lowest point. I figure it's my way of giving back."

"Your friend Devon must be a special guy."

"Dev gave me my big break in the art world, but he wasn't the one who rescued me from the gutter. That was . . ." He frowned, rubbing his temples. "His name was . . . Michael." He blew out a breath. "God, why can't I remember anything else about him?"

Very carefully, Lily set down her wine. "Would you both excuse me for a few minutes? I'll be right back."

Fast as she dared, she ducked into a powder room off the

foyer and locked the door behind her. Bracing her hands on the counter, she hung her head and let the tears flow.

This was so fucking unfair. When her mission was complete, she'd find one good reason to kill Dietz. Slowly.

A quiet knock jolted her from her contemplation of Dietz's demise. How long had she been standing here?

"Lily, are you all right?"

Jude. At least he couldn't tell she'd been crying.

"I'm fine, just freshening up." That seemed safe enough. Most men had no clue what women did when they "freshened up."

"Are you upset with me? Did I say something wrong?"

"No! Give me a second."

Quickly, she splashed some water on her face and used the small hand towel to pat it dry. She fanned her face to try to erase evidence of her tears and red eyes; she was glad her makeup was spare. Ready, she opened the door and stepped out.

Jude stood there, mouth turned down at the corners, brow furrowed. "Whatever I said, I apologize."

"Don't be silly! Can't a woman take care of business without everyone coming unglued?"

"Lily . . ."

"All right. If you must know, the idea of what you've suffered gets to me." Not a lie. "Hearing your story, the good you've done, made me a little emotional. I'm fine."

His expression softened. "Oh. Well, that's ancient history and there's no reason for anyone to feel sorry for me. I have a good life, and now more than ever, I have reason not to squander what I have left. Even if I do have bad days."

Which only served to ramp up her misery. "I'll keep that in mind."

"Hungry?"

"I could eat."

He offered his arm. "Why don't we retire to my suite? The guy from the shelter just left with their portion of the food, so we're free to dine in peace."

"We?"

"You, me, and Liam," he said, tone thick with suggestion.

Never had she been so at war with herself. Mind, body, and soul. She wanted these men, yet she knew what she had to do—allow them to seduce her.

Then do her job.

"Sounds promising." She took his arm and they went upstairs.

In his suite, he helped seat her at the same table where he'd eaten with Tamara. Just before he *ate* Tamara.

The table was already set with a bottle of wine chilling in the middle, glasses, bowls, plates, and cutlery. Jude sat and she took the place on his right, leaving the spot on her right for Liam.

Mind racing, she thought ahead to the evening before them. There was no question what the two men had planned for her tonight. How would she keep the two different drugs at the ready and time the doses? In addition, making sure each of the drugs went to the correct man was essential. A mistake would mean disaster.

She'd wait until they were feeling loose. Offer to refill their glasses. But how—

"You're thinking too hard," Jude said with a smile. "I can almost hear the wheels grinding."

"Busted."

"Well, stop. We want to spoil you and we need your cooperation to succeed."

"Yes, sir."

His lips quirked. "Good girl."

Liam rolled in with his cart of food, jeans slung low on his hips. "Chow time."

"Good, I'm starving," Jude said, patting his stomach.

"You're always hungry."

"You should know."

Liam blushed, cutting a look at Lily. "I'm not the only one."

The sexual tension was thick as molasses as Liam served the meal. The Chardonnay he poured, however, was one of her favorites, which was a shame. After tonight, she'd probably never touch it again.

Dinner progressed amid comfortable, idle chat. Her nerves gradually gave way to the growing lust palpable between the three of them, her senses simply no match for being sandwiched between two potent males. They smelled so good, heat practically radiating from them. Each so sexy in his own right, yet so different.

At last they pushed their bowls away and Liam gestured to the small plates on the cart. "Dessert? I made cheesecake."

"Yeah, but I've got an idea," Jude said. "You're going to be our plate."

"Me? You mean you're going to . . ."

"Yep. Lily and I are going to have you with dessert. Strip and get on the bed. Now."

Making a strangled noise, Liam did as he was told. His clothing hit the floor and he crawled onto the bed and lay on his back, cock at full salute.

"Lily, undress and help me with the cheesecake, if you would."

Fascinated by the prospect of devouring the handsome young man, she shed her clothing as well and grabbed a plate. She got on the bed and scooted next to Liam, setting the dessert on the covers next to them. Jude followed suit and joined them, sitting on their friend's other side, his excitement evident. He was clearly running the show and they waited to see what he'd say next.

Jude waved a hand in her direction. "Take a nice amount of cheesecake on your fingers and coat his cock with it. Balls, too."

Oh, my. "And then?"

"You're going to enjoy your dessert, honey. What else?"

"Good God," Liam groaned, but it wasn't a complaint. "You're an evil man, boss."

"Tell me that in thirty seconds."

"I won't be able to speak by then!"

"That's the idea."

Intrigued and more than a little aroused by the prospect of driving Liam out of his mind, Lily grinned, scooping a dollop of the confection with a bit of the strawberry topping. Grabbing the base of his cock with one hand to hold it steady, she used the other to spread the stuff on his shaft. It warmed and melted some as she worked, making a coating of goo, covering him completely. Even his sac, which had drawn taut at the attention.

"Okay, I'm done. Shall I eat him?"

"Let me have your fingers first," Jude said.

She complied and he grasped her wrist, then proceeded to lick every bit of cheesecake off the digits. The feel of his warm tongue rasping off the cream was incredibly erotic. Her pussy clenched at the sight and sensation, and she could only imagine how great it would feel to Liam.

"Mmm, delicious. Your turn."

Taking her cue, she bent and tasted the head of the younger man's cock. He whimpered, muttering something unintelligible, jerking his hips. Obviously he liked it, so she laved with more enthusiasm, loving every bite of his strawberry-cheesecake cock.

"You taste so good," she praised, licking his balls. "Delicious."

"Oh, God," he moaned. "Lily . . ."

"Yes, sweetheart?"

But before he could answer, Jude ran a palm up the other man's leg to the juncture of his thighs. "Let's taste him together," he suggested, tone husky.

Jude dipped his head, suckling Liam's balls while she took the sweet cock into her mouth, pulling harder now. The object of their attentions made helpless noises, thrashing his head back and forth on the pillow.

"You two . . . if you don't stop, it's going to be over!"

Jude lifted his head. "Well, we can't have that. Damn, I wish we had a way to torture him for a while without allowing him to come."

"We do," Lily said, loving the idea. "Wait here."

Hurrying to her room, she raided her stash of toys and quickly returned carrying several items. She laid them on the bed and pushed Liam's chest when he tried to sit up and look. "No peeking."

"Does that go for me, too?" Jude asked.

Liam rolled his eyes. "Man, that was lame."

"Sorry, couldn't resist."

"Jude, you're going to help," she said, placing a small leather strap in his palm. "Know what this is?"

He fingered the item, mouth curving upward. "Yep. Want me to do the honors?"

"By all means."

Jude lifted the other man's balls, taking great care to wrap the leather strap behind them and around the base of his cock.

"A-a cock ring? Oh, crap," Liam groaned. But he spread his legs wider in a silent invitation for more.

"We have to be sure you won't come before we're ready," Lily said. "Now for the next little device. Lube?"

Jude gestured to the nightstand and she removed it from the drawer, squirting a generous amount on the small butt plug in her hand. "Liam, raise your hips."

He did, and she parted his ass cheeks, nudging his hole with the tip of the plug. "Be a good boy and relax for me."

She began to push it into his channel.

"Oh . . . oh, Jesus!"

"Good?"

"Y-yes!"

"I wish I could see," Jude pouted.

"He's beautiful, his skin flushed, body spread for us." When the plug was seated to the base, she observed her work with satisfaction. "There. Two more finishing touches, and he's ready."

"Two?" Liam croaked. "I'm gonna die!"

"Shush," she said, rolling his nipples between her thumbs and forefingers. "You'll like this, I promise."

Once his nipples were coaxed to rigid peaks, she took a pair of small clamps connected by a length of thin chain and sprang the serrated teeth onto one.

"Ah! Christ!" Liam writhed, pain giving way to pleasure.

"One more." She snapped the second one into place, liking how his cry gave her a sense of power. "Liam, get up on your knees and hold out your wrists."

He obeyed and she grabbed a length of rope, wrapping it to bind his wrists together, then tying the other end around a spindle in the headboard. Addressing Jude, she eyed her handiwork.

"He looks scrumptious, bound and filled, at our mercy." She flicked the head of Liam's penis. "He's so hard, red and leaking. What shall we do with him now?"

"Lily, spread more of the cheesecake on his cock."

Liam angled his head and watched, wide-eyed, as Lily reapplied the confection and Jude again sucked her fingers clean.

"Now hand me the dessert and get underneath him, on your back," Jude said.

She pushed it across the bed to him until the edge of the plate touched his fingers. He smiled and scooped some as well.

"Go ahead and sample more of our boy while I spread this all over your pussy."

Oh, yes! She positioned herself between Liam's spread knees and swallowed his cock once more, loving his unfettered delight as he cursed, thrusting between her lips.

Cool cream touched her heated flesh, oozed, sinfully naughty. "Let me see how you taste," Jude said.

When his lips nibbled her labia, tongue flicking out to lap her, she gasped around the shaft in her mouth. This was wicked, like nothing she'd ever done before. Liberating. Exciting.

She renewed her efforts at sucking Liam as Jude did the same to her. The three of them writhed together, the temperature reaching the boiling point at warp speed. She was dripping wet now, in heat, pushing into Jude's face as she devoured the hard cock, taking him down her throat again and again.

"Jude . . . get inside her, please! I'm not gonna last much longer."

His friend obliged, leaving her for a moment, and she almost protested. A condom wrapper crinkled, and then Jude was there, shoving inside her. Deep and hard. Grasping her hips, he began to shaft her. He wasn't gentle, and his actions set the tone.

They fucked her, down and dirty, one man filling her mouth, the other her pussy. She was along for the ride, taking every forceful thrust, her cries of ecstasy muffled. Spiraling higher, losing control.

Reaching up, she fumbled, and managed to release Liam's cock ring, freeing him.

Liam shouted first, stiffening, and slammed his cock down her throat, the headboard creaking as he strained in his bonds. Salty cum sprayed and she swallowed rapidly, not wanting to miss a drop.

Jude went next, buried himself deep in her burning channel with an exultant yell, pumping and jerking. The awesome sensation of having two gorgeous men being so turned on by her, filling her with their cum, drove her over the edge.

She cried out as her pussy spasmed, bathing Jude's cock, fire flashing through her body. It was the most wondrous feeling she'd ever experienced, being shared by these two.

As they all floated to reality, she blurted, "Do you guys do this often?"

"What? Share a woman?" Jude asked, pulling out.

"Yes." She blushed. Why, she didn't have a clue. She was no pure, naive virgin.

Scooting from between Liam's legs, she sat up and untied his wrists.

"No, we don't," Liam answered. Removing the butt plug and nipple clamps, he set them on the nightstand and got comfy.

Propped on the pillows, he gazed at her, sexy as hell. "We have, but seldom."

"I never would have guessed. You guys blew my mind."

"*Your* mind? Sheesh! My brain is mush," Liam complained good-naturedly.

"You were fantastic, Lily," Jude said softly. "Sexy as hell, the way you put Liam through his paces. What did we do to deserve such a special woman?"

"Oh, God." Tears stung her eyes.

Jude thinks I'm special.

"I don't know what to say." Do. Not. Cry. She was glad Jude couldn't read her now.

"Say you're not going anywhere for a good long while."

"I'm not," she said quietly.

Jude leaned closer. "Kiss us, baby."

They closed in on either side of her, seeking her mouth. She melted into them as two sets of lips met hers, hot tongues spearing her mouth, tangling together. Suckling, an affirmation of what they'd shared. A promise of friendship from Liam.

Of something much more from Jude.

A promise she couldn't let him keep.

Lily broke the kiss first, heart heavy. "You guys relax while I go next door to my room and clean up. When I come back, I'll pour us more wine, so don't move."

"Hurry back," Liam said. The two men got comfortable and closed their eyes, leaving a spot for her in the middle.

She practically fled, as though she could outrun the horrible act she was about to commit.

How could it feel so wrong to take out a traitor to the U.S., something she'd done countless times in the past?

Ruthlessly, she squelched the running dialogue of doubt before it drove her crazy. In her room, she grabbed a nightshirt and carried it to the bathroom, where she hurriedly washed the rest of the sticky dessert from her sex. Then she yanked the shirt over her head and went to one of the locked cases in her walk-in closet.

Checking to make certain the men had stayed put, she heard their voices in Jude's room. Satisfied, she bent to her task and opened the case. Nestled in foam rubber were all sorts of toxins and their antidotes. Liquid in tiny bottles, fast-dissolving pills, capsules, syringes.

Sorting the options rapidly, she decided against using a liquid, normally her preferred choice. In this situation, hiding the bottle or syringe after doctoring the wine, then ducking back to her room to rid her hand of it, would be difficult. Her actions might seem suspicious.

She'd have to go with the pills and hope they performed as fast as she remembered. Carefully, she extracted the pill she would put in Jude's wine. This particular poison was slow acting and the effects were compounded with each dose, killing the victim gradually. He'd suffer badly before he died.

After the first dose, he'd become ill, vomit. Believe he had the flu; then he'd feel better. With the second, he'd vomit blood, maybe have a nosebleed. After the third, he'd begin hemorrhaging inside, his organs toast. Without the antidote, he'd die in a couple of days, whether he got the fourth dose or not—that one was a mere formality.

Her stomach hurt and dinner threatened to rebel, but she managed to keep it together. This untraceable poison was the correct one for the job because he must appear sick and in declining health. Which he would be, and the symptoms mocked so many illnesses, no autopsy would ever learn anything helpful.

From another bottle, she removed a simple sleeping pill for Liam, harmless but strong. He'd be out cold for the rest of the night.

She locked the case again and took one tablet in each palm, taking scrupulous care to keep them separated. As she walked back into the room, Liam grinned.

"About time. Did you fall in?"

"Something like that." She walked straight to the table, glancing at the pair. Both were reclined, Jude with his hands behind his head, Liam's eyes closed. She filled each man's glass half-full of wine and quickly dropped the tablets in their respective glasses.

In a tiny burst of fizz, each one was gone in ten seconds, in the time it took Lily to pour her own glass. Steeling her nerves, she took their glasses over to the pair, handing them off. She returned for hers and crawled onto the bed with it, wedging herself between their naked bodies.

"To us," Jude said, holding his glass out for them.

They clinked theirs to his and drank. Lily was hyperaware of every swallow, the life pulsing through the two men. Of their heady male scent, their beauty. Of life being destroyed.

They talked of inconsequential things, sipping the damned wine until Lily thought they'd never finish. She wanted this done; the sooner the better.

Finally, Liam's eyes drifted shut for good in the middle of their conversation. In moments, his hand fell to the bed, stem of the glass in his limp fingers.

Jude reached out. "Liam?"

"He's sleeping."

"Guess we wore him out, huh?" His voice was tired. Slurred.

"Yeah, we did," she said, aching inside. "Why don't you get some rest, too?"

"Wanted to . . . make love to you . . . again."

Not fuck. Make love.

Those were the last words he spoke before his glass hit the floor.

Nine

Lily snatched the glasses and rinsed them in the bathroom sink, then placed them on Liam's cart. Next, she returned to her room, donning loose warm-ups and a pair of tennis shoes. When descending into a strange basement area, one never knew what to expect.

A thumb drive went into the pocket of her warm-ups, in case she located the two remaining files. Last, she grabbed a flashlight and walked through Jude's bedroom again, pausing to study the figures on the bed. An emotion very much like grief forced its way into her throat, foreign and bitter.

Both men were so handsome, sculpted chests and stomachs, strong arms, long legs. Jude could've been hers for the taking if circumstances had been different.

But life was rarely fair.

She'd learned that the day a traitor had killed her father.

In Jude's closet, she went to the panel and pressed the molding. As before, it slid open easily. All she had to do was infiltrate the enemy's den.

Testing the rungs, she found them stable and began her

descent, flashlight in one hand. Down, down into the bowels of the house until her shoe met solid floor.

She turned on the flashlight and stared at her surroundings in awe. "Holy shit."

This setup could rival NASA's with all the monitors, keyboards, and other technical crap she couldn't begin to name. Against one wall stood a rack of clothes in various styles, and another entire wall bristled with weapons of every kind imaginable, both legal and not so legal.

Rifles, scopes, pistols, hand grenades. A fucking rocket launcher!

Fishing around, she found a light switch on the wall next to the ladder and flipped it, flooding the room with light. She turned the flashlight off and set it at the foot of the ladder for when she left.

How the hell was she supposed to find one file in this massive setup? By searching each hard drive, methodically ruling it out until the correct one was found. This could take all night.

Disheartened, she set to work, booting up the machines. The password was no problem; she used SHADO's bypass code the top brass shared only in need-to-know cases. This being one of them, in order to get the dirt on their own man.

Running the virus-search program she'd used to locate the other files, she resigned herself to the boring task. Four hours later, she was on the next-to-last machine when the message popped onto the screen.

VIRUS LOCATED.

She bolted upright, blinking at the screen for a few seconds before it registered. She'd found it.

A few commands later, she had the worm isolated, but like

the others, it wasn't a readable file. The damned thing was encrypted, not her area of expertise. Oh, she could figure it out, but it would take her several days to crack. Days she didn't have, with Dietz phoning tomorrow.

But if she could stall him . . . yes. She might be able to put Dietz off long enough to take a good look at this little gem that had him sweating. She wasn't sure how she'd avoid him, but she'd manage.

Feeling better with this plan, she downloaded the file to the thumb drive, double-checked to be certain it was there, then destroyed the worm on the hard drive. Poof. Gone as if it had never been.

She started to fry all of Jude's computers, but knew once the house was empty, SHADO would just send in a cleanup crew anyway, so there was no need.

She shut everything down again and, after taking a last look around, grabbed her flashlight, turned off the light, and made her way back upstairs. Emerging in the closet once more, she wondered if this was how Alice had felt after going down the rabbit hole and coming back. Like traveling between parallel universes.

After secreting the thumb drive in one of her locked cases, she undressed and again settled herself between Jude and Liam. She wanted to retreat to her own room and hide, but they would be concerned to awaken and find she hadn't wanted to stay.

So she remained there.

But sleep didn't come for a very long while.

· · ·

Jude came awake as though from a deep, dark tunnel. The first thing he became aware of was that he ached all over. Bone deep.

His head hurt, too, but not like one of his migraines. No, this was different.

He rolled to his side, and that's when the nausea began. Low and ominous, in the pit of his belly. Roiling like a stormy ocean.

"Oh, God."

He was going to throw up. Any second.

Scrambling off the bed, he stumbled in the direction of his bathroom. He didn't have time to grope for his cane, didn't care.

Hitting the doorjamb hard with his shoulder, he grunted and fell inside, crawling. Felt desperately for the toilet because he couldn't stop—

There. He shoved the lid open and lost the meager contents of his stomach, heaving until he sat with his forehead on the rim, shaking and miserable.

"Liam? Guys?"

Nothing. From somewhere in the house the aroma of breakfast cooking finally made its way into his consciousness. Another round of vomiting greeted that smell and he groaned, willing the floor to stop moving.

The minutes stretched on forever as he sat, weak as a baby, waiting for the sickness to pass so he could head downstairs. He couldn't recall the last time he'd been ill. Hadn't had the flu in years. But that had to be the cause, with the allover pain, feeling like he'd been dropped from a high-rise.

After a bit, he pushed up and fumbled along, made his way to where he thought he'd left his cane. It had fallen on the floor beside his bed and he bent to retrieve it. When he stood, dizziness nearly toppled him.

He breathed through the waves and paused long enough to put on a pair of shorts, then lurched across the room and into the hallway. Deciding against the stairs, he took the service elevator Liam used for his rolling carts, damned glad it would put him out near the kitchen.

The doors slid open and he walked the remaining few feet with cement shoes, sicker than he'd been in his entire life. He knew he'd made the kitchen when he heard Liam call out his usual cheerful greeting. Jude just couldn't understand the words.

"Liam," he rasped. "I'm sick. . . . I hurt so fucking bad. . . ."

His body folded and he couldn't stop his fall. He heard Liam's startled shout as he hit the floor, cheek on the cool tile. Felt strong arms cradling him.

And he slid into blessed oblivion.

. . .

Lily was hanging out with Liam in the kitchen, watching him cook breakfast, when Jude staggered in.

He looked like death.

"Hey, big guy! Ready for some bacon—" Liam turned and his eyes widened at the sight of Jude disheveled, white as a sheet.

"Liam," he rasped. "I'm sick. . . . I hurt so fucking bad. . . ."

"Shit!" The younger man lunged for Jude as he crumpled to the floor, but he was too far away.

Jude's head smacked the tile with an awful thump, cane clattering from his outstretched hand. Carefully, Liam pulled Jude into his arms, smoothing the long auburn hair from his face.

"Jude!" he cried, pressing shaking fingers to the side of the other man's neck. "Oh, my God, his heart is racing. His pulse is too fast."

Lily dropped to her knees beside them, checking for herself. "I agree. I think we should take him to the emergency room. I'll drive."

A safe bet, since the doctors wouldn't find anything in his

blood. They would be puzzled, but would say he'd picked up a bug and send him home, telling them to put him to bed.

Liam only nodded, face panicked. He stood, lifting his burden, practically carrying the larger man by himself to the Mercedes while she turned off the burners under their breakfast.

Between the two of them, they managed to get him into the back seat of the car, Liam cradling his head in his lap. Jude's friend was inconsolable, widening the crack in her heart.

"Please be okay," he whispered, over and over. "Don't you die on me and leave me all alone. Not now."

They arrived at the nearest hospital in fifteen minutes, Lily screeching to a stop outside the ER. The first dose had hit him harder than she'd thought it would; the third would probably kill him outright.

A doctor and a couple of nurses came running with a gurney and whisked their patient inside. Liam stared after them, devastated. Lost.

Only then did she realize her face was wet, too.

. . .

"Mr. St. Laurent?"

The greeting was strange. Distorted. He was underwater, struggling to the surface. Almost there, but not quite.

Blackness.

Next time, he was more aware. Heard them discussing blood tests. Heart rate. Other terms that escaped him.

"Mr. St. Laurent?"

He licked his dry lips. "Yes."

"Good, you're back!"

Whoop-dee-fucking-do.

"I'm Dr. Cline. How do you feel?"

"Chewed up and shit out," he croaked. "What happened?"

"That's what we'd like to know. Other than an elevated pulse and a bit of a temperature, we can't find a thing wrong with you," he said, sounding both positive and concerned at the same time.

How did doctors do that?

"Flu?"

"Nope. We did tests for types A and B, and got nothing. No infection, either. At this point, I'm leaning toward some sort of bug you've picked up that our tests aren't catching," the doctor said. "There're so many different strains of things going around, it's a process of elimination sometimes."

"You gonna keep me here?"

"Honestly, I don't see why you can't go home. Get plenty of bed rest for a couple of days, drink lots of fluids, take ibuprofen. If you aren't up to speed in two days, see your private physician and he'll order a whole battery of tests to start narrowing this down."

"All right. Can I go now?"

"Let us get your paperwork together. As soon as the nurse brings it, and if you can walk without getting dizzy, you're set to go. I'll send in your friends, too. They seem quite anxious."

That news warmed him some. "Thanks."

"Don't mention it; just get well."

Shortly after the doctor left, more people shuffled to his side. He didn't have to wonder for long who was there.

"Jesus Christ, I thought you were going to die on me," Liam said, obviously upset. A hand squeezed his shoulder.

Jude mustered a smile. "Nah, I'm too mean to kick it anytime soon."

"We're glad you're better," Lily said.

She sounded weird, and his smile faltered. "Me, too. I still hurt, but not as bad."

"Think you can walk?" Liam asked.

"I'll try."

"Good, because you're one heavy SOB."

The checking-out process took ages, but finally they were on their way out, his friends on either side, guiding him. The dizziness and nausea had faded to a dull annoyance, and he was glad. But the aching in his bones was something else. He didn't complain, though, saw no reason to worry them.

He dozed on the way home and it seemed seconds had passed before they pulled into the drive. By the time they got him inside, up to his room, and undressed, he felt like he'd run the Boston Marathon.

"Sorry, guys," he said, settling under the covers with a sigh. "This isn't the way I planned to spend today, especially after such an awesome night."

Liam stroked his hair. "Don't worry, boss. Just rest."

Unable to do much else, he did.

. . .

Lily turned away from the sight of Jude lying there, dusky lashes resting on his pale cheeks, smudges under his eyes. She didn't know if she could do this. Carry this out to the end.

One thing for sure—either way, this was her last assignment as an assassin.

The decision had been surprisingly easy. Watching Liam curled up in a chair in the corner of the ER, arms around his knees, sweet face wretched with worry, she'd known.

After this, no more.

Leaving the two men alone, she pocketed her cell phone and went outside on the pretext of taking a walk. The gardens out behind the pool would hide her well enough and afford some privacy.

She already had one message from Dietz and it wasn't wise to disappear on him. Stalling him would have to be done another way—by lying her ass off.

Placing the call, she was numb inside rather than nervous.

"What do you have, Agent?"

Nothing but contempt for you.

"I administered the first dose, and it affected him more strongly than I'd believed. He'll be dead by the third."

"Excellent. What else?"

"I breached his war room, and it's quite a setup. Looks like the cockpit of a frigging airplane. If he's hidden one of the files there, I wasn't able to locate it yet. It will take a few more days."

"Agent Vale," he said casually, "I do believe you're lying to me."

Her gut lurched. "I'm not. I worked all night at each of the hard drives. His shit is well protected."

"You've never needed a few days to complete a task."

"I do now."

A weighty silence.

"I want that file on Friday. Find the bastard."

She ended the call without saying good-bye, and hung her head. The urge to phone Michael again was overwhelming, but she'd had no success so far and she didn't see that changing. She couldn't give SHADO's code for an emergency when she didn't even know if there *was* an emergency.

Soon, very soon, she was done.

. . .

A true nightmare this time, not a memory.

He was lost, stumbling along a dried, barren lake bed.

Well, barren except for the fish. Miles of fish, as far as the eye could see, mouths gaping, gills expanding, as they struggled for breath that would never come. Eyes popping out. Staring. Scaly, stinky bodies baking in the scorching heat.

Mesmerized, he halted and stared down at one of the dying fish.

"Join us in the boneyard," it said. "You belong here."

He stumbled backward, intending to run. But his feet were stuck, sinking into the ground. . . .

"No!"

"No!" Jude shot upright, gasping. Horrible images from his sleep gave way to blessed reality and he shuddered, willing them to abate.

"Jesus Christ, what *was* that?"

The virus, or whatever, must've really done a number on him.

After he showered and dressed, he felt much better, weird fucking nightmare aside. Almost human. The dizziness and nausea of yesterday's attack were gone, and he wasn't hurting as much. He was more tired of lying around than he was from the twenty-four-hour bug he'd gotten, and he was ready to do something. Anything.

Liam had stopped in his room earlier and told Jude he'd be

out by the pool if he was needed, so Jude headed there first. Might as well ask his friend a question while it was on his mind.

"Hey, man!" Liam called out. "Damn, you look a zillion times better than yesterday."

"I'll take your word for it," he said, poking fun at his lack of sight. "But I'm up and around, at least."

"Pull up a chair."

Jude found one without too much problem. Liam had stopped jumping up to help him weeks ago, letting him learn to cope. He sat and got right to the point.

"Do you recall when you brought me home after the accident?"

"Jesus, like I could forget. Why do you want to talk about that?"

"I don't. I just want to know if you remember what you did with the clothes I had on that day."

His friend paused, then asked slowly, "Why would you want to know?"

"I've lost my grandfather's lighter. You know, the antique I used to carry around in my pants pocket?"

"Oh. Well, I suppose it's probably in your closet. When you had the accident, you were coming home from one of your trips and had a duffel bag. I tucked away everything you had on you into the bag and stuck it on the top shelf."

"All right, I'll search there. Thanks."

"You're not going to start smoking again, are you?"

"Is that why you hid it from me?" He ribbed his friend. "You were afraid I'd resume the habit?"

"I did not hide it! Not on purpose."

"I know you didn't. I'm kidding." He sat back, soaking up the sunshine. "Anyway, the lighter is sentimental. It's all I have left of Pop."

"I'll help you look if you want."

"I can check the closet. If it's not there, I'll take you up on the offer."

"Sure."

Something else was bothering him. "Is Lily okay with what happened between the three of us? She's made herself pretty scarce around me," he said, worried. He could've sworn they had a real connection going. That she felt the same things he did.

"As far as I know, but . . ."

"But?"

"You're right. She has been sort of quiet. Now that you mention it, she's been disappearing for stretches of time, like an hour or so," Liam said thoughtfully. "I saw her talking on her cell phone in the gardens, too. When she came back, she seemed distant. Almost like she was someone else."

The back of Jude's neck prickled. "Did she mention who she was talking to or what the conversation was about?"

"No, and I didn't want to pry. She's not exactly keen on discussing her life outside of here."

"That's not so unusual. Plenty of folks don't want to air their laundry." He thought back. "I did get that her father is dead, though."

"Really? That's too bad."

"Yeah." Jude stood, grimacing at the leftover ache in his body. "Well, I'm going to go poke around for that lighter, since I've got nothing better to do."

"You could paint, now that the glass guys are finished replacing the window and the mess is cleaned up."

He shook his head. "Later. I think my muse packed and left for the Congo."

"You're just in a slump. It'll come back, my friend."

He really didn't think so, but didn't want to upset Liam any more. "Probably. Enjoy your soak."

Inside, he went back to his room and headed into the closet. The top shelves were high, barely reachable, but he managed to feel around, discarding several containers. At last, his fingers brushed a bag with handles and he grabbed it, dragged it down.

He didn't remember the bag, or what he'd been wearing the day Liam was allowed to bring him home. Didn't recall much of those black days at all.

Except wishing he were dead.

Now he just wanted to find his balance, his place in a world turned upside down. He had no clue what Pop's lighter had to do with that or why it would make him feel better to hold it again, but the drive to find it was an itch under his skin.

Tossing the duffel on the bed, he sat down, unzipped it, and stuck a hand inside, checking the contents. A belt, something cotton. The material had arms—a T-shirt. A pair of sunglasses. A pair of jeans. He sniffed the clothing and detected a hint of fabric softener. They smelled clean, and he guessed these were extra clothes from his last mysterious trip. The pockets were empty and he laid them aside.

He continued fishing and found another set of clothes. Slacks of some kind and a button-up shirt. These were rumpled, smelled a bit musty. Liam should have given these to the housekeeper to launder, but he doubted his friend had been any more eager to deal with what had happened than Jude had been.

The shirt's pockets were empty, as were the pants. At the

bottom of the duffel, however, he found a small lump. Jude's fingers closed over the rectangular metal object he hadn't touched in months.

Pulling it out, he held it tight, unable to reason out the excitement and relief that washed over him. His reaction made no sense. The old Zippo wasn't particularly valuable or even all that attractive to a collector. But he clung to the thing like a lifeline, suddenly assailed by a vision.

He leaned back in the squeaky vinyl chair so thoughtfully provided by the shitty motel and shook his last Marlboro out of the pack, narrowed eyes never leaving the screen of his laptop. He lifted his antique Zippo lighter from the corner of the scarred desk and stuck the cigarette between his lips.

He lit up and inhaled, letting the rich smoke curl through his lungs in a futile attempt to soothe his nerves, on a whole variety of levels.

There was a jackal in their midst, and he couldn't reach Michael.

With a low, cynical laugh, he stubbed out the cigarette he hadn't really wanted in the cheap plastic ashtray. The prickle on the back of his neck warned him that the joyless screw he'd indulged in last night could very well be the unremarkable period on the end of an otherwise exciting life. And if so, he wanted to know why, nosy, self-destructive bastard that he was.

Jude clutched the lighter to his chest, sweat rolling down his temple as the scene shifted.

He dropped his face into his hands. In the wake of this terrible exercise of connect the dots, he'd be goddamned lucky if he didn't wind up at the bottom of the Atlantic. In five different oil drums.

Because a traitorous, murdering bastard was coming for him. No doubt about it.

If he had a whisper of a prayer of avoiding a grisly fate, he had to work fast.

His fingers flew on the keyboard, precious seconds being whittled away.

The door to his motel room burst open, hitting the inside wall like a gunshot. He spun, the SIG from the desktop already in hand, arm leveling at the leader of the traitor's cleanup crew.

Too late. A pop split the air, and pain blossomed in his chest. He stumbled backward, managing to get off a shot, the explosion deafening in the tiny space. The leader went down with a grunt as he trained his gun on the second man, tried to squeeze the trigger. And couldn't. His arm fell limp and useless to his side.

"Holy fuck, I'm losing my goddamned mind," he rasped, wiping the sweat from his face. "I'm an artist. A painter. I open shelters for the abused. I don't kill people, I don't play espionage games in crappy hotel rooms."

Do I?

Merciful God, this was worse than he'd thought. What sort of man was he? What had he been doing on all those trips? And why?

"Jude? How are you feeling?" Lily asked, her soothing whiskey voice cutting through the growing panic.

"A little out of sorts," he said with a shaky laugh, sliding the lighter into his jeans pocket. He hadn't heard her come in, but her presence was a balm on his nerves.

"What are you doing?" Her slight weight dipped on the bed next to him.

"Just sitting here . . . reflecting."

"Oh? On what?"

He almost told her. He wanted to confide in her, but fear, self-doubt, held him back. "Nothing important. At loose ends and wondering what to do with myself, I guess."

"Right this minute or in the future?"

"Take your pick."

Scooting closer, she brushed his hair from his face. "You look flushed."

"I'm fine." Unable to help himself, he pushed into her touch. Kissed her palm.

"I'm not so sure about that. Jude, I want to tell you something. I know all about loss," she said quietly. "Losing a part of yourself that hurts so badly you're sure you'll bleed out. And I'm not speaking of things like memory or sight, though those losses aren't small."

"Your father's death?"

She froze. "How did you know about him?"

"I don't, really. But when you mentioned him the other day, you spoke of him in the past tense."

"I see." She dropped her hand, and he immediately missed the contact. "Yes, my greatest heartbreak was my father. He was a shining light to everyone around him, kind and brilliant. He was a scientist, patriotic to the core, developing revolutionary new weapons technology that would've changed the face of American defense. And he was murdered for it before he could realize his dream."

"Lily, I'm so sorry," he said, reaching for her hand.

She took it, curling her fingers around his. "So am I. I lie awake nights fantasizing about all the different ways there are to make traitors pay, men like the ones who snuffed his wonderful light. Is that wrong?"

"No." He pulled her close. "In your position, I'd likely go one giant step further. With no remorse."

"I'm glad you understand."

She sounded so sad, he wanted only to erase her pain. She'd shared a part of herself he suspected she'd never divulged before, and he felt honored. Closer to her than to anyone since the day he'd met Liam, and still . . .

This was different. These burgeoning emotions inside him, the connection to the woman at his side. He couldn't name them, didn't care to.

But in his own way, he'd show her.

"Let me make love to you," he said.

Her breath tickled his ear. "Please."

She'd given him a gift. Now he'd give her one in return.

Something he'd given no other woman.

Ten

Watching Jude shed his jeans and shirt, Lily trembled inside. A profound bond had been forged between them. Not the one he imagined, but a bond all the same.

She'd had to explain to him about her father, allow him the opportunity to understand her motivations even if he'd never know the truth about why she needed absolution.

What part of him greed and evil hadn't destroyed understood that she'd brave hell itself to eliminate men like those who'd murdered Brandon Vale.

Men like Jude.

Hard to believe; he was so beautiful. Muscles rippled under taut skin as he tossed his jeans aside, his cock hard and leaking. Green eyes glittered with desire, his strong jaw clenched. She couldn't help but respond to him, crave him inside her. Her sex burned, nipples ached.

"I need you," she heard herself say. "Now."

"Your wish . . ."

She took his wrist and guided him to her. He pushed her

onto her back and unzipped her skirt, pulled it down. Brushed her slick sex, ever so lightly.

"Sweet. Already hot for me."

Next, he helped her off with her blouse, plucked each of her nipples to points. He grazed one, then the other, sucking while raking his fingers through her long black hair.

One palm skimmed her belly, delved between her thighs. He stroked, spread her dewy moisture over her sex, rubbed her clit. Sent electric sparks zipping to her nerve endings as she opened her legs wider, inviting more.

His lips lowered to hers in a kiss so gentle it brought tears to her eyes. As they kissed, his fingers parted her flesh, dipped inside, stroked in and out, preparing her.

"I want to feel you with nothing between us," he whispered into her mouth. "No barriers, just our skin. I'm clean—I swear. Liam's the only one. . . ."

"I'm healthy, too. Jude, *please.*"

He crawled over her, positioned himself between her legs. His cock probed her opening, pushed into her heat. Deeper, every bump and ridge massaging her inner walls. So good, so right.

When he was fully seated, he braced his arms on either side of her head, cradling her close. Holding her as though she was precious to him, he began to move. She wrapped her legs around his waist and lifted her hips to feel each stroke to the fullest.

His back muscles flexed and rolled under her hands. His auburn hair curtained his face, full lips parted. Driving deeper, he tilted his head back, throat exposed. She couldn't help but bite and kiss him there, tease the vulnerable area with teeth and tongue.

She reveled in him. His movements, his musky male scent.

This wasn't the wild, explosive fucking of before, but something far more meaningful.

"Mine," he murmured, burying his face in her hair. "Mine."

She'd never been so complete. Cherished.

This man was truly making love to her.

Thrusting in slow, sure rhythm, he drove them to the peak. Overwhelmed her like a spring storm, replenishing a barren desert. Strong and true, his passion carrying her with him over the edge.

"Oh, baby, yes," he moaned, big body shuddering. "Yes."

She arched into him, his name on her lips, clinging tight. Never wanting to let him go.

They came down together, Jude stroking her hair, kissing every inch of her face, petting and loving. He was such an affectionate man, in bed and out.

But only because he didn't recall being any different.

Slipping out of her, he rolled to his back and gathered her into his arms. She settled her head on his chest, listening to his heartbeat. He kissed her head, voice low and rumbly. Protective.

"Don't even think of going anywhere."

"Right now?"

"Or tomorrow, or the next day."

She swallowed hard. "No worries there."

"Good." He let out a big yawn. "God, I'm tired already."

"You're probably still recovering from being sick. Do you still hurt?"

"Some, but not too bad."

She bit her lip, pondering her next question. Per Dietz's orders, she wasn't supposed to ask, or do anything to jog his memory. Now she wondered.

"Jude . . . tell me about the nightmares. About the killing," she said softly.

He went still under her. "Why?"

"Because I care about you." She paused, caressing his chest. "Do you think they're based in fact? Maybe you were, like, working for the government or something." Oh, that was pushing it. Dietz would be furious.

"I don't know what to believe," he said tersely. "And I don't want to talk about this."

Well, that went about like she'd expected.

"Fair enough. I'm sorry. Why don't you take a nap?" she suggested.

"Will you stay?"

"I have work to do, but yes. For a while."

"All right. Lily?"

"Hmm?"

"I'm glad you came into my life," he said. "I just thought you should know."

Did the guilt never end? "Thank you. I—I'm glad, too."

He hugged her close, but in moments, his breathing evened out into sleep. The drug still doing its work. When she was sure he was out, she left his embrace, went to the bathroom, and washed up. God, she could smell his cum and wanted to rub it all over herself. Wallow in it like a cat. Instead, she finished and began to dress.

She refused to think of what had just transpired between them. The depth of emotion, of their connection. It was all for nothing, meant nothing in the end.

She'd best not forget that.

Leaving him, she fetched the thumb drive from her closet and went down to the office. She closed the door and sat at her desk, wiggling the mouse to wake up her computer.

Inserting the drive, she waited for the box to pop up containing the file and got busy. Or tried.

The program was a maze to her. To an agent experienced in breaking code, however, this one would be child's play.

Did she dare call someone to help with this? If so, whom could she trust?

There were a couple of agents she'd trust with her life. The problem was, she wasn't willing to risk theirs. Nor could she take a gamble on saving the worm to her computer's hard drive, or making copies.

Dietz's pompous comment that he knew everything rang in her head. He'd threatened Liam, and she knew he wasn't spouting bullshit.

So she examined the file from one end to the other, played with the code every which way, but she wasn't good enough to crack it. Even so, instinct warned her against letting go of this copy.

Disheartened, she shut down the program and pocketed the thumb drive again. Friday, when Dietz called to tell her where to make the drop, she'd be "out of pocket." Put him off a little longer while she continued to try to reach Michael. She'd go to dinner with Jude and his fancy friends, try to unwind. Forget all of this, for a time.

Pretend that here she'd found a life and a man of her own to love.

. . .

"This is why I haven't gone out," Jude grouched, fussing with his tie. "How am I supposed to get through an evening in a fine restaurant when I can't even dress myself?"

Christ, he sounded like a snot-nosed little kid. But he couldn't help it—he was scared shitless.

"That's the whole *point*, remember?" Lily reminded him, swatting his hands away. "Getting out and proving to yourself that you have the option if you want."

"I'd rather stay here. Liam's cuisine is better than any four-star establishment, which is why I hired him in the first place."

"This was your idea."

"No, it was *Devon's*. But I agreed." Dammit.

"What do he and his wife look like? Are they attractive?"

He knew she was only trying to distract him from being nervous, and he loved her for it. Still, he decided to play along.

"They're striking. Like Brad and Angelina, only she's a redhead. Devon has that blond, spiky, just-rolled-out-of-bed look and carries it off like a Hollywood leading man. Geneva is about an inch taller than he is, even without heels. A true Amazon beauty."

"They sound lovely," she said, patting his tie. "Are they nice?"

"They're . . . magnetic. They'll draw you in before you quite know what's happening. If their sexual allure doesn't have you dripping wet by the time we arrive back at their place, then you're made of solid ice. No hope for you."

He hadn't meant to say anything, but he felt he should warn her now. In case she wasn't game for an adventure.

She leaned in, nuzzled his jaw. "Don't you know by now I'm game for anything?"

"Good." He grinned. "Maybe we can skip dinner?"

"Not a chance. I'm starving."

"Liam can make—"

"Let's go before you wimp out." She grabbed his arm.

"Wimp? I've got your wimp right here in size ten extra long."

That earned a laugh as she dragged him downstairs. Liam saw them off at the front door, his tone a bit down.

"You guys have fun."

"Hey, you should bask in your time off," Jude said, turning toward him. "It's not like you get a night away from the stove very often."

"I guess."

That wasn't convincing at all. Frowning, Jude reached out, touched his shoulder, then skimmed upward and cupped his face. "What's wrong?"

"Nothing, I'm just being stupid. Not used to being alone and it's kind of weird, that's all." His friend's voice brightened, too cheerful to be sincere. "I'm good. Get out of here so I can put my feet up and hog the cable."

Jude almost relented. Nearly said to forget it, they'd stay home. But the nagging doubt passed and he let it go. Liam could handle one night to himself.

"Next time, it's a date with you, me, and Lily," he said. "Deal?"

"You bet," he said, without much enthusiasm.

"Great. Don't wait up."

Out front, Jude held the door while Lily climbed into the limo, then got in after her. Settling close, he held out his hand for her to take and gave his driver directions to pick up the other couple.

As the car pulled away, Jude told himself the finger of dread trailing down his spine was nothing.

Nothing but his imagination.

. . .

Lily watched the city lights roll past, taking mental inventory. The second pill was in her purse, ready for the opportune moment. Her cell phone was off, had been all day, preventing Dietz from reaching her. He could get in touch personally if he wanted, but he'd wait. Chew her ass out when she least expected it.

She tried to forget her agenda for a while, concentrate on pretending to be normal. A woman on the town with three dynamic people.

When the limo stopped and the other couple climbed in, Lily saw Jude was spot-on. Devon and Geneva were stunning; these two belonged on the red carpet at the Oscars.

"Jude!" the blond god exclaimed, pumping his hand with enthusiasm. "God, it's been ages!"

"It has. Too long," he answered, smiling.

"Hello, Jude." Geneva greeted him with a hug and a kiss on the cheek before turning curious, friendly eyes on Lily. "You must be Lily. It's wonderful to meet the woman who's captured Jude's affections."

"Nice to meet you, too," she said warmly. Lily glanced at the men, who were engaged in brisk conversation, catching up. "But I doubt it's possible to capture a free spirit."

"He is that. But he's also loyal. Once he lets you in, he'll do anything for you."

Lily nodded. "He certainly seems devoted to Liam and projects like the shelter."

A wistful look crossed the other woman's face. "Yes. He's an incredible man, but I have a feeling you're only just scraping the surface of learning how much."

Geneva's gaze went right through her, as though she saw the secrets Lily worked so hard to hide. The conflict tearing her apart.

"You'd be right."

"Speaking of Liam, how is he?"

Lily studied her serene expression, wondering if that was more than a simple note of polite inquiry she heard. "Okay, though he seems a bit down lately. Especially tonight."

Something like regret or worry broke through her calm, then was quickly hidden. "Oh? Has he said why?"

"No. You'd have to ask him, but good luck there. We've tried, with no success."

"I—I'm sorry to hear it."

The ride progressed smoothly, the conversation turning to happier, lively topics. The other couple made sure to include Lily, asking her opinions on whatever they discussed, no matter how trivial. They were charming and energetic, and Lily indeed found herself falling under their spell, exactly as Jude warned.

Lily gaped at the restaurant when they arrived. It was exclusive, expensive, with a two-year waiting list. The establishment, notorious for admitting only the upper echelon of society, radiated wealth and snobbery.

No wonder Jude hadn't wanted to come here, of all places, for his first public dinner since being blinded.

But when Lily took his arm and led him inside . . . the management's reaction to him was as though a deity from Mount Olympus had deigned to join them for the evening.

"Mr. St. Laurent, how fabulous to see you!"

"Mr. St. Laurent, you're looking well!"

"We have your private table, right over here. Come this way, but do be careful!"

Stunned, she watched them fawn over Jude. It was like witnessing the parting of the Red Sea. She'd never seen anything like it in her life.

Behind her, she heard Devon chuckle as they were shown to the best table in the restaurant. Un-frigging-real.

After they were seated, Lily leaned to her left and whispered in Jude's ear, "You didn't tell me you're a celebrity."

He shook his head, looking embarrassed. "I'm not. I have lots of money to spend and I'm a good tipper, that's all."

"I don't see them treating anyone else like they're visiting royalty."

"You'll have to look harder, then. I'm nothing special, just a guy."

"Don't let him fool you, Lily," Devon said, blue eyes twinkling. "Our Jude is one of a kind and everyone knows it except him."

"Oh, for God's sake. Can we change the subject?"

His friends laughed affectionately and let him off the hook, launching into talk of the art world. Lily did her best to follow along, but the names of the artists and society figures meant nothing to her. Those people weren't her crowd—not that she had a crowd—and were as far removed from her as the Middle East.

Wine flowed and appetizers were served, Lily taking it all in. Jude looked sinful all in black, hair pulled back into a short tail. Unlike many blind people, he didn't wear sunglasses, which she learned was because he could discern between light and dark, and could sometimes make out vague shapes. Shades would hamper that small ability.

When dinner was served, Jude squeezed her hand under the table. "You're quiet. Are we boring you to death?"

"Not at all. I'm soaking in all of this. I can't believe some people live like this every day."

Jude cocked his head. "Didn't you rub elbows with the elite during your stint at the governor's mansion?"

Ah, shit. A misstep.

"Yes, but though my title was the same, my role was very different. I didn't often get to mix business with pleasure by attending elegant, private dinners, or by socializing on the town with my boss."

"Good point."

"And are you, Lily?" Devon asked with a mischievous grin. "Mixing business with pleasure tonight?"

Beside him, Geneva gave her and Jude a catlike smile, toying with the necklace that plunged into the impressive cleavage of her skimpy black dress. Oh, this couple was good. Just like that, the sexual tension between the four of them could've been cut with a knife.

"I believe I am," she said, eyeing him in appreciation. He was no Jude, but he was very sexy.

"Then might I suggest we finish our meal and skip dessert? We'll take you on a brief tour of the gallery since it's on our way back, then have a nightcap at our place. If that sounds good to both of you." There was no mistaking Devon's true invitation.

The image of this handsome man taking her, burying his cock inside her, made her pussy wet and tingly. "Fine by me. Jude?"

"Christ, when can we leave?"

Devon laughed and they enjoyed their meal, not rushing, but not lingering too long, either. After some haggling, each wanting to pay, the men agreed to split the bill and they were soon in the limo again. They cruised toward the gallery and arrived within twenty minutes.

Lily had thought the outside gorgeous, but the inside was palatial. One did not come by to "pick up a little something" for the house unless one pulled at least seven figures a year. For the first time, Lily pondered just how much was Jude's net worth.

The tour was grand, but at some point Geneva took mercy on her. "We all know what you really want to see," she said. "Let's show you Jude's floor."

He had his own *floor*? Holy crap.

As they stepped off the elevator and her eyes lit on one of his large paintings, her mouth fell open. "My God, these are . . . exquisite."

Jude's paintings were a celebration of human sexuality, a tribute to the beauty of human form. People of all shapes, colors, and sizes. Men and women. In repose, touching tenderly, making love. The forms had no faces and the renditions were not realistic portraits but, rather, blurred. Impressions and suggestions instead of too much detail. She didn't have to know a lot about art to recognize the truth.

The man was a master.

Or had been before Dietz had destroyed his sight.

Geneva touched her arm. "Aren't they special? No one captured the joy of eroticism like Jude. They're priceless."

"Yes, they are."

Lily glanced at the man in question to see him lounging against the wall, letting them look. How must this hurt him to never again take pleasure in his work, or in any aesthetic beauty around him?

Lily admired each one, but grimaced at the two Liam had told her about that must've been from his "dark" period before his blindness. These angry, volatile renderings she hurried past.

As she neared the end, one in particular caught her eye. This one was more detailed than the others. It was of a young man with a mop of black hair, longer in the front than the back, wearing an impish smile and nothing else. Gray eyes danced, shone with love. He lay on his back, legs spread, one knee cocked, hand reaching out, as though beckoning his lover to join him.

"Liam," she breathed.

"Yes," Geneva answered, a catch in her voice. "Our Liam. Devon and I commissioned this one for our private residence, but decided to display it in the gallery. It's not for sale, nor will it ever be."

Our Liam. Could this be the reason behind Liam's funk of late? Were they the ones he'd been meeting secretly? Was he in love with this vibrant couple? It would explain a lot. She didn't know what to say.

She turned back to the painting. Jude's love for his work was evident in every brushstroke, in the way he saw the younger man, the way he would always remember him.

Lily's throat tightened with emotion. No one who could feel so deeply was as bad as Dietz claimed. No matter what Jude had done, there was good inside him.

Turning away, she pretended to examine the rest of the paintings through watery eyes. A few minutes later, they were on their way again, heading toward the Sinclairs' town house.

If either of them noticed how profoundly she'd been affected by Jude's work, they were too kind—or savvy—to mention it.

. . .

Liam popped a bowl of popcorn, grabbed a Diet Coke, and slouched in his favorite chair in the media room. He tried to get into the third *Lord of the Rings* movie. Tried to forget that Dev and Geneva were having a great time without him. Were probably tangled up in a steamy four-way with his lusty friends.

Christ, he wasn't needy or clingy. He just wanted to be secure in his place in Dev's and Geneva's hearts, but knew the couple needed their space. They didn't do live-in, permanent lovers. Liam understood. He *did*.

Fuck that. He was miserable. Sometimes he got so goddamned lonely waiting for the phone to ring, or for the message to appear in his e-mail.

We miss you. Come tonight. Now.

Or how about this one? *Don't ever leave us again.*

He'd long despaired of that ever becoming a reality.

But with Lily's arrival, hope had blossomed that finally things might change. Like she was some sort of omen or something. Jude might have a reason to quell his wandering spirit. Lily would make him happy, and it would rub off like magic dust on Dev and Geneva. Make them realize what they had with Liam was more than just explosive sex.

That they loved him.

His biggest fear—that the two most important people in his world besides Jude would move on, without him. Wouldn't need him anymore, wouldn't want him in their lives. Like tonight.

Liam would rather die than see that day come.

The movie hit a quiet part and a noise caught Liam's ear. A thump, a scrape. He bolted to his feet, bowl sliding off his lap, scattering popcorn everywhere. Whirling, he fixed his gaze on the door to the media room and the hallway beyond.

Another faint noise, coming from downstairs.

"Fuck me," he whispered.

He couldn't stay here. The media room was a trap, no other way out. Leaving the movie going, he crept to the door, gathered his courage, and peeked out. The hallway was clear, so he tiptoed to the top of the stairs, looked down. The foyer was empty, no shadows moving, but he wished he'd left on more lights.

Was his imagination running away with him? He'd stayed here alone many times over the years, for weeks on end. He wasn't the nervous type, had never had a single problem with an intruder.

But he had one now. Another thump, toward the living room window, made his heart kick into overdrive. Hurrying downstairs as quietly as possible, he crossed to the phone in the alcove off the foyer, the one with the landline, picked it up, and punched 911, then laid down the receiver. He couldn't hang around to talk to the dispatcher. He had to get out of the house.

Digging into his shorts, he palmed his cell phone, hands shaking. The noise was right in his path to the kitchen, where he'd laid the keys to his Porsche on the counter, and to the garage beyond. Which fucking way? If he ran out the front door, the closest escape, he'd be in the open without the relative safety and speed of his car.

Dammit, he'd have to try for the car. He inched through the foyer and peered into the living room. One lamp was on, providing a pool of soft light. He didn't see anyone and decided to take the risk.

He hurried through the room and was halfway across when a man stepped casually from the dining room to block his path.

A goddamned big man, wearing a black ski mask and holding a billy club.

"Fuck!"

Liam spun and ran. Faster than he'd ever run, for the front door. The man huffed behind him, gaining. Just as his hand reached the knob, the club slammed into the back of his head with a sickening crack. Pain exploded in his brain and he fell, the man grabbing him. Throwing him to the tile, the cell phone skittering away.

Liam cried out and scrambled on his hands and knees, panic-stricken, trying to escape. But the brute was on him again, a knee in his back pinning him down. He grabbed Liam's hair and smashed his head into the hard floor once. Twice.

Through a haze, Liam saw blood splattering on white marble. His blood. He fought, but the man had him down, delivering several blows to his back. Each one agony, radiating through his entire body.

"Please, stop! I have money! Please—"

"This isn't about money," the man growled. "It's about teaching someone a lesson. Sorry, kid."

"What? Why?"

The knee moved to his back, and a cord wrapped around his neck. Strong hands yanked backward, tightening the cord, digging into his throat. Cutting off his air.

Can't breathe. Oh, God, no. Help me.

I don't want to die.

Gazing across the tile, he saw the crimson pool widen around his head, spreading outward. Felt his body relax, weightless, the pain fading.

Then his vision faded, too. Soft blackness enveloped him,

carried him away from the horror. Away from the murderer, the pounding, someone yelling the word *police*.

Too late.

Jude.

Dev . . . Geneva . . .

Don't forget me.

I love you.

Eleven

ily and Jude were ushered into the Sinclairs' living room, which Lily was amazed to find even more elegant than Jude's. Done in sleek contemporary with plump white sofas and chairs, tons of glass, and priceless art, it was somewhat aloof for Lily's taste. But it was no less mind-boggling.

The best feature was the huge glass see-through fireplace separating the living room from another room, perhaps a den or study. Too bad the weather was too warm to enjoy the ambience.

Devon lit a few candles instead, bathing the room in a seductive glow, then walked to the wide wet bar. "Nightcap, anyone?"

"Chardonnay for me, darling." Geneva kicked off her heels and lowered herself to one of the sofas. "Jude, come sit with me and get comfortable."

Using his cane, Jude joined her, obviously familiar with their layout, yet moving carefully, as though he hadn't visited in a while. "Bourbon and Coke for me."

"I'll have the same as Geneva." Lily parked on the smaller sofa that was positioned to form an L shape with the other, a square glass coffee table in the center.

While Devon prepared the drinks, Lily watched, fascinated, as Geneva curled against Jude, already making her move. The other woman began to loosen his tie, kissing his jaw.

"You're entirely too dressed, handsome."

"Not for long if you have your way, I'll bet." One of his arms went around her, skimming her spine through the thin material of her dress.

"You know me well. We've missed you."

"The feeling is mutual."

She slid the tie from around his neck and tossed it to the coffee table. His jacket went next, which she draped over the arm of the sofa. Then she started on the buttons of his shirt.

Devon placed the two glasses of wine on the table, his lips tilting up. "The poor man just arrived and you're already devouring him?"

"I'm hungry for dessert," she said, parting Jude's shirt, pushing it off his shoulders. She rubbed his chest, plucked at his nipples. When she reached for the buckle on his pants, he made a sound of approval and relaxed, spreading for her.

Lily was mesmerized, hardly aware of Devon returning with the bourbon and colas and settling beside her. A muscular arm went around Lily's shoulders, his breath hot on her neck.

"Have you seen Jude fuck another woman?" he asked softly, kissing the shell of her ear.

"Yes, one of his models in his suite." She shivered, knowing she'd just admitted to spying on Jude. But from his groan of approval, he didn't mind. Then again, Jude had practically invited her to watch.

"And how did that make you feel, pretty Lily?"

"I—I burned. It made me . . ." God, she couldn't think.

"Wet?" Devon unbuttoned her blouse slowly. "Did it make your pussy ache, your body long to be with them?"

"Yes." Her blouse parted, and he cupped one of her breasts, grazing the nipple with his thumb.

"Watch them, Lily," he murmured. "See how explosive they are together. It's liberating, isn't it, being a part of Jude's world? Your every wicked fantasy will be realized, and there's nothing wrong with that."

While Devon played with her nipples, Geneva lifted Jude's cock and balls from his pants. The redhead pulled the pants off his hips and down his legs as he sat exposed, acquiescent to her wishes. His heavy genitals plumped on the sofa, his erection stiff, the whole package making an exclamation point.

Geneva knelt between his thighs and licked the tip, swirling it and making her lover's hips jerk. She sucked the cap, then inched him deeper, fondling his balls as he rested his head on the back of the sofa, apparently in heaven.

Devon's hand slid under Lily's short dress, finding her mound. With a whimper she spread, giving him access, her senses quickly becoming overwhelmed by the couple's skilled seduction. He stroked and petted her pussy, keeping her on edge but not allowing her to go over.

"Keep watching. I want you primed for me," Devon said, blue eyes glittering.

Lord, the man was gorgeous with his blond hair artfully spiked, long dusky lashes, full kissable lips. She wanted him so much. But the other couple captured her attention again, sending her blood pressure higher.

Geneva deep-throated Jude, swallowing him again and again, slurping noisily. Just before he lost control, she pulled off, leaving him flushed and desperate, his erection almost purple with need. But he didn't have to suffer for long.

"Condom?"

"Pants pocket," Jude said hoarsely.

She expedited the matter efficiently, rolling the condom down onto his shaft. Standing, she shed her black dress and straddled his lap, grabbed the base of his penis, brought the head to her entrance.

"Yes," Devon hissed.

Lily groaned with them as the lovely woman sank onto his cock. Everything about the couple was beautiful: her pale, slender limbs, her spine arching, glorious red hair cascading to her ass. Jude's cock impaling her, fingers gripping her slender waist, his sexy face etched with desire.

"Devon, please," Lily begged.

"Not yet. Soon."

Jude held his lover firm, fucking her, cock disappearing and withdrawing. "Always so good, honey. Ahh, yes, give me your sweet pussy."

She did, raising and lowering herself, increasing the tempo of their strokes until she was bouncing on his lap. Helpless noises of pleasure escaped from them both as they fucked with abandon, flesh slapping.

"Gonna come," Jude panted. "Come with me."

Two more thrusts and he stiffened, shouting his release. Geneva ground onto his cock, crying out with her orgasm, and they trembled together, Jude making several more quick pumps into her, milking the rest.

"Now, Lily. Come over here," Devon said, taking her hand. He pulled her up and led her to a thick rug in front of the fireplace. Candles glowed on the hearth, making the scene inviting.

Her body was on fire as he pulled the dress over her head and studied her in bold admiration. Then he guided her to lie on the rug and parted her legs, lying between them on his stomach.

Sure fingers exposed her, baring her to his tongue. He used it expertly, slipping it into her channel, lapping every inch he could reach.

"Oh, yes," Lily said, unfurling for him. "Like that. Don't stop."

Turning her head in a daze, she saw Jude and Geneva kissing, his cock still buried within her. Lily felt hot, so hot she might melt in her skin.

"What do you want?" Devon asked, gazing up at her with a sly smile.

"What?"

"You're still watching them. Tell me—us—what you want." He gestured to his wife and Jude. "What's the point in being a foursome if you don't explore?"

"I—I—"

"Tell me, Lily."

"I want them to come over here. I . . ."

"Yes?" His tone was patient, encouraging.

"I want to be devoured," she whispered.

Devon's eyes flashed dark with arousal. "You want three mouths worshipping your body? Taking you somewhere you've never dared?"

"Yes." She was going to combust. "Then I want you to fuck me hard."

"Good girl. Geneva?"

"We heard, darling. Here we come, pun intended."

Geneva led Jude over, situating him on one side of Lily, herself on the other. Devon's low voice set the tone for the scene.

"Lily, raise your arms above your head and cross them at your wrists, as though you're tied," he said. "It's an act of trust, of giving up all control to us. We won't do anything to hurt you and will bring you only pleasure. But we *are* going to ravish you, do anything we please to your delicious body, and you're going to surrender completely. Do you understand?"

"Y-yes!" Just the simple act of positioning her arms that way made her feel more vulnerable than she'd ever been.

Geneva stretched out beside her, cupping one of Lily's breasts, gently rolling the nipple in her fingers. "She's lovely, Dev. All spread for us."

"So hot," Jude agreed, skimming her stomach. He bent to her, kissing and nibbling.

Devon returned to his mission of eating her pussy and suddenly, three mouths were indeed making a feast of her. She closed her eyes and gave herself over to them, let the tide sweep her away. Jude was right—in some instances, not being able to see heightened the other senses. Every touch, kiss, and caress felt so big. So much *more*.

Twin mouths suckled each of her nipples, greedy. Her clit pulsed in time to the manipulations of tongue and lips. She was nothing now except a mass of erogenous zones being tasted, a banquet. A carnal sacrifice.

Just as she began to unravel, the lips feasting on her pussy disappeared. She made a sound of protest and in seconds, her bottom was hoisted upward in strong hands. The blunt head of a cock found her entrance and she opened her eyes to see Devon crouched there, expression filled with lust. Sexy as the devil.

He pulled her forward, speared her deeply, in one smooth thrust.

Lily pushed onto him, frantic. "Oh, yes!"

"Hard and fast?"

"Fuck me into the floor," she begged.

She didn't have to ask twice. Holding tight, he pumped into her, gave her all he had. He pounded into her, driving her wild, and she met him stroke for stroke.

As she reached the pinnacle, the pair working her nipples swooped on her mouth, claiming it in a three-way kiss. Tongues teasing, playing.

Lily's orgasm detonated and she bucked, flying high, riding wave after wave of pure molten flame. Her descent to reality was gradual and she lay gasping, becoming aware of three grinning faces surrounding her.

"Well," she said with a shaky laugh. "You guys sure know how to devour a girl."

They all laughed as well and Devon said, "You made a request and we aim to please."

"Which you do quite marvelously," she praised, sitting up.

Devon winked. "Thank you. What shall we do now? Enjoy our nightcap and perhaps recuperate for round two?"

"I'm easy," Jude quipped.

Geneva patted his arm. "We know."

Jude opened his mouth to reply, but cocked his head. "What's that?"

"Don't hear anything," Devon said, then paused. "Oh, wait, I do. Someone's cell phone. I think it's coming from Jude's clothes."

"I'll get it." Geneva got up and walked to the sofa, fishing in Jude's shirt pocket. Retrieving the phone, she came back and pressed it into his hand.

"Thanks." Jude flipped the device open. "Hello? Yes. Who is this?"

Time crawled to a stop as everyone watched the satisfied, happy light die, his face turning ghost white as he answered some questions, listened.

"Oh, God, no."

The bottom dropped out of Lily's stomach.

.   .   .

Jude answered the phone, expecting anyone on earth besides the man who greeted him in a somber tone.

"Is this Jude St. Laurent?"

"Yes. Who is this?"

"Mr. St. Laurent, my name is Detective Dan Phillips. Do you own the home at 5573 Cherrywood Lane?"

"I do."

"And you have a young man by the name of Liam O'Neil living in your home; is that correct?"

He hesitated, taken completely off guard. "That's right. What is this about?"

"Mr. St. Laurent," the detective began, voice sympathetic, "you were listed as the emergency contact in Mr. O'Neil's wallet. I'm very sorry to inform you of a break-in that occurred at your residence tonight. Mr. O'Neil was attacked by the intruder, but managed to call 911. He was taken to the hospital but—"

"Oh, God, no." Jude felt light-headed, the blood drained from his head into the floor. "How is he? Please tell me he's all right."

He heard Lily and his friends rise and move toward him.

"I'm sorry, sir, but I honestly don't know. I'm still at your residence with some other officers, trying to piece together what happened."

Which meant Liam wasn't able to tell them. Panic clawed at his heart, a knot of fear in his throat. "Where was he found? What did this bastard do to him?"

"All I know is the responding officers found him lying facedown in the foyer, and the assailant had already fled. The paramedics took your friend away soon after. I wish I could tell you more, but the hospital will be able to provide you with the answers on his condition."

The detective was hedging. Didn't want to tell him how bad Liam was hurt.

What if . . .

No. Liam wasn't dead. He would not accept that.

"Thank you, Detective," he heard himself say from a distance. "Do what you need to at the house. I'm sure you or your officers will talk to me and Liam, eventually. I'll be at the hospital and I want a full report of exactly what happened tonight."

"I'll come by as soon as I wrap up here."

Jude hung up and stood, trying to think what to do next. "Lily, get dressed. We have to go."

She grabbed his hand. "What's happened?"

"Someone broke into the house tonight and attacked Liam," he said, voice cracking. He clutched his head, barely registering Geneva's horrified gasp, panic threatening to overwhelm him. "The police won't even tell me if he's okay."

"Oh, honey," Lily breathed. "We'll go to him, fast as we can. I'm sure he's fine."

"Here're your clothes," Geneva said, pressing them into his hands. Tears were evident in her voice. "We're going with you."

"Damned straight." Devon's voice, strained. "Let's hurry."

Jude opened his mouth. Couldn't speak for the giant lump in his windpipe.

Lily helped him dress, sliding the shirt onto his shoulders, holding out his pants. Clothing rustled, everyone deadly silent.

He left his shirt untucked, slid his feet into his shoes. Someone handed him his jacket, tie, and cane; then Lily dragged him out the door, holding his hand.

All four of them jumped into the limo and Jude gave the driver the name of the hospital closest to his house, praying it was the correct one. He'd been too upset to ask.

The ride seemed to take hours. Jude left everything in the limo except his cane and Lily led him into what he assumed was the emergency room.

"Liam O'Neil," she barked with authority. "Was he brought in here?"

"And you all are?" The receptionist—Jude assumed—sounded bored.

Lily didn't hesitate to lie, her voice cool and firm. "Family. We're his sisters. These are our husbands."

"Oh, let me see what I can find out."

Footsteps receded. Jude clung to Lily's hand, quietly going out of his mind. Liam had seemed so sad earlier when they left. What-ifs thrummed in his head, each one a blow to his stomach.

What if they hadn't left Liam alone?

What if they'd taken him along?

What if he died?

Devon's voice, rife with grief and self-recrimination, broke into his bouncing thoughts. Soft, but not far enough away to keep Jude from overhearing.

"What have I done? I took him for granted and now, because of my selfishness, he may never know—"

"Shh," Geneva whispered. "Don't do this to yourself. He'll know, honey."

"Not if we don't get the chance to tell him! My God, Geneva, I love him as much as you do," he rasped. "He *has* to be all right."

What the—oh.

His friends had fallen in love with Liam—and obviously Dev had been the one greatly conflicted about the fact. Falling for one of their toys was a huge no-can-do in his friend's rule book. Until now. When the hell had this happened?

And Liam feels the same. No wonder he hasn't been himself, especially tonight, watching me and Lily usurp his place.

Jude chose not to comment. What could he say at the moment? The couple already felt bad enough. After ten minutes—twenty?—the receptionist returned, betraying no hint of whether to expect good news or bad.

"The doctor will be with you shortly."

At least they knew Liam was here. Being treated. That had to be good news, right?

Lily's small hand pressed against his chest. "Calm down or you're going to bring on one of your migraines. And if that happens, you won't be any comfort to Liam. He's been through a terrible ordeal and he's going to need all of you."

Jude took several deep breaths, tried to do as she asked. "You're right. It's just so hard not to lose it," he said, pulling her into his arms. She rested her head in the crook of his shoulder, hugging his waist. They remained like that a while, holding each other, seeking solace, giving it in return.

No other woman had ever touched his soul the way Lily did. She felt right in his arms. If only he wasn't such a screwed-up mess, he might pursue something more.

"Are you Mr. O'Neil's family?"

"Yes," Jude said as Lily pulled away.

"Come with me and we'll talk somewhere private," the man directed kindly.

Private. Didn't necessarily mean bad.

Several twists and turns later, a door shut behind them all and Lily guided him into a chair. The doctor wasted no time getting to the crux.

"First, I want you to know that Liam will recover."

"Thank God," Devon said hoarsely.

If Jude hadn't been sitting, he would've fallen from sheer relief. "What are his injuries?"

"Well, he sustained several contusions on his skull and back, and suffered compression of his larynx—"

"In English, goddammit."

The doctor paused. "He was beaten and strangled."

Geneva whimpered. "Oh, Dev . . ."

Those two words hammered into Jude's brain like railroad spikes. Some son of a bitch had put his hands on Liam. Had hurt him. Jude's hands clenched into fists.

"How bad is he?"

"His appearance is worse than his condition. We ran a CAT scan and his brain was fine. He has no internal bleeding, which is great news. However, he has a couple of head injuries that required stitches, a concussion, multiple bruises on his back, and a nasty ligature mark around his neck. His larynx is probably swollen, and talking will be painful for a few days."

"Probably?"

"He's only been awake briefly and he was still in shock. To my knowledge, he hasn't tried to speak. I'd like to keep him overnight for observation, but he should be able to go home tomorrow. Barring any complications, of course."

Go home. As horrible as this was, Jude latched on to that with everything in him. Liam would get to come home. He would recover.

"Can we see him?"

"Sure. He's being moved to a room at the moment, but as soon as he's settled, I'll have a nurse give you the room number."

"Thank you." He reached out and offered his hand. The doctor shook it, then showed them out with instructions to make sure Liam rested for the next few days.

Like he and Lily were going to allow him to lift a finger.

Another interminable wait. If Jude still had his sight, he would've paced, distracted himself by watching the people bustling in and out. As it was, he sat in an uncomfortable plastic chair and fidgeted until a nurse finally gave them Liam's location.

He couldn't get there fast enough. When they entered the room, he didn't have to see to know his friend looked bad.

"Oh, Dev," Geneva choked. "Our poor angel."

Lily pushed Jude into a chair and he reached out, but she caught his hand. "Careful, he has a bandage on the right side of his head and his face is bruised. Here."

She moved his hand and he stroked Liam's silky hair, recalled the way the damnable strands always fell over those laughing gray eyes. He let them slide through his fingers, agonizing that they'd almost lost him. A few more seconds, a bit more pressure on his delicate throat, and this wonderful life would've been snuffed forever.

He's right here, breathing. Safe.

He grazed Liam's cheek and moved downward, careful of his neck, and laid his palm on the younger man's chest. Just felt it rise and fall in reassuring rhythm, heartbeat strong.

Someone shifted on the other side of the bed, and he could sense the person touching Liam, too. "He's all right, darling," Dev said to his wife. "He's going to be fine."

Liam stirred, twisting. "No . . ."

The fear and pain in his battered voice tore out Jude's guts. Gently as he could, he held his friend's hand and squeezed. "Shh, it's me. Lily and I are here. So are Dev and Geneva. Don't try to talk."

"Hurts."

"I know it does," he said, holding back tears. "Try to sleep."

"Jude," he whispered brokenly. "Why? I've never . . . hurt anyone. . . ."

"I know you haven't. You're a good person, my best friend and—oh, God, don't cry. Please, Liam."

But there was no turning the tide. Harsh, rasping cries shook Liam's body and Jude couldn't take it. He could not sit by and listen, simply do nothing. He started to rise, but Lily caught his arm.

"Wait. Dev is going to him," she said quietly. Then, to his friends, "Watch his IV."

Jude heard his friend lie down on the bed with Liam. Nobody

gave a flying rat's ass how it might look to anyone else who came in. The younger man collapsed against Dev and sobbed as though his heart were shattered.

"I've got you," Dev murmured, over and over. "We're right here, Geneva and me. We'll never leave you alone again. Never."

Well, that might be hard to manage in normal, daily life. But Dev would do anything, Jude knew, if it meant the safety and well-being of the gentle soul in his arms.

Several minutes later, Liam was spent, limp and exhausted. "Is he asleep?" Jude asked quietly.

"Yeah, he's out," Lily answered.

Rage seethed in his blood, replacing the panic of earlier. "The motherfucker who did this had better pray to his God for whatever mercy he can get. Because when I find him, I'm going to tear him limb from goddamned limb."

. . .

When the nurse fussed about visiting hours being over, Jude struggled to convince Geneva and Dev to leave. They were devastated about Liam's attack, but Jude pointed out that Geneva needed her rest. Especially if they planned to speak with Liam regarding their relationship with any degree of coherence. They promised to return first thing.

To the watchful nurse, Jude announced that he and Lily were staying, and unless she could provide around-the-clock security for Liam, she could kiss his ass.

Watching the two men doze, Lily wiped the tears from her face. Jude was sitting in a chair, his top half resting on the bed. His hair had worked free of the leather tie and spilled over the pillow next to his friend. Liam's good side was nestled into Jude as much as possible, bandage peeking from under a fall of black hair. His face was bruised, a little swollen.

But the worst was the strangulation mark around his neck. Mottled and purple, it bisected his throat in a thin line. He must've been so terrified, convinced he was about to die.

After all of this was over, she prayed Jude and Liam would forgive her.

Dietz was behind the attack on Liam, no question. Threats were one thing, but he'd crossed the line. Harmed an innocent. His actions smacked of desperation, and where there was a desperate man, there was a guilty one.

She didn't know how all the pieces fit as of yet, but she knew one thing—Jude St. Laurent was a good, honorable man. Yes, he was frightened by the memories that were trying to surface. Some of them were bound to be bad. But she'd bet her life none of them included betraying his country.

Jude's brain had been swept by Dietz and his henchmen. Dietz did not, under any circumstances, want Jude to remember his past with SHADO. Was burning to recover the files as quietly as possible. Which could mean only one thing.

Jude had made a discovery, had locked Dietz's balls in a vise. Dietz had taken him out of commission, but kept him alive for a reason.

The files. Six worms Jude had sent to different places as a safeguard. Evidence? Maybe.

Somehow, she had to learn what was in the file. She needed time to think. To plan.

Her gaze strayed back to the bed. Jude's rage over what had

happened to his friend was a terrible thing to witness. As she'd seen through his paintings at the gallery, this man loved. Deeply. And was loved in return by many.

How could she have been so blind? Even Jude saw better than she did.

Sitting up, she wondered how long they'd been there. The police would be by before it got too late, wanting to speak to Liam. Make their report. If she hurried, she'd have time to slip out and make a call before they arrived.

With a furtive glance at the pair, she crept out and rode the elevator to the main floor. She went and stood outside, a few paces from the front entrance, and turned on her cell phone.

No more messages from Dietz. No doubt he was confident she'd call. She hated to oblige him.

He answered on the third ring. "Took you long enough. Then again, I suppose you've got your hands full at the moment, putting your cute little boy toy back together."

"What's wrong with you, you sick fuck?" she snarled. "He's an innocent young man who's never harmed a soul. He has nothing to do with whatever games you're playing."

Careful. Don't let him know you're on to him. He'll expect you to be angry about Liam, but he's arrogant. Make him think you still believe Jude is guilty; keep him confident.

"You were warned to do your job, so I was forced to get your attention. Don't be a maverick and your lover doesn't get hurt again."

"I have things under control," she said, letting him hear she was pissed. "I've found five out of the six files, but I haven't had time to contact you today. We had an engagement this evening and I might have managed to get it to you later if you hadn't sent in your goon."

"I told you to have the file for me by Friday. You failed."

"I did *not*. It's still Friday for another hour," she pointed out. Fucking bastard.

Silence.

"All right. A point conceded in your favor," he said calmly. "Though I expect in the future you won't keep me waiting."

She ignored that. "I'll have the file to you first thing in the morning." Then she would have time to copy it tonight, continue working on cracking the code. "Meet me at the same park?"

"No need. My man relieved you of your thumb drive before he took care of your lover." Dietz sounded amused. "Careless of you to leave information that could start another world war lying about in your closet like a pair of shoes."

No!

"It was hidden and locked up," she said, seething.

"For all the good it did. What sort of spy can't locate and liberate a simple thumb drive?"

Lily felt ill. Her best chance to find out the truth, gone. She had no clue where Jude might've hidden the last file.

What am I going to do now?

Somehow, he had to remember. It was the only way.

"Is everything on track with eliminating St. Laurent?"

Time to test how good of a liar she was. "I gave him the second dose a short time ago, before we left on our date. He's asleep in Liam's room and will be very sick when he awakens. I need to get him home soon, away from the hospital."

"Excellent. Wait another week, then give him the third dose. Make it strong enough to kill him—I'm tired of waiting."

"Yes, sir." *I'll kill you instead.*

"I'll be in touch."

Lily stuck the phone back in her purse.

"Not if I can help it, dickwad."

Twelve

ily returned to the room and drew up short. A uniformed officer and a man in plain clothes were inside, standing at the foot of Liam's bed. The guy not in uniform had a shield clipped to his belt. A detective, then.

Jude was back in his chair but had a protective hand on his friend's arm, and a forbidding scowl on his face that did not bode well for the next person who upset Liam.

The cops barely glanced at her as she walked in and took a spot on Liam's other side.

"—heard a noise," Liam was saying, his ruined voice a hoarse whisper. His expression revealed his misery at having to recount the attack. "I went out to the top of the stairs . . . heard it again. Knew I had to get out."

"So you went downstairs?" the detective asked.

Liam nodded, wincing in pain at the slight movement. "I called 911 . . . left the phone off the hook. Wanted to get to my car in the garage. Get out."

He reached for a plastic cup on the nearby tray. Lily handed it to him and they all waited while he took a few sips of water. Talking this much had to be painful.

He lowered the cup to his lap. "A guy stepped out of the dining room. Cut me off. Big fucker . . . all in black, wearing a ski mask." The cup in his lap trembled violently and Lily grabbed it before it spilled, set it back on the tray.

She propped her arm on the pillow beside him, stroked his hair. "It's okay, sweetie. You're safe now. Go on."

"I ran—he chased me. Caught me, hit the back of my head. Threw me down." He paused, swallowed hard, composing himself. "He hit me with a billy club a few times, slammed my head into the floor. And then he wrapped a cord around my neck. Started choking me and . . . I thought I was dead."

A dangerous, animal noise rumbled in Jude's chest. She had no doubt that if he ever found out Dietz was behind this, he'd make the man suffer.

For one crazy moment, she came close to blurting Dietz's name to the cops. Telling them who she was, everything. But that would be suicide. SHADO did not exist anywhere on record. The cops would think she was insane with her tale of espionage, and they would all be dead by morning.

"Why would anyone want to kill me?" The devastated look in his eyes was almost more than she could bear.

"That's what we hope to find out, Mr. O'Neil," the detective said. "Could he have been a burglar you surprised? Maybe after jewelry or electronics?"

"I don't know, I . . ."

"Do you remember something?" Jude asked.

"Yeah. I told him I had money and he said . . . it wasn't about money." Liam's eyes filled. "He said it was about teaching someone a lesson."

The officers exchanged a look.

"Did he say anything else?" the detective asked.

"No."

"Any idea what that means?"

Liam glanced at Jude, then looked away, picking at the bed-covers. "No."

A few more pointed questions later, the cops left, no closer to answers than when they'd arrived.

Liam studied Jude. "This has something to do with you and your mysterious trips, doesn't it?"

Jude hung his head. "I don't know. I wish I could remember. I'm so sorry."

Do I tell him?

No. His memory needed to return naturally. No telling what damage could be done if she suddenly hit him with the truth.

Liam shook his head. "Forget it. We'll be okay."

"Will you? Be okay?" Jude clasped his friend's shoulder, giving it a squeeze. "I know about Dev and Geneva. How you feel about them."

Liam's bitter laugh emerged as a wheeze. "Do you? Too bad they don't feel the same."

"You should've seen them, buddy. They were frantic when we heard about your attack. Dev is beating himself to a pulp for not telling you how they feel—"

"Guilt." Liam's lips compressed into a thin line.

"No, love."

"Whatever. The fact is, they were with you two last night.

Not me. If I hadn't been hurt, they wouldn't have realized their great *love* for me," he insisted, voice almost gone. "I don't want to see them right now, *either* of them. Take care of it, Jude."

"If that's what you want," Jude said slowly.

"It is."

"Just promise me one thing, my friend." Jude paused. "Don't throw away a chance at true love. Even if the road isn't nice and smooth."

Liam's expression became determined. "Me? I'm not throwing away anything. If they want me, they'll have to fight for me."

*   *   *

Damn, he hated hospitals and he was glad to have Liam home. No one ever got any rest there, what with all the poking and prodding every hour. His friend was exhausted, fear and shock taking their toll.

Not to mention his brooding over his lovers, who, after a round of arguing with Jude, had honored Liam's wishes.

Liam said sadly that they gave up too easily. Maybe he was right.

He and Lily brought him in through the kitchen and paused long enough to make him take a painkiller. The doctor had prescribed a mild sleep aid to help him rest at night, if needed, but they'd cross that bridge soon enough. Right now, they all could use a nap.

As they trekked through the dining and living rooms, approached the foyer, Liam must've reacted badly, because Lily soothed him. Kept him walking past.

Jude thanked God Lily had the presence of mind to have him phone the housekeeper, get her in here to clean up before Liam came home. The woman had reported that the tile was smeared with his blood. Jude called the window and glass service again as well, who made another trip to fix the broken window where the intruder entered the house.

"Where are we going?" Liam asked, nervous.

Lily tried to sound upbeat. "We're going to get you tucked into bed, sweetie. You need some real rest."

"M-my bed?"

"Yes, why?"

"No. Don't m-make me s-stay down here alone," he rasped, pleading. "What if . . . he comes back? I can't—can't—"

Oh, Christ. The guy was about to have a panic attack. How could he have been so thoughtless?

"Easy does it," Jude said firmly. "Of course you don't have to stay down here. We'll just take you upstairs and put you in Lily's room for now. Sound good?"

"O-okay."

Upstairs, Lily got Liam into bed, fussing over him. "Do you want us to stay?"

"Yes," he said, barely audible. "If you guys don't mind."

"Mind? Don't be silly! Strip, Jude. We're going in."

He shed his clothes and slid under the covers with a tired groan. They sandwiched Liam between them, holding him close, doing their best to let him know he was loved. Protected. He snuggled in with a sigh and almost immediately fell asleep.

As Jude drifted off, he silently cursed Geneva and Dev for not fighting harder for the man they loved. This distance between them wasn't good. Liam should be with *them* right now, not settling for his second choice.

Everything was fucked-up and he didn't have a clue how to make it right.

. . .

Lily sat at the computer, cursing the loss of the file, and not for the first time. She'd made two more covert trips down to the war room, and come up empty. All weekend, watching Liam slink around the estate like a pale ghost while Jude worried himself sick, she'd agonized over what to do. Dietz would be in contact again in a few days, and by then he'd know Jude wasn't getting the poison.

She had a plan. It was a sucky plan, but better than nothing.

One last time, she tried phoning Michael Ross. When Simon started in with his usual song and dance, Lily cut him cold.

"Listen to me, and hear what I'm saying. If you don't tell Michael to put his sorry, baggy ass on the phone, I'm going to be on your doorstep in an hour. And if I have to go to all that trouble, I *will* come in whether I'm invited or not."

In less than thirty seconds, a tired voice said, "I'll have you know my ass is not baggy. It's so tight you could bounce a quarter off it. What the fuck gives, Lily?"

Now that she had his attention, she wasn't going to waste a second. "You have a traitor in your midst, Michael. And no matter what line of bullshit Robert Dietz fed you, it isn't Jude St. Laurent."

"Jude? What the hell are you talking about?"

Lily closed her eyes and pinched the bridge of her nose. "Jesus H., you're so far out of the loop, you're on Pluto."

"I'm in mourning here," he said coolly. "If there's a point, get there or hang up."

"I'm sorry. I meant no disrespect, but we have a serious problem here. And before you tell me that's why you left Dietz in charge and to go to him, he *is* the problem."

"How so?" At least she had his attention now.

"A couple of weeks ago, he ordered me to eliminate Jude. Said he had hard evidence linking him to the theft and sale of a weapon of mass destruction to one of our enemies."

"But . . . that theft occurred three months ago. It was kept hush-hush, no press."

"Right. It was stolen right about the time Jude sent six worms containing information on the theft to six different hard drives. Dietz then had Jude picked up, his brain swept of all memory of being an assassin, or of SHADO. He declared Jude the mastermind behind the theft, but wouldn't kill him outright because he didn't know where all of the files had ended up. Jude wouldn't tell, even under torture."

"He kept Jude around for insurance?"

"Yes, temporarily. In the meantime, he ordered me to find all the files to keep the press from getting wind of the theft. I'd found four of them and we figured the other two were here somewhere, in his home."

"So he finally lost patience and sent you in to locate them and eliminate your target."

"Yes."

"But now you're convinced Jude is innocent."

"Right again. Dietz is getting desperate to see Jude dead, and is getting nasty. He's already hurt one of Jude's good friends, a man I've come to care for, in order to keep me in line."

"I see." He was silent for a moment. "What have you done with the files you've found? Given them to Robert?"

"Yes, five of them, which I'm sure he's destroyed. Actually, I'd kept the last one to try to decipher and he stole it when he orchestrated the attack on our friend. There's one more, but I have no idea where it could be. I've searched every inch of this place."

"Lily, Robert's actions are questionable at best. Suspicious. But what makes you so positive Jude isn't guilty?"

"You're asking me? He was one of your best."

"Even the best can go bad."

"Not Jude," she said firmly. "I'd stake my life on it. Dietz is frantic to get rid of Jude before the mind sweep breaks down. Jude is already recalling stuff about his jobs and it's only a matter of time."

"You realize, without proof, it's your word against Robert's?"

"Michael, *Robert* is the one with the burden of proof. He's the one hot to kill a good agent, after ruining his sight and derailing his life. What right did he have to make a decision like that without your approval?"

Take the reins. Please, for God's sake.

"All right," he said after a long moment. "I believe you. You're a damned fine agent and so was Jude. Neither of you has ever let me down."

She sagged in relief. "Thank you."

"But we have to tread carefully on this. If Robert is the one behind the weapons conspiracy, then we need solid evidence. We need that remaining file, or for Jude's memory to return. Preferably both."

"What do you want me to do?"

"Get Jude out of the country, fast. Go someplace warm and tropical, hole up for a bit, and try to jog his memory. Carefully, because there's no telling how he'll react if he *does* recall everything.

And let me know where you're going. Only me. If something goes down, one of us will call the other and we'll meet at the safe house in Tennessee."

"What will you be doing?"

He gave a humorless laugh. "I'm going to keep an eye on Dietz. And while I'm at it, I'm going to take my company back."

"I'm glad, Michael."

"It's past time, apparently. Get back to me with your destination as soon as you know it."

"I will, and thank you."

"Don't thank me yet. The fat lady is nowhere near the stage."

He hung up and she set the phone down, burying her face in her hands. Thank God. Finally, someone on their side. That someone being the boss, and one of the most powerful, fair men she knew. Things would be fine now.

If only he could keep tabs on Dietz.

Lily spent an hour on the Internet, researching tropical resorts, discarding one after the other until she hit pay dirt—a fabulous adult-only resort in Los Cabos that catered to the sexually adventurous. The place sounded like heaven.

She spent another half hour on the phone with the resort, wrangling for a last-minute reservation, but in the end wound up with their best luxury suite, boasting a built-in hot tub, a fully stocked bar, and all sorts of other naughty goodies.

Last, she booked a flight for the three of them. No way in hell were they leaving Liam here, since he wasn't ready to deal with Dev and Geneva. He needed this impromptu vacation as much as, if not more than, she and Jude.

Done, she went in search of the men and found them reclining by the pool in shorts and no shirts. She drank in the sight of them, such a striking pair. Even the bruises on Liam's back and throat didn't detract from his beauty. They, along with the head wounds, were already starting to heal, but would take a while to completely disappear.

The inner scars would take much longer.

"What's up?" Liam glanced at her, trying to smile. His poor voice was still scratchy.

"Los Cabos, that's what."

"Huh?"

Jude inclined his head toward her with a puzzled smile. "Mexico?"

"Bonus points for Edgar."

"Funny. What *about* Los Cabos?"

"Reservations. Ours. For two weeks," she said, taking in their stunned faces. "At a five-star adult resort that redefines the word *debauchery*."

"Holy shit," Liam said, mood lifting. "When are we going?"

"Pack your bags, gentlemen, because our plane leaves at nine in the morning." She grinned. "And I'm going to be on it with my favorite guys."

. . .

Los Cabos gleamed like a jewel, with pristine sands and blue green water, the fresh salty air inviting.

Or at least that's how Jude imagined it—except for the breeze, the rush of waves on the shore, the call of gulls, lively conversation. Those enabled him to form a better picture. But what was so special about a place you couldn't see?

The woman you're with, big guy.

The bellboy rolled their bags to their suite and brought them in, exclaiming about how much they'd love their stay, all the fun activities to do, the nightlife, blah, blah. Jude figured the guy wanted a good tip, so he gave him a fat one.

That shut him up and he scurried away, leaving Jude and his companions to explore their new surroundings. Jude had to admit, at first he hadn't thought this was such a good idea. Well, a great idea with bad timing, maybe. He hadn't taken a vacation in years, and certainly hadn't planned on one now.

And then there was Liam. Battered and heartsick, his sleep broken by terror, he was only just beginning to heal. Jude had almost nixed the tropical excursion, but after the way his friend lit up like a Christmas tree at the idea, depression lifted, Jude had relented. This could be just what they all needed.

"Hoo-boy!" Liam exclaimed in a scratchy voice. "I love it here already!"

"What is it?"

"There's a bowl of condoms on the coffee table! Purple, red, green, blue . . . ribbed, lubed . . . flavored!"

"You are such a horn dog," Lily teased. "You'll probably have tried them all by the end of our stay."

"Me? I'm as pure as a nun. Sex, ewww."

Jude chuckled. This was the Liam he knew.

Lily twined her fingers through Jude's. "You guys want to change, check out the bar, and get a drink, then walk down to the beach?"

"Great!"

Jude pictured him pumping his fist. "Sounds good. I am a little thirsty."

Jude brought his cane even though Lily helped to steer him from their suite and through the resort the short distance to the outdoor bar. Here, he discovered, the drinks were served in plastic cups so the patrons could conveniently carry them all over the resort.

They sidled up to the counter and a bartender spoke from directly in front of Jude.

"What's your poison today, guys?"

Liam didn't hesitate. "I'll have a *Sex on the Beach.*"

"You are so cliché," Lily said, giggling.

"Am not! They're good—you should try one."

"We just got here, cutie. I want to be conscious when the sun sets." Ignoring Liam's snort, she addressed the bartender. "I'll have a Corona with a lime."

"A rum and Coke for me," Jude said.

"Coming right up."

The man moved away to his task, while Liam continued to ogle their surroundings.

"Oh, man. This place is awesome. Thanks for bringing us here, Lily."

"You're very welcome. What would you like to—"

"Holy crap! Topless volleyball," he breathed in reverence. "Can we go down there?"

"We are, in a minute. Hope they're wearing sunscreen," Lily joked.

"You want to play?"

"I'll pass, thanks. Jumping around with my parts jiggling isn't my thing."

"But you don't have anything to jiggle," Liam said, laughing.

"You little shit," she replied with fake menace. "Just see if that gets you any nooky."

"Oh, there's plenty of that around here if you cut me off."

"Careful, you have to live with me."

"Sorry." He didn't sound sincere.

Their drinks arrived and Lily pushed Jude's into his hand. "Here you go."

"Thanks." He took a swallow, relishing the cold burst of the dark flavor on his tongue. "This is good."

"Mine, too," Liam said. "Well, I'm going to watch the volleyball game. Come on, you two!"

Jude heard the barstool scrape and figured he must've taken off. Lily laughed, leaning into Jude's side.

"Good grief. Don't you ever let him out of the kitchen?"

Jude thought about that. "Not enough, apparently, considering he's been sneaking around with Dev and Geneva. In fact, I'm not sure he's ever been on a real vacation."

"That's just criminal. If it was up to me, I'd spoil him all the time. I'd spoil both of you."

Did he detect a hint of wistfulness?

"You two have bonded quite well."

"And have *we*? Bonded?"

He reached for her. "Do you really need to ask?"

"Yes," she said, taking his hand. "I feel . . . like there's more going on between you and me than great sex—not that there's anything wrong with consenting adults playing fair and square. But I . . ."

"Tell me." His heart quickened. He very much wanted to hear what she had to say on the subject.

Just then, a man next to them ordered a drink.

"Walk with me," she suggested.

He let her pull him away from the bar, getting that she wanted a little more privacy. He toyed with his rum and Coke, happy and a little nervous, too.

"This is new territory for me," she went on. "In my limited experience, it's not wise to get too attached to someone you care about. To let those feelings grow into more."

"You've been hurt," he said, squeezing her hand.

"Not in the way you mean."

He took a guess. "You're talking about your father again."

"Yeah. It's not that I consciously shut out people on purpose. Or at least I don't think so." She sighed. "I'm not doing a very good job of explaining myself."

"You're doing fine. I think I know what you're trying to say."

She gave a rueful laugh. "Well, you're a step ahead of me."

"Let me give it a shot—you came to work for me, a man who shares your sexual preferences, and you thought you'd won the lottery. But you didn't expect our fun to develop into real feelings. And that scares the shit out of you."

"You're a mind reader."

"No, I just feel the same way."

"You—you have feelings for me? Real ones?" She sounded vulnerable, unsure.

"How could I not? You're smart, beautiful. You blow my mind in bed. But more than that, you've been a rock for me. In the short time we've known each other, you've gotten under my skin like no one else has." Pausing, he pulled her to face him before going on.

"Do you remember the first time we made love?"

"Yes. How could I forget?"

"You'll never know how much that meant to me. I want to spoil *you*, make you happy. Learn all the things that make you laugh. Or make you sad. I'm falling for you, Lily, and I want to let this grow," he said softly, skimming up her arm.

"Oh, Jude." Her voice shook with emotion. "I want that, too."

"But there's something you need to know up front." He took a deep breath. "About my nightmares. More and more, I'm convinced they're memories and if they are . . . I might be . . . an evil man. Or at least might have done horrible things. You can walk away now and never have to find out."

"No. You're not evil," she said, brooking no argument. "I'm absolutely positive you're one of the finest men I know. Period."

"You can't know—"

"I do." She sounded a bit on edge now.

"How?"

"Tell me something." She paused. "How do you feel in these dreams, when you're committing these supposedly evil acts?"

"Mostly? Cold. Locked down inside."

"Justified?"

"I . . . yes," he said slowly. "I think so."

"Anything else?"

"No—wait, yes. Tired. Ready to throw in the towel." How strange.

"As though the time has come to quit," she said, sounding certain. "You're burned-out."

A chill crept down his spine. "How do you know this?"

"Have you considered that you may have had a second job? Something covert? In that case, you aren't a monster at all, but a victim of something bigger than yourself."

"That's pretty far-fetched." But even as he protested, he wasn't so sure.

"Just think about it, all right? And focus on recalling what details you can."

"I—sure. I can do that."

"Good, handsome. Kiss me."

"Gladly."

Why did it seem like she wanted to distract him? Of course, there were worse ways to end the disturbing conversation. Cupping her head, he claimed her mouth, lips moving against hers, gentle. Then he delved deeper, sliding his tongue inside to taste the beer and lime, salty sweet, and more intoxicating than all the liquor in Los Cabos.

When they parted, she took his arm. "Come on, let's catch up with Liam. I want to watch him go nuts over topless volleyball."

He accepted the change of subject without comment, for now. Such a serious issue couldn't be avoided forever.

"People leaping around half-naked? Christ, what a sport. This part of being blind sucks, big-time," he complained.

"I'll give you a play-by-play."

"Gee, thanks."

"And a live reenactment, later."

"Now you're talking!"

As she led him toward the mad revelry, Jude thought maybe he could luck out. Have everything a man could want or need.

Love. Companionship. Contentment.

Awesome sex.

If only Lily was right, and he wasn't the monster he feared.

. . .

Lily had to tell him the truth. Despite Michael urging her to take it slow with him.

Not once had she considered it a real option before now. She'd been too focused on the case itself, not the man. Once the mind sweep failed, and it would very soon, he'd remember his job at SHADO. He'd recognize her name as that of a fellow spy.

And he'd know that, best-case scenario, she'd come here to deceive him. At worst, he might believe *she* was the one behind the sweep. That she was involved in Dietz's schemes.

Eventually, he'd realize she was sent to kill him.

He'd never forgive her, and the knowledge slammed her hard. Made her want to spill the whole story and throw herself on his mercy. But she'd lose him anyway.

She'd come so close just now to telling him that he was an agent. That the nightmares weren't crazy ramblings. Then he'd demand to know how she knew, what the hell was going on, and the rest would unravel.

She wasn't ready. Selfishly, she wanted to cling to him as long as possible, to pretend for these next few days that he was hers. That he wouldn't order her to leave when he learned what she'd done.

Pushing away the melancholy, she glanced toward the volleyball game and smiled in spite of herself. Liam was right in the thick of it, laughing, soaking up the attention from the ladies. He moved a bit stiffly from the sore, bruised muscles on his back, but he looked good.

"He's having a great time," Lily remarked. "He's got more energy than anyone I've ever met. Even when he's still healing."

"I hope this trip is good for him. And that Dev has come to his senses by the time we go home."

Home.

Some things just weren't in the cards, no matter how badly one might want them. Or how hard one fought.

Lily settled them into beach chairs under an umbrella and tried to forget about secrets. Lies.

And how they'd soon destroy a life she hadn't known she wanted until she met Jude.

Thirteen

J ude relaxed in a lounger on the resort's patio area, soaking
in the revelry around him. Not wild and crazy, but lively,
friendly. The folks they'd met today had been nice, some curious
about Jude's blindness.

To the few who dared to ask outright, he gave them the simple
explanation of being in a car accident. Most left it alone, but two
or three had commented about the heightened-sensuality angle,
and the true anonymity of the partners he'd enjoy at a resort like
this one. Though he'd give anything to have his sight back, he had
to give them that point.

Especially now, with certain murmurs and moans of pleasure
drifting to his out-of-the-way spot on the fringe of the activity.
With the setting of the sun and the arrival of evening, inhibitions
loosened and vanished.

Whispers of "Lick her there" and "Stretch him wide" washed
over him like a low electric hum, heating his blood, thickening his
cock. Where in blazing hell were his own companions? The
debauchery around him began to get to him and he spread his
legs some, adjusting his growing dick in his swim trunks.

208 • Jo Davis

"My, my," a female voice purred close to his ear. "Who disappeared and left a stud like you alone and wanting?"

"I'm here with my two friends, but they've obviously found something to keep them busy."

She skimmed his bare chest, nipped his shoulder. "The pretty young man and the petite woman with long dark hair," she said. "I've seen you with them today. I see one of them now."

"Which one?"

"Your lady friend. She's on the opposite side of the patio in the darkness with her legs spread and one of the hunky bartenders lapping her cunt." Her exploration continued to the waistband of his trunks.

"Oh, God." His cock went hard as a steel pole.

"He's really getting with it, eating her while two of his friends have her ankles, keeping her open for him." She delved inside, wrapped her fingers around his scorching flesh. "Your young man went off down the beach with two hot girls some time ago, and here you are, in such a sad state. Let me help you, and we'll give them a show in return."

"Yes," he hissed. He'd been on a slow simmer all day, and with his friends partaking of their own pleasures, he wasn't about to refuse.

"Let's get naked, sweetheart," she said with a laugh.

Jesus, this place was getting to him, sending his libido into hyperdrive. To be in a haven solely for adults who shared the same attitudes about sexual freedom was a heady experience.

"What's your name?" he asked.

"Brenda. Yours?"

"Jude."

With those preliminaries done, Brenda took his hand and pulled him up. As soon as he stood, they were all over each other, devouring each other's mouths, tongues spearing. Searching.

With his help, her skimpy bikini top went first, then the bottoms. She yanked his trunks down his legs and off, then knelt as he widened his stance for her.

Grabbing the base of his cock, she guided the head to her lips. Licked and teased, tasted the drops of pre-cum oozing forth.

"We're gaining quite an audience," she informed him, pleased with herself. "Oh, your lady friend is watching, too."

"Fuck, yeah. Let them all look their fill." Jude fisted his hands in her hair, cut in a chin-length bob. He wondered at the color, then decided he didn't care. Hot, dirty sex with a total stranger was what he craved tonight. Knowing Lily was enjoying the same, while observing him, aroused him beyond belief.

"You're so huge." Lick. "Hung like a bull."

"Suck me, honey," he growled.

She obliged and his entire length was sheathed by a warm, wet cavern. Her clever tongue bathed the ridge underneath his shaft, mouth sucking. His balls were manipulated, rolled in her palms, as she worked him.

"Ahh, yes. Like that—suck it."

Losing himself, he fucked her mouth harder, hitting the back of her throat. She took him easily, no novice at servicing a man this way. So good. The sounds of sex around them drove him higher.

When the familiar buzz began in his balls, hummed at the base of his spine, he tugged gently. "Need inside you. Now."

She pulled off him with a last slow lick and stood. "Can't wait. Damn, you're so freaking sexy. How do you want me?"

"I think there's a low wall nearby. I want you to face it, brace yourself, and spread your legs for me. I want everybody to be able to see me fucking you."

"Fuck, yeah," a man groaned. "Do her."

"Condoms?" she asked.

"In the pocket of my swim trunks. Put it on me."

The package crinkled and she smoothed the rubber over him quickly. His cock twitched. He'd always been turned on by a lover doing it for him, though he was in no coherent frame of mind to reason why.

"Make sure we're visible," he said as she led him into position, hardly able to contain his release at the image of fucking Brenda in public. "Spread wide and poke your ass out. I want your pretty pussy exposed to me. To *everyone*."

"Shit, yes." She moved into position. "Take what you need, handsome."

First, he'd treat her with the same consideration she'd showed him. Crouching behind her, he rubbed a hand up her leg, to her ass cheeks. When he parted her and rimmed her taut little back entrance with his tongue, she gasped, nearly coming unglued.

"Oh, God! That's good. . . . Tongue me. Lick me."

He tongue-fucked her, plunging into her tiny hole. Inhaled her earthy scent. After a few moments of attention there, he moved lower. Tasted her slit, her readiness for him. She was sweet and plump, dripping, and he feasted on her, licking and nibbling until she was grinding onto his face. Sobbing and begging.

"Please, fuck me! Do me, now!"

Several voices moaned their own pleasure to punctuate the demand.

Ready to burst, he rose over her, grabbed her curvy hips. Carefully, he brought the head of his cock to the opening, worked between her lips. In one smooth motion, he buried himself deep inside her. Reveled in their bodies, connected, hot and sweaty. He felt dark and nasty, gave himself to the glorious feeling of being buried in his lover's cunt. Owning her, for this brief space of time.

For all to see.

Especially Lily.

He imagined them, two attractive strangers moving together in this beautiful setting, sharing their bodies. He wondered whether Lily was as swept along by the tide of lust permeating this place.

The thought did him in and he fucked her hard, hips pumping rapidly. He couldn't get enough of his cock pounding her sheath, her little cries, her body wild underneath him.

"Fuck, yes!" she yelled in time to his strokes. "Yes, yes! Harder . . . almost there . . ."

His balls exploded and he filled her with a hoarse shout, buried to the hilt. She shattered and vibrated around his cock, on and on. For a few seconds they remained in place, breathing hard. Coming down.

Finally, he pulled out with a bit of regret. "Thank you, Brenda. You were incredible."

"Back at you." He heard the satisfaction in her tone. "You incinerated me."

"Did our audience survive?"

Brenda chuckled. "I think you sent a few of them over the edge. Your pretty friend just left—alone, by the way."

He was suddenly anxious to get going. Quickly, he tied the condom and pulled on his trunks, putting the rubber in the pocket to discard later. He considered staying a while longer until he recovered and going for another round, but the urge to return to Lily was stronger.

As naughty and exciting as his tryst with Brenda was, it had taught him something very important—if he had any doubt before, he now knew where his heart lay.

He wanted to return to the woman he loved most.

No matter how hard they played, he knew he could count on her to be there.

As though sensing their time was at an end, Brenda didn't try to coax him to stay. She handed him his cane, which had been parked by the lounger, and kissed his cheek.

"Let me see you to your door," she insisted. "The paths are confusing even for a sighted person, and I'd hate to hear you'd injured yourself."

Touched by Brenda's thoughtfulness, he agreed, giving her his suite number. They had a nice walk, filled by her friendly chatter. She and her husband had an open marriage, and indulged in staying here once a year to keep things spicy. Apparently, the hubby had his own fun planned for tonight.

That's what I want, he thought. Someone who's mine and whom I can count on to keep things exciting. *Yet she knows whose arms she belongs in.*

Soon, they were at his door. "Perhaps we'll run into each other again?" he asked.

"Maybe so," she said playfully. "You never know."

They left it at that and he dug out his card key, letting himself in and shutting the door behind him. The suite felt empty, the silence total.

"Hey, I'm back! Hello?"

Since his friends weren't back yet, he took a leisurely shower, washing away the ocean and the great sex. Once he was clean, he flopped onto the bed he was sharing with Lily and flipped on the television, only halfway paying attention.

Where the hell was Lily? He'd assumed she was headed to their room, but apparently he'd been wrong. Damn, he wanted to talk about their steamy encounters on the patio. Public sex was a first for him! That he could recall, anyway. And maybe talking would lead to more.

He hoped Liam was all right, too. Despite the younger man's assurances, Jude worried about him. Being a couple of thousand miles from where the attack occurred had obviously helped him feel safe, though. If he said he was fine, Jude would go along. For now.

The drone of the television began to lull him to sleep, the day catching up to him. Fighting the airport, the flight. Sand and surf. Sex. Man, they'd really packed a lot into today.

He was hardly aware of the remote slipping from his hand.

. . .

Lily rolled over and stretched, blinking at the bright sunshine streaming through the gauzy curtains. A soft snore buzzed beside her and she glanced over to watch Jude sleep peacefully.

The sunlight set his hair on fire, bathed his rich golden skin. Long lashes rested against his high cheekbones and his lips were parted a bit. He lay sprawled on his back, one arm over his head, legs tangled in the sheets. A slice of naked hip was just visible, tantalizing her with thoughts of what was beneath.

When she'd crept in last night, he'd barely stirred. Part of him was awake now, however, poking at the sheet draped across the target area. The man was insatiable, even unconscious.

Thinking back to last night, she recalled the decadence of having the attention of the handsome bartender and his two friends. The two had her spread for their buddy, who feasted on her pussy with amazing skill, when she'd seen the cute, curvy blonde with the bobbed haircut approach Jude.

Watching what he and the girl were doing—knowing he

obviously wanted Lily and everyone else to see—while Lily's three studs spoiled her brought her one intense orgasm after another. Oh, the talents of the three men were pleasing enough, but it was dreaming of Jude that sent her into orbit.

Beside her, Jude shifted. Then his lashes fluttered open and she found herself looking into striking green eyes. Was he awake? Did blind people know their eyes were open when they first awoke? What a strange thought.

"Good morning," she said, brushing a strand of hair from his eyes. "How was your night?"

He rolled to face her, a slow smile spreading across his face. "Good morning. It was very naughty," he said, voice rumbling. "How about yours?"

"I have a feeling you already know."

"I might've heard something."

"From your cute blond acquaintance?"

He reached out, skimmed her arm. "Was she blond? I'd wondered. Though not for long, since I was too busy to think about it." He seemed to enjoy provoking her.

"You're incorrigible."

"That's why you love me," he teased.

Something inside her went still and quiet. In a very good way. "Yes, it is."

Leaning over, he gave her a slow kiss. Not with too much heat, but lazy and comfortable. When he pulled back, a frown wrinkled his brow. "Is Liam back?"

"Yes, don't worry," she said, hugging him. "He returned a few minutes after I did, and he's fine. Our Casanova was whistling."

Jude pulled back and smiled in relief. "Good. I want him happy, and if this trip helps him recover, I'm satisfied, too."

"He's not the only one having fun," she pointed out, caressing his broad chest. "You're doing pretty well in that department."

"Mmm, you bad girl. You really love to spy, don't you?"

"You have no idea."

His lips curved up. "Since I don't have that luxury, where did you run off to last night? I came back here to find you and fell asleep waiting for you. Did your three admirers treat you right?"

That was sweet of him. A little pang pricked her heart at the thought of him waiting. "They did. After you and your blond friend were finished, we went to the indoor spa and took turns pleasuring each other. Juan—the bartender—went down on me outside, so I returned the favor. Afterwards, his friends were so aroused they needed some attention."

"I can imagine," he said, grinding his cock into her mound. "And did you give them some?"

"Of course. They were so patient, so hard from watching me and Juan. I sucked both of their cocks . . . at the same time," she said with a grin.

His jaw dropped open. "The hell you say! Both?"

"Oh, yes. They were quite a tight fit, but the effort was well worth the results. I had them both sobbing like babies before I was through with them."

"Christ, I can imagine," he muttered. "Did any of them fuck you?"

"Would that bother you?"

A strange expression crossed his face. "I don't know. Yes and no, I guess. It turns me on, but at the same time . . . it makes me jealous," he said in wonder. "I know that's a double standard, but I can't help it. And at the same time, it makes me hotter than a torch."

"Confusing, isn't it? I feel the same way. We're quite a screwed-up pair, aren't we?"

"I'll say."

Clearly, he was done talking, because he nudged her thighs apart and his erection breached her sex. His cock slid into her, the invasion welcome, his strong body flexing. Moving over her, thrusting deep again and again.

"Lily, baby . . ."

Jude made love to her, cradling her against his chest, making her feel cherished. She trusted him, knew this was different than some hot, random encounter for him. He'd said he was falling for her, and she felt the truth in every movement. Every touch.

Far too soon, he propelled them to the edge and over. They clung together, shuddering, riding out the tremors until they lay replete. He peppered her face with kisses, nipped the sensitive skin of her neck until she giggled and squirmed, happier than she'd ever been.

She gave herself to the high, refusing to think about Dietz and how pissed he must be that she'd vanished. About whether Michael would be able to expose the man for the evil traitor he was.

She just held on and prayed that, for once, she'd have something left worth fighting for when this was over.

. . .

Dietz wore a hole in the carpet of his office, seething at the unacceptable turn of events.

Why, of all times, did Michael fucking Ross have to take the helm again? Dietz had been summoned to their leader's office and relegated back to his old, mundane duties quite abruptly, with barely a word of thanks for all he'd done to keep things running smoothly.

Lily Vale. The bitch must've figured out the truth. Gone running to Ross—right before she gathered her two fuck buddies and left the goddamned country.

Dietz would find them. And when he did, she and her friends would all pay.

The chirp of the phone cut his inner tirade short. He took a few cleansing breaths before picking up. "Dietz. Make it worthwhile."

"Got them," Tio said. "They went and took themselves a little Mexican holiday.."

Yes. "Where?"

"Los Cabos. At an adult resort that could make a celibate priest rescind his vows. You'd love it."

He doubted that. Sex was highly overrated. Brief. Power was eternal. Power wrote history books. "You know what to do. Fail me and you'd better buy a ticket to somewhere remote, where even the devil will never find you."

"I'll take care of it," he said, unruffled.

"Be discreet."

"I will."

"Follow the plan exactly."

"I'm on it."

"And don't get caught by the Mexican authorities with your gear. I assure you no one's going to pull strings to get you out."

"Do *you* want to get your hands dirty? If so, I'll leave you to it."

The cocky bastard would, too. Just take off and leave Dietz to deal with finding a replacement. "Of course not. Contact me when it's done."

"Yep. Later."

Dietz hung up and lowered himself into his chair behind his desk. The game wasn't over yet.

He still had a move or two to execute.

· · ·

"Liam has a fan club. Good Lord, look at all the girls following him around! Couple of guys, too."

Jude laughed, digging his toes into the sand. "I'm not surprised. What are they doing?"

"Playing topless Frisbee."

"Jeez, I think we've created a monster. He hasn't dragged himself in before two in the morning in the past three nights."

"I know. Has he given you any details?" she asked, curious.

"Nope. I hinted for some scoop and he played coy with me, the little turd. Wouldn't give up a thing."

"Same here. Know what I think?"

"What?"

"I think our angel with the crooked halo is playing with us."

"Really?" There was an intriguing idea.

"I'm almost positive. You can't see the sly looks he shoots our way, but I can. I think he's angling for something, and he's waiting for us to give it to him."

"Like a good paddling?" The thought had merit.

"Or a good sound fucking. And I think it's working, because I, for one, am tired of watching him flirt with everyone in the resort and waiting for him to remember we're alive!"

Jude thought for a moment. "Well, it's getting late. If we don't do something, he'll be gone again."

"What do you suggest?"

"Time to take our friend in hand. Get his attention, would you?"

A few moments later, Liam ran toward them while calling back to his new friends. "See you later! Hey guys, what's up?" Something of their exasperation must've shown in their expressions. "Is there a problem?"

"You," Jude told him, pushing to his feet. "You're coming with us."

"What? What did I do?" he asked, confused.

"Don't ask questions," Lily instructed. "Just do it."

"What is this? Am I, like, being kidnapped or something?"

Jude smiled as they made their way toward their suite. "You're being punished."

"*Seriously?* No way!"

"Way."

Liam snickered, getting into the game. "What's the charge, Officer?"

"Operating a runaway dick without a valid license."

"Omigod!" The younger man hooted with laughter. "Jude's got a sense of humor under there. Who knew?"

"I'm not laughing, kid."

"Yeah, you are. On the inside. So what are you gonna do to me, huh? Cuff me and make me spread 'em? Do a full body search?"

Lily opened the door to their suite. "He's enjoying this way too much."

"Nah, he hasn't even started yet," Jude said. "Liam, turn on the bubbles in the hot tub, low. Then strip and get in."

"Some punishment," he drawled. "I'll try not to shake."

"Oh, you will, but it won't be from fear."

"You think so? Bring it, big guy."

"Lily," Jude said, grinning. "You know those items we bought in the gift shop today? Would you be a sweetheart and get those for me?"

"Oh! You bet." To Liam, she said, "I hope you saved some strength for tonight, cutie. You're so going to need it."

. . .

Lily hurried and retrieved the plastic bag from the bedroom. She couldn't wait to see Jude try this stuff on Liam. Their friend was in for a treat that would blow his mind.

When she returned to the living room area, the two men were climbing into the elegant sunken hot tub near the patio doors. Stripping off her suit, she laid the bag beside the rim and climbed in, giving a groan of bliss.

"Oh, that feels good." She settled in, watching excitedly as Jude pulled Liam close, the younger man practically sitting in his lap.

"And we're just getting stared, baby. We're going to give our lover the attention he obviously needs."

Jude cupped the back of Liam's head and swooped in for a fierce kiss, almost violent in its intensity. Liam returned it wholeheartedly, giving a soft whimper.

Lily understood, or believed she did, why Liam had stayed away. It wasn't just some game on his part. He wanted them, but hadn't wanted to cling. The attack, plus his troubles with Dev and Geneva, had shaken his confidence and he'd distanced himself, waiting for Jude and Lily to come to him. To need him.

She was blown away by the raw honesty of the emotion between them. Two sexy guys together were hot enough, but when there were real, true feelings involved . . . the act became beautiful. Pure.

Jude broke away first. "Stand up and bend over at the waist, bracing your hands on the edge of the tub."

Liam complied, and Lily was treated to a great view of his sleek body, tight ass, and lengthening cock.

"Lily, hand me the new lube, the leather strap, and the plug, please?"

"Plug?" Liam squeaked. "Not that! You *know* it drives me crazy."

Jude gave a feral grin. "You don't know the half of it."

One by one, she fished the items from the bag and handed them over. Jude set each one on the rim next to him, then grabbed the vanilla-flavored lube. Flipping open the cap, he used his fingers to pry apart his friend's ass cheeks and dribbled some of the oil into his crease, onto his hole.

"Oh, that's cold!"

"We'll warm it up. Push your ass toward me, buddy. That's it. . . ."

Jude poured a generous amount on his fingers and began to work it into Liam's entrance. Liam moaned and his cock rose to its full glory, red and glistening with droplets. But if he thought that was good so far, he was in for a surprise.

Removing his fingers, Jude picked up the plug and coated it generously with the lube. When he parted Liam's ass again and nudged the entrance with the tip of the plug, the younger man almost blew right then.

"Oh! Shit! I can't—"

"Sure, you can. The plug isn't any bigger than the one I used before, and it's not nearly as big as me. But you'll be filled and it will drive you crazy."

"B-but I want *you.*"

What an adorable pout, which was clear in his voice. But Jude wasn't diverted from his mission, and began to push the device slowly into his channel.

Lily stared, fascinated, as the small phallus split their lover's flesh. As he writhed, completely giving himself over to what was done to him.

"That's it," Jude said, soothing him. "All the way, take it for me."

"So full."

"I know. There you go; it's in."

It was in, to the base. Liam continued to make helpless noises in his throat while Jude picked up the thin leather strap.

"Now turn around and face me for a second," he said.

Liam did as he was told, careful not to slip. When Jude reached for his cock holding the leather, he blinked. "What are you doing?"

"Putting this cock ring on you. Hold still."

"Damn, you're a sadist."

"Exactly." Jude looked pleased with himself. "It'll display your package and keep you nice and hard while I paddle your pretty ass."

"Wh-what?" His eyes rounded. "Oh, no. Uh-uh. You're not—"

"Turn around and grab the rim again," Jude ordered sternly. "You wanted this attention—this punishment—and now you're going to get it."

Swallowing hard, the younger man did as he was told, presenting his bottom. Angling her head to see him from the side, Lily noted his erection was harder than ever. He did want this, even though he was nervous.

"Lily, hand me the paddle." She complied, and he gave his palm a few experimental whacks as Liam flinched. "Lily, I'll need you to let me know if I'm marking his skin too deeply."

"All right."

"Liam, you'll need to tell me when you've reached your limit," he said, smoothing the other man's buttocks with his palm. "But you'll need a safe word."

"Why? I trust you."

"That's good, but when sexual pain is involved, sometimes a person can get caught up saying *no* when they mean *yes*. Or they forget their own limits and can't verbalize that they really are ready to stop. Does that make sense?"

"Yes," he said.

"Good. Pick a safe word, one you wouldn't normally say. If you say that word, I'll stop, but otherwise not before I'm ready."

"Okay, um . . . sailboat."

"Fine. I'm going to start lightly. Ready?"

"I guess so."

Lily couldn't tear her gaze away as Jude swung. The paddle slapped Liam's bare ass and he yelped, more in surprise than pain, she figured. Jude delivered another swat, then another, each increasing in force.

"Oh! God . . ." Liam pushed his rear toward the blows, cock bobbing on the water, high and hard.

As she watched, fascinated, he seemed to settle into a zoned-out head space. His cries increased in volume, but they were cries of pain mingled with ecstasy. His ass had turned a bright red and Lily wondered if she should intervene.

"Jude! Fuck! I—I . . . stop, please!"

"Do you really want me to stop?"

More blows, Liam yelling hoarsely.

"No. Yes! Stop!"

"Use your safe word."

Another blow. One more.

"Sailboat! Ah, God." Liam slumped forward, hanging on to the side, head on his arms.

Jude stopped and laid aside the paddle. "You did well, my friend. Are you still hard?"

"Jesus, yes," he croaked. "I'm going to die."

"Sit on the rim on the tub."

"Why on the rim?" he asked, squirming.

"One, so you don't get too hot in the water while you wait. Two, sitting on the lip will keep the plug shoved up inside you, keep you nice and open for me."

"While I wait? What will you be doing?"

Jude smiled. "You're going to sit there and be tortured more while I make sure Lily gets some attention of her own."

Lily blinked. Oh, boy.

It was her turn to squirm. Because she knew what was left in the bag.

Fourteen

"Hand me the bag and assume the same position Liam did, sweetheart."

"Yeah, it's only fair," Liam grouched, cock and balls thrust forward in their confines.

"What are you going to do?" she asked, pulse fluttering as she handed it over.

"If I told you, it wouldn't be a surprise." Fishing inside, he removed the dildo. Thick, long, and veined, the thing was unbelievably realistic.

Well, except for being black as ebony.

Turning around, she spread herself as Liam had done, excited but not terribly concerned. She'd used her own dildo before, so this would be pleasurable. No big deal, but very nice.

What she did not expect was for Jude's fingers to part her ass cheeks. To begin the same preparation on her hole.

"Oh, wait a minute—"

"Shh, just relax. Trust me," he said. "I won't hurt you."

"But that thing is huge! Bigger than you, and that's saying a lot."

"Not to worry, I'll make sure you're ready. You're going to look so pretty with me working this big, black cock in and out of your ass. Won't she, Liam?"

"Fuck, yes. What are you waiting for?"

Her entrance was massaged, slowly and gently. Stretched bit by bit, his slippery fingers becoming two, three, then four wide. She felt a pinch at first, an uncomfortable burn, but afterward, the burn became heat that filtered to her pussy. Made her clit throb and her knees weak.

"Okay, you're ready. Easy, baby. I'll take this nice and slow."

His fingers slid out and a blunt tip pressed against her hole. She gasped when it pushed inside, feeling like the head of a baseball bat. Enormous. So wicked.

By inches, he pushed it deep, all the way to her womb. So big she felt it there, brushing inside her. God, she might explode just from this, even if he never moved it again.

But she held back her orgasm, gripping the edge of the tub as he began to fuck her ass with the toy.

"Good girl. Is she beautiful, Liam?"

"Gorgeous," he breathed. "A goddess. All that black hair falling down her back to tickle her ass, while you split it with a black cock. That's why you bought it, didn't you? To match her?"

"I did. Damn, I wish I could see."

"Me, too. But take my word, she's smokin'. You don't have to see to know that."

Jude increased the strength of the strokes, plunging the cock into her hard and fast. She was teetering on the brink, just barely.

And then he rubbed his lube-slicked fingers against her clit, kneading it furiously. "Ah! Yes!"

She shattered, bucking, as he wrung every last drop from her. Bracing her forearms on the side of the tub, she panted, coming down. She winced as he slid the toy out, leaving her feeling quite empty.

Boneless, she slid into the water again and flopped against the side, anxious to see what Jude would do next.

"Remember when you said you wanted to see me fuck Liam?" he asked.

"Yes." She swallowed. "I never got to."

"Now you will."

"I'm in pain here," Liam whined, stroking his poor bound cock. "Put me out of my misery."

Wading over to him, Jude groped for his arm and pulled him up. "Turn around and spread for me, but this time bend all the way over and rest your arms on the side of the tub. I want you completely open to me."

"Jesus, yes."

Liam assumed the position and Jude got behind him, smacking one sore ass check with his open palm. Liam yelped in surprise.

"Do you let anyone else bury their cock in your ass, besides me and Dev?" Jude demanded playfully. "Do you let any of the other men have this?"

"Sometimes," he said, voice shaking. "But it's just not as satisfying with anyone else, you know? Same with Lily and Geneva. I play, sure, but no other women can compare to them."

Jude looked pleased. "What about here, at the resort? You're out late every night."

"I've partied, had a great time, but I haven't fucked anyone. Not even a blow job."

"Why haven't you?"

"Because I just wanted to *feel* wanted. I've done my share of fooling around, but the four of you are special to me," he whispered.

Lily was touched by Liam's loyalty to his lovers, and she hoped Dev and Geneva came to their senses soon. Reaching between Liam's cheeks, Jude slowly withdrew the plug and laid it aside. Slicked his length with lube.

When he mounted the younger man, his big cock taking control, parting the tender flesh, Lily thought she'd never seen anything more erotic. She had a perfect view of Liam's hole stretching impossibly wide, hugging the shaft as it sank deep inside him.

"Ohh, Jude," he said, voice breaking. "God, yes, that's so good. Love you inside me."

"Beautiful man. I love being inside you." He seated himself to the balls. "Filling you, fucking you."

"Making love to me?"

"Always."

Jude began to move, shafting him with long, sure strokes. Playing the body underneath him like a fine instrument. Owning him down to his soul. His ass muscles flexed as he drove faster into his lover, head thrown back, auburn hair drifting around his shoulders.

Gradually their moans elevated in volume, passion carrying them away. Liam began to hump frantically, pulling on his own cock.

"Jude, let me come! Please!"

"Oh, yeah," he said, reaching around Liam. He peeled off the cock ring and tossed it aside. "Come with me. Let me feel you."

Liam stiffened with a cry and began to spurt rope after rope of milky white cum against the side of the hot tub. Jude went next, slamming deep and holding him close, pumping into his ass. Finally, he slumped over Liam's back, kissing him between the shoulder blades.

"You were so good."

"We're good together."

Jude smiled. "Yes, we are."

He pulled out and as Liam turned, he pulled the younger man in his arms for a kiss full of passion. They licked and suckled tongues for several moments before breaking reluctantly apart.

"Wow," was all Lily could say. "That rocked."

"Anybody up for round three?" Liam quipped.

She and Jude laughed.

"See, he's a total horn dog," Jude said. "I'll never be able to keep up with him."

Liam touched his face in affection. "You keep up with me just fine. Don't ever change a thing."

"Not a chance."

Lily joined them and they soaked together for a while, none of them in any hurry to get out.

And that was fine by Lily.

. . .

From the heavy foliage, Tio frowned at the clueless trio, adjusting the bulge in his jeans.

Too bad this assignment was so pressing. He'd love to hang around this place for a few days of wild pussy. But he had his orders and though Tio considered himself a tough son of a bitch, Dietz was the one in control. He was fully capable of making Tio disappear from the face of the earth with one phone call.

So he'd do his job, tomorrow. A pathetically easy job at that. Glancing at Agent Vale and the boy toy, he discounted the dude. He wouldn't matter in the long run.

All that mattered was that St. Laurent would not leave Mexico alive.

And Vale would take the fall.

. . .

Jude awoke with the familiar pressure in his head, crushing his temples in a vise. God, he'd prayed the migraines were gone for good.

The nightmares had been worse. More blood and death, and, just as bad, the feeling of how dead he was inside. Like he was putting in time on the planet, waiting for his expiration date. Tired and jaded.

The pressure grew worse and with it came the sickness. He rolled onto his side, curling into the fetal position to try to escape the agony. No use.

In bed beside him, Lily stirred. "Jude? Are you having one of your headaches?"

"Yeah," he rasped. "Medicine's in my overnight kit. Haven't needed it."

"I'll get you a pill." Shortly, she was back. "Oh, sweetie. I'd hoped those were gone, since you hadn't had one in so long."

"Me, too." He sat up, taking the pill and a glass of water, and downing the medicine. "All I need is a nap and I'll be good as new."

She stroked his hair, kissed his temple. "I was going to take a shower. Will you be all right?"

"Go ahead, I'll be fine."

Jude heard the water running, voices in the bathroom. He wished he could join them, suggest a group shower.

Wasn't happening this time. All he could do was lie there and fight the nausea until the medicine kicked in.

He must've drifted. The next thing he knew, Lily was bent over him asking if he wanted them to bring back anything for breakfast. The idea of food made him ill.

"No, thanks. I just want to sleep. You guys have fun."

"We'll check on you in a little while," Liam said, sounding worried.

He muttered something and they left. He was asleep before he knew what hit him.

When he awoke next, he felt a little better. No more nightmares. The headache wasn't as bad and he thought he might be able to sit up. Perhaps order something to eat and have it delivered to the suite.

His stomach rumbled, glad about that plan, and he pushed out of bed. His legs were steady, the slight dizziness bearable, and he padded into the living area to use the phone, leading with his cane.

Since he hadn't learned to read Braille, even if the hotel had had a menu for the visually impaired, room service read him some of their most popular options over the phone. In the end, he went with an omelet, toast, and juice. He wasn't sure coffee would settle.

After his shower, he found a pair of clean shorts and pulled them on, followed by a T-shirt. Recalling a snippet of his nightmare, he went to his duffel and fished until he found his grandfather's lighter. For some reason, he hadn't wanted to leave it at home.

Tapping his way back into the living room with the cane, he located a large chair and sat down, holding the Zippo.

Lifting it up, he used his thumb to flip the old lid up, and back down with a brisk snap. Up, and down. Up. Down.

He'd done this before, many times. But not at home in Cortlandt. Everywhere else he went. Flipping the cap, trying to talk himself out of smoking. All those places in his nightmares, whether a faraway sandy hell or a dense jungle. Always flipping.

A sense of foreboding began in his gut. Crept in and ate at him like acid. Something was very, very wrong with him. Wrong, period. He didn't know himself. Wondered if he ever had.

Was Lily right? Did he have some sort of secret job?

A knock interrupted his dark musings and he made his way to the door, calling out. "Yes?"

"Your breakfast, Mr. St. Laurent."

He opened the door. "Great, I'm starved," he said, being friendly.

"Well, this ought to hit the spot," the man said. "I'll put it on the table over there for you. Want to charge it to your room?"

"Sure." Digging in his wallet, he pulled out a marked bill for the tip. After the man set his tray down, he held out the money. "Here you go."

"Thanks, have a great day."

The waiter left and Jude went over to the table, famished now that his migraine was under control.

The omelet was excellent, but the juice was a little sour. Maybe they'd given him something made out of exotic fruits rather than the average orange juice he'd ordered. He took another sip. Nope, not orange, but what the hell.

He polished everything off and felt pretty darned good.

For about five minutes.

His stomach did a slow roll. Suddenly, his skin felt clammy

and hot by turns. Then agony gripped his gut and twisted. Like the day he'd gotten sick from the bug he'd picked up. Only this was much worse.

Jude shoved to his feet and staggered, the vertigo so bad he fell. He tried to stand. Fell again.

So he crawled in the direction of the bathroom, panting through the ripping pain in his stomach. Sharp lances speared his brain as well, the pain that was nothing at all like his headaches.

The attack was so sudden and fierce he could hardly think. But about the time he hung his head over the toilet, he realized his mistake; he should have brought the goddamned phone with him. Called the front desk for help.

He retched violently, lost his breakfast. Just lay draped over the toilet like a sacrifice, waiting for his body to turn completely inside out.

Sweat popped out on his forehead and his nose began to run. On reflex, he swiped at his nose and was startled to find it kept running. A lot.

Shit, he had a nosebleed.

What the hell was causing this? Even tainted food wouldn't have hit his system so quickly. No, this was . . . unnatural.

Almost as though he'd been slipped something. By the nice employee who brought his tray? *Come on, Jude, that's ridiculous!*

Your breakfast, Mr. St. Laurent.

He gasped, clinging to the bowl. No!

To make Liam feel more secure, Lily had made the reservations under assumed names. The resort did not have his real full name. And he hadn't told his last name to Brenda, either.

"Oh, God."

What was going on? He had to get help.

Jude crawled down the hallway, stopping now and then to clutch his gut, his head.

He collapsed before he reached the living room, blessed darkness swallowing him whole.

. . .

Breakfast was great and Liam had decided taking a stroll down the beach would be fun. Lily wanted to get back and check on Jude, but they decided a quick walk wouldn't hurt.

Hand in hand, they left the restaurant and passed through the patio area, and started down a pretty, winding path to the beach. Tropical plants and flowers encroached on the walkway, and a lizard jumped from a leaf.

They were almost to the end when Lily glanced through a break in the foliage and spotted a big, dark-skinned man dressed in one of the resort's uniforms duck his head and take off down another path. Nothing strange about that. The employees were everywhere.

Something about this man, however, prickled the back of her neck.

Liam tugged on her hand. "Whatcha looking at?"

"Huh? Oh, nothing. I just saw an employee who seemed familiar."

"There's a ton of them. I'm sure he's been around." He started pulling on her. "Come on, let's go find a crab!"

Laughing at his infectious enthusiasm, she took off jogging with him toward the beach.

. . .

How long had he been out?

A few minutes? An hour?

Jude pushed up to his hands and knees, found he still couldn't stand, and sat instead, leaning back against something. The wall in the hallway, he realized.

His bones ached as though being ground into dust. He'd always had a high tolerance for pain, but this . . . if he had the energy, he'd scream. The muscles in his joints were on fire, felt scoured raw.

Reaching to his face, he swiped under his nose. The blood was sticky, drying, not flowing anymore. That was something, at least.

His head hit the wall with a *thunk*, eyes closing. Despite the ice pick stabbing his brain, jumbled thoughts began to sort themselves.

The man who'd brought his breakfast. Had he put something in the juice? Jude had gotten sick immediately. But he'd been hit with this illness before, and that man had been nowhere around.

What did this have to do with the nightmares and the suspicions Jude held about himself?

Flipping the lid of the lighter. Something just out of reach. What?

"What, goddammit?"

And then, a crack in the dam. Growing dangerously wider, revealing truth after ugly truth he would have chosen never to remember.

Jude—using his alias of John Sandborn on this assignment—leaned back in the squeaky vinyl chair so thoughtfully provided by the shitty motel and shook his last Marlboro out of the pack, narrowed eyes never leaving the screen of his laptop. He lifted his antique Zippo lighter from the corner of the scarred desk and stuck the cigarette between his lips.

He lit up and inhaled, letting the rich smoke curl through his lungs in a futile attempt to soothe his nerves, on a whole variety of levels.

Something was royally fucked about this order from Dietz—the one he'd turned down flat not one hour ago, thus hurtling his illustrious career with the Secret Homeland Defense Organization down in screaming flames as nothing else could've done. Especially with Michael Ross grieving, secluded, and out of the picture. Indefinitely. SHADO's take-no-bullshit leader, and Jude's staunchest ally, had been brought to his knees by his wife's death—and, blinded by the loss, had left a jackal in charge.

Jude held his pounding head. Dietz. Robert Dietz. Tall, sandy hair. A weaselly fucker.

SHADO. Michael Ross. What the fuck?

Oh, Jude had lost his edge in the last year—he was on his way out and everyone knew it—but with Michael's support, he might've held on a bit longer. Might have . . . what? Managed to retire and slip quietly away to a foreign beach where he'd spend his days trading tequila body shots with a naked beauty or two?

With a low, cynical laugh, he stubbed out the cigarette he hadn't really wanted in the cheap plastic ashtray. Flipped the lid on his lighter. Open and shut. Snap. Snap.

The prickle on the back of his neck warned him that the joyless screw he'd indulged in last night could very well be the unremarkable period on the end of an otherwise exciting life. And if so, he wanted to know why, nosy, self-destructive bastard that he was.

He continued to pick apart the classified information on the screen, more vital for what it didn't say than for what it did. The facts seemed complete on the surface, and the job appeared to be highly justified, a no-brainer, as it involved protecting American citizens from terrorism through the machinations of a trai-tor. Absent was the usual moral dilemma he weighed with each assignment before executing a flawless kiss of death.

"Kiss of death?" Jude whispered. "I'm a killer? Sweet Jesus, no."

Why had he been chosen? The fact was, his days had been numbered before Dietz dumped this dossier into his lap, and with it an order that should've gone to another operative. One who wasn't beginning to crack around the seams, who hadn't nearly botched dispatching his last tango.

Which meant SHADO needed a fall guy, and who better than a man who'd become unstable and therefore expendable?

But Dietz had made a couple of mistakes. For one, Jude wasn't so far gone that he hadn't clued in on the almost imperceptible discrepancies between the information they'd fed him and his own sources. Just a little more time, and he'd solve the puzzle. Second, he'd prepared long ago for just such an emergency. An elaborate ace up his sleeve even an asshole like Dietz would appreciate.

If only Jude could make sense of this maze of half-truths.

As afternoon melted into evening, he poured two fingers of Jim Beam into a Styrofoam cup and ignored the rumbling in his stomach. The whiskey blazed a path to his gut and, unfortunately, to his groin. His unsatisfying encounter the previous night had left him hungry for the darker, richer pleasures to be found at home, where the sharing of flesh was like savoring various types of wine. Some sweet, others crisp with more bite. All heady.

God, he missed Liam. His friend hated it when Jude disappeared for weeks with no explanation. Worried himself sick. And what Jude wouldn't give right now to be buried balls deep in that tight ass—

"Stop, you idiot," he muttered.

He refocused his mental energies. It wasn't only his life on the line here, but the lives of thousands. Danger, closing in on Americans from all fronts. Hell, just last month there was that theft of—

The answer came, ripping the breath from his lungs. His heart slammed against his rib cage, and for one moment, the cold assassin was nothing more than a frightened man. Horrified and nowhere near prepared for the path set before him.

Jude slumped, curled in on himself. "No. I don't want to remember. Please."

But the dam had burst wide, and there was no stopping the flood.

"Sweet Christ." Elbows on the desk, Jude dropped his face into his hands. In the wake of this terrible exercise of connect the dots, he'd be goddamned lucky if he didn't wind up at the bottom of the Atlantic. In five different oil drums.

Because Dietz was coming for him. No doubt about it.

If he had a whisper of a prayer of avoiding a grisly fate, he had to work fast.

Clicking the X in the top right corner of the laptop's screen, he closed the classified file and opened another. Fingers flying, he activated a program he'd hoped never to use, but was damned glad he'd put into place. Next, he composed a simple coded message a ten-year-old couldn't decipher, yet not so difficult a trusted operative couldn't, either.

"Okay . . . got it." He blew out a deep breath. It wasn't perfect, but would have to do.

Last, he opened his e-mail and hit Send. He waited, every muscle tense, while the new files, along with the classified one, shot to six different destinations and burrowed into six different hard drives. A high-tech worm that would make any hacker cream in his shorts—and just might save his ass.

Action complete.

"Thank fuck." Jude attacked the keyboard again, clicking rapidly. His instincts screamed Get out, but he didn't dare leave the last two tasks undone.

Precious seconds were whittled away, scraping his nerves raw, as he accessed the script file he'd written to initiate the virus that would destroy his hard drive. The final box popped onto the screen, and he executed his CTRL+F+U command.

Jude gave a grim chuckle at the double entendre in his chosen three-finger salute and wiped the sweat from his brow. Time to make like a ghost.

The door to his motel room burst open, hitting the inside wall like a gunshot.

Jude spun, the SIG from the desktop already in hand, arm leveling at the leader of the traitor's cleanup crew.

Too late. A pop split the air, and pain blossomed in his chest. He stumbled backward, managing to get off a shot, the explosion deafening in the tiny space. The leader went down with a grunt as Jude trained his gun on the second man, tried to squeeze the trigger. And couldn't. His arm fell limp and useless to his side.

The second man crossed the room, a smirk on his ugly, pockmarked face. Cold overtook the pain, spreading from Jude's chest to his limbs. Numbing every muscle. Looking down, he stared in fascinated horror at the dart embedded in his left pectoral.

He swayed, speaking quickly. His life depended on it. "Tell your boss I know everything. I put safeguards in place, and he'll never find them without me," he rasped, the drug freezing his vocal cords, fast. "If I die . . . the whole world will know . . . what he's done."

Jude's legs buckled and he slumped to the floor, completely nerveless. Aware, but paralyzed, along for the ride and at their mercy. A nightmare.

A pair of heavy-soled leather boots appeared in his line of vision as the second man paused, obviously peering at the laptop. "You smart-ass sonofabitch," Crater Face hissed.

Jude pictured the cartoon gopher dancing across the screen, shooting the finger at the henchman, and a hoarse laugh barked from his dry throat. The boots backed up a couple of steps.

Jude's last image was a snapshot of the man's right shitkicker rocketing toward his face.

And Jude had awakened in a strange hospital. Had been told he'd been in a terrible car accident.

Blind. Confused.

All a lie.

"I work for Michael Ross at SHADO. I'm a fucking *assassin*," he rasped. "And I was set up. Betrayed."

By Robert Dietz, the motherfucker.

Thank God for Liam and—

Lily.

Lily Vale.

Agent Lily Vale. Fellow assassin. Black widow.

They'd never formally met. But he'd brushed past her at SHADO's compound, seen her at meetings and debriefings. He'd been intrigued at the thought of getting closer to her, but their assignments had always taken them in opposite directions.

Until now.

Jude began to laugh. Harsh, bitter laughter, agony spearing his chest, and not just from the poison she was feeding him.

Dietz had sent her to find the files.

And eliminate him.

How pathetic am I? How sad is that?

He laughed until tears streamed down his face, and the laughter became something else, splitting his chest in two.

The irony killed him. He'd spent months after the "accident" wishing he would've died.

And Lily, who had breached his defenses, made him fall in love, was going to see he got his wish.

Fifteen

Lily pushed into their suite, listening to Liam ramble about their find.

"Did you see the size of the pincers on him? Boy, was he pissed when we dug him out—oh, God! Jude!"

Liam dashed past her and ran to the man slumped in the hallway, dropping to his knees. "Jude? Talk to me." He patted the other man's face, shook his shoulders. "Shit, we never should've left him alone."

Lily jogged over and knelt beside them, noting the stains from what had been a pretty bad nosebleed. A chill went down her spine. "Do migraines cause bleeding?"

"I don't think so. Jude's never have. Hey, buddy?" he called louder.

Jude shifted, eyes fluttering open. His face was pale, lined with pain. "Liam . . . get out of here."

The younger man frowned. "What? I'm not going anywhere. Did you hit your head?"

"No. I want you on the next plane to New York."

"What? Why?" Liam's face blanched in hurt. "Never mind that, let's get you cleaned up and in bed."

Jude waved him off. "Give me a few minutes."

"I'll get you a wet cloth," Lily said.

"Don't bother," he replied. Cold as the Arctic.

Liam shot her a concerned look.

Fear crept in, forming a chunk of ice in her gut. "You're bleeding."

His laugh was scary. Sarcastic and angry. When he lifted his chin, she swore he could see into her soul.

"I don't have a high tolerance for toxins, Agent Vale. But then, you know that already, don't you?"

The bottom dropped out, the earth tilting on its axis.

"You—you remember," she said hoarsely.

"Fat lot of good it does me, huh? Give me the third dose and I'll be dead before Dietz whisks you out of the country." His expression twisted into a snarl. "Are you fucking him, too? What are you getting out of helping a traitor?"

"What in the holy freaking hell is going on?" Liam was starting to appear frightened. "All of a sudden you guys are talking a different language."

For the moment, they were too wrapped up to answer him.

Lily laid a hand on Jude's chest, desperate to make him understand. "I'm not a traitor."

"Save it, honey. Tell me you didn't slip me poison." His face was hard.

"Once! But that was before I knew you were innocent!"

"Of what?" he asked in disbelief.

"Of the theft of the weapon. Dietz took advantage of

Michael's absence and pinned the whole thing on you," she said quietly. "My mission was to—"

"Worm your way into my life, fuck me if necessary, locate the files, then watch me die slowly." He gave a sad, bitter laugh, the sound strangled. "Yeah, I get it."

"When I figured out what Dietz had done, and after Liam was attacked to blackmail me into complying with him, I forced Michael to listen," she insisted.

Liam stared at her, rocked back on his heels and brought his fingers to his still-healing throat. "I was attacked to teach *you* a lesson."

She grabbed Liam's hand and squeezed. "I'm so sorry. I know this doesn't make much sense right now, but it will soon."

"I'm starting to get some of the picture. This has to do with all of Jude's trips, doesn't it?"

"Yes, in part." Addressing Jude again, she said, "I told Michael everything and he suggested we leave the country and lay low for a while. I never gave you a second dose, Jude. I swear it."

"Then the guy who delivered my breakfast wasn't working with you?"

"No. You got sick right after you ate?"

"As a damned dog. A lot worse than before."

Liam clutched her arm. "Lily, on our walk, you were look-ing at that big guy in the resort uniform. You said he looked familiar."

The pieces fell into place, and her fear grew. "Oh, God, I should have recognized him! He's one of Dietz's men. And if his men are here, we've got to get the hell out. Now, before they realize we're escaping."

"And after we get gone, someone's going to fill in the gaps for me," Liam said. "Jude, can you walk?"

"I don't know. I'll try."

It took both of them to get Jude into the bedroom and lower him to sit on the bed. His face was white, beaded with sweat. His breathing was too fast, and he was clearly in agony.

"Liam and I will pack only what we absolutely need into one bag. A couple of changes of clothes, and leave the rest here. Clothes can be replaced."

Lily grabbed a duffel and stuffed in some clothes for herself and Jude. Liam hurried back in, face pinched in anxiety.

"Is this too much?" he asked.

"No, that's fine. Anything else we need, we'll have where we're going."

Liam paused. "We're not going home?"

"No. I'm phoning Michael, our boss, and giving him the heads-up that things here are FUBAR and we're taking off for the safe house in Tennessee. Michael and some of our trusted men—the ones not working around Dietz—will meet us there for reinforcements."

"Reinforcements," Liam repeated, in a daze. "Groovy. Shit."

"They'll have our doctor come with them to take care of you," she said to Jude.

He nodded. "How are we getting to our ride?"

"Rental. I'm going to the front to secure a car, and while I'm there, I'll make a point to say Liam and I are going sightseeing since you're not feeling well. Then we all make tracks. Michael will give us the rendezvous point."

Liam, bless his heart, was trying so hard to keep calm. "I take it we're not flying commercial."

"No. Helicopter. Fast, efficient, and totally under the radar."

"Fantastic. I've never escaped a foreign country with a posse of arch villains on my ass."

Jude managed a sideways smile at his friend. "And you thought your life was boring."

He snorted. "I just want it on record with the Powers That Be that I never once complained about that."

While Liam distracted Jude, Lily used her secured, SHADO-issued cell phone to dial Michael's house. On the third ring, Simon answered.

"Ross residence."

"Simon, this is Lily Vale."

He sighed dramatically. "Miss Vale, I'm sure—"

"Pass a message to Michael, and I guarantee he'll want to speak with me. It's urgent."

"Carry on," he said, reluctant.

"Tell Michael that Lily Vale said *Granny's apple pies make big thighs.*"

"I say! What a lot of nonsense," he huffed.

"Just do it or you'll be job hunting tomorrow."

"No need to be rude. One moment."

Michael came on the line within seconds. "Lily?"

"Dietz's men are here. One of them posed as a resort employee and slipped Jude a second dose of the toxin. Probably meant to pin it on me. He's in trouble, boss. We're *all* in deep shit."

"All right. I'll send Kelly along with the copter—he and one of our pilots are in south Texas and they'll be able to reach you within the hour. He'll back you up until I can get to the safe house with the team."

Blaze Kelly was a damned fine agent, and a good man to have at your back. Lily knew Michael might be slightly delayed getting the others mobilized, and she'd feel safer with Blaze there.

"All right. We'll be rolling in fifteen. Where do we meet them?"

He gave her a location not too many miles from the resort, which was both good and bad. Good that they didn't have to travel long to get there—bad because neither would Dietz's men, if they pursued. While they waited on the copter, there wasn't really anyplace to hide.

"Be careful, Lily, and tell Jude . . . tell him I'm so damned sorry for fucking up his life."

"It's not your fault." But it was, a little. "You can tell him when you arrive at the safe house."

"I will."

Lily hung up, pocketed the phone, and zipped the duffel. "Ready. You guys stay here. I'll get the car and bring it as close to—"

She turned to see Jude leaning against Liam, eyes closed. He was coughing into a tissue, the sound rattling ominously.

"Just hurry," Liam said, voice raw with emotion. "He's really sick."

She nodded and hurried out, heading for the check-in building and the front desk when what she really wanted to do was throw herself in their arms and beg for forgiveness. Even if Jude believed her involvement to be what she claimed—that of an agent following a superior's orders—he'd never forgive her for endangering Liam.

His dearest friend had nearly been killed. Because of her.

No, because of Dietz, the bastard!

But to Jude, there would be no difference.

Renting the car went smoothly and while she took care of the paperwork, she discreetly scanned the lobby. She didn't see the big man or anyone who appeared to take too much of an interest, but then, agents were trained to blend into their surroundings.

After making sure most in the vicinity heard she and Liam were going "sightseeing," since their lover was ill today, she grabbed the keys and moved the car to the lot closest to their suite. Then she walked back, twirling them and humming a little. As though she hadn't a single care.

In the bedroom, Lily paused, considering how to do this. Jude was barely hanging on to consciousness, Liam's arms around him. The tissue in his hand was flecked with blood. He was bleeding internally, the drug breaking his system down.

A wet washcloth lay on the bed, telling her Liam had tried to clean him up. At least the blood was gone from his face.

Blinking back the tears, she steeled herself mentally. If she lost it now, they'd never get out of here alive.

"We're going to have to just support him between us," she said. "There's no way to finesse this. If they see us, we're screwed."

"I'm ready." Liam slung the duffel bag over his back, then draped one of Jude's arms around his shoulders. Lily got the other.

"Jude, try to help us a little. On three."

At the count of three, they stood, hauling him to his feet. God, he was heavy. They half carried him out into the sunshine, the beautiful scenery that had seemed so perfect now surreal. Even sinister.

On the way to the car, they met a couple, who did a double take as the strange trio passed them.

"Too much to drink, huh?" the man said with a knowing chuckle.

Jerk. Why did some people feel they had to comment on things that weren't their business? Liam said, "Yep," and they kept going.

"Tryin' to help," Jude mumbled.

"You're doing fine. Almost there."

"Goin' for a ride, buddy," Liam said. "Hang on."

"Wanna go home."

The plaintive note in his voice got to her. She wouldn't tell him that wasn't an option anytime soon, for treatment of the poison alone. As an agent, he already knew.

But he would go home one day, if it was the last thing she did.

. . .

Tio approached the front desk in his "borrowed" uniform, striding straight up to the young guy behind the counter as though he had good cause to be there.

"Hey, man," Tio said. "The lady Janet Booth, who's in the big suite with two guys? She asked me to take her a tray from the kitchen and I can't find her anywhere," he said. Learning Lily's alias had been a cinch.

"You new? I haven't seen you around here," the guy said, eyeing him.

"Yeah, just started. Look, I've got food getting cold and that means an unhappy customer. I was just wondering if she'd been through here. I need this job, you know?"

The other man's hesitance was put by the wayside. "Yeah, I hear you. These rich snobs can be a handful." He waved a hand toward the parking lot. "Miss Booth rented a car for some sightseeing with one of her friends."

"Not both?"

"Seems one is ill. Too bad."

"Sure is. Thanks." He turned and strode for the suite, disliking the unease this news caused. The closer he got, the more the dread increased.

Using the stolen master card key, he let himself in and stalked down the hallway, noting the droplets of blood. Good, the shit was working. So he ought to find St. Laurent in bed, slowly dying and not even knowing.

But the room was empty.

Quickly, he checked the closets, the bathrooms, and the other bedroom, finding them almost empty, save for a few clothes and toiletries. Two rolling suitcases were still there. By all appearances, they might have just stepped out.

If Tio hadn't given St. Laurent enough of the toxin to kill a lesser man.

The trio had definitely *not* gone sightseeing. He phoned Dietz, who answered right away.

"Yes?"

"They're gone," he said by way of a greeting. "St. Laurent is sick, so they haven't gotten far."

"Dammit!" Dietz's anger vibrated through the airwaves. "I have an idea Michael is sending someone to pick them up. I'll find out where the rendezvous is, which safe house, and get back to you."

"You think he's going to tell you any of that shit now?"

"I have a mole who will. Stand by."

In less than ten minutes, Tio was on his way to shoot three fish in a barrel.

.   .   .

Lily drove, forcing herself to go at a normal pace. Being stopped by the Mexican police would be a disaster. Besides, if she got there too fast, they'd look suspicious parked in a car in a rural area for too long.

"Do you have a gun?" Liam asked from the backseat. Jude's head was in his lap, big body folded uncomfortably.

"Not with me."

"Why the hell not? If you're some sort of ninja woman, shouldn't you take one everywhere?" Liam sounded close to panic.

"Covert agent," she corrected. "And I don't have one now because we flew commercial. They don't like finding weapons on a person these days. Makes them cranky."

"The bad guys will have one!"

"If so, they bought it once they arrived."

"That was not reassuring."

"I'm sorry. But the helicopter will be here soon. They're on our side and they *will* be armed."

"Thank God."

As she reached the pickup spot, she slowed and turned off the road, driving a good ways down it before shutting off the ignition. The only sounds were the tick of the cooling engine and Jude's harsh breaths.

"Lily? Is Jude going to . . . ?"

She turned in her seat, gazed into his worried, handsome face.

He'd never looked younger than he had at this moment, terrified for his friend's life.

"No. He's going to be fine. Our doctor is on his way with Michael, and he has the antidote. It's not a magical cure," she cautioned, "but it does help neutralize the effects of the poison so the body can begin recovery."

He looked forlorn. "So it's not a sure thing."

In the distance, Lily thought she heard something. "Listen."

"I don't hear anything."

But as the noise grew closer, the *whump-whump* of rotor blades was unmistakable. "They're coming. Be ready to haul Jude out of there and book it."

The noise grew deafening and the craft burst into view. It was the most beautiful thing she'd seen.

"Jesus, they fly that piece of crap? It looks like something out of the Vietnam era," Liam said in dismay.

"It is. You won't care how pretty it's not when it saves your bacon." The copter set down about forty yards away, the blades kicking up a dust storm because the pilot hovered, ready to take off again. "Let's go."

As she got out of the car, Lily recognized Blaze Kelly leaping from the open side door of the copter. The tall, muscular man had an M16 slung across his back, his dark, wavy hair blowing around his face.

She got their duffel, put the strap over her shoulder, and helped Liam get Jude out of the car. By the time they got Jude upright, Blaze was there.

"I've got him," he shouted above the noise.

With that, he hoisted Jude in a fireman's carry over one shoulder, as though he weighed nothing. The man was damned strong.

They took off, Liam jogging beside Blaze, Lily a couple of steps behind.

Just as they reached the belly of the copter, a popping noise came from behind them. A sting in Lily's arm made her cry out and she whirled to see the big man from the resort standing by his own vehicle, firing at them.

"Get in!" She pushed Liam in the back, forward and down, sending him sprawling onto the floor of the copter. She scrambled in after him, shielding him with her body.

"Fuck! He's shooting at us!" Liam yelled.

"Stay down!"

Blaze spun and yanked the M16 into position one-handed, never losing his grip on his fallen comrade. In a move that would've done Sylvester Stallone proud, he opened fire on the enemy, sending him diving for cover.

Satisfied, Blaze climbed into the craft. They were lifting into the air, spinning away, by the time he laid Jude carefully on the floor, on his back.

"Michael said he's been poisoned?" Blaze called out above the racket.

Lily nodded, feeling nauseated.

"Sorry, we're not equipped to treat poisoning, just a few things for wounds."

Inspecting the stinging arm, she held it up. "Like this?"

"You've been shot?" Liam exclaimed. "Shit!"

Yes, indeed. In the fleshy part of her arm above the elbow. Though it bled profusely, it technically wasn't too bad. Amazing how wounds so small could cause such pain and make her stomach flip.

"That I can take care of, temporarily," Blaze said.

Grabbing some alcohol, swabs, and bandages, he cleaned and bandaged her arm—both the entrance and exit wounds. She supposed she should be thankful it wasn't worse, but right now she was too wiped too care.

She wanted to get the man she loved to the safe house. The man she loved who'd never love her in return after this.

But now was not the time to give in to the black hole waiting at her feet. They weren't out of the woods, but when this was over, she'd crawl off and hide. Cry herself dry.

After that, she had no idea.

Michael would probably fire her when all was said and done. So she'd quit before he had the chance.

The flight took forever, the trip made longer because of a stop to refuel, and she was convinced they'd all be deaf before they arrived in Tennessee. Talking was too difficult, so they did it only when necessary. Liam sat by Jude, clutching his shoulder, giving him what comfort he could.

Lily no longer had the right.

The copter finally descended, coming to rest in a valley surrounded by rolling hills. A pretty log cabin sat in the middle of the picture like a postcard, inviting.

They landed and jumped out one by one, Blaze carefully gathering Jude and carrying him inside. She and Liam trailed the big man through the house to a bedroom, where he laid Jude down and stepped back. Outside, the copter took off again.

"I heard he's been through motherfucking hell," Blaze said, turning questioning golden eyes on hers. Not accusing, but cautious. Like the jury was out for him.

"He has," she said around the lump in her throat. "Part of that is my fault."

"Oh, I don't know. When you trace this thing back to the root—Dietz and his greed—I think there's plenty of blame to go around. We all accepted him, answered to him as our second-in-command. Even when the signs began to show, no one did anything. The problem was overlooked until . . . well, this."

This was Lily, shot. Jude lying pale and still, lashes rested against his cheeks, dark smudges under his eyes. His hair spilled like blood around his head. His sleep was unnatural, his chest barely rising and falling.

Perching on the edge of the bed, she checked his pulse. Too fast and shallow. He might recover at this point, or he might not.

Look what I've done to you.

"You guys want something to drink? I can check the fridge," Blaze offered.

"No thanks," she said.

"Me, either."

"All right. I'm going to stand watch outside. Oh, take this, just in case." He pulled a SIG from the small of his back and laid it on the nightstand. "Yell if you need me."

When the agent was gone, Liam looked her straight in the eye, no trace of his warmth or humor present. "I think it's time you told me a story, don't you?"

"I deceived you both, from the start. I was sent to kill him."

Liam sucked in a shocked breath and hung his head. He didn't say a word, just listened as the whole fantastic, ugly truth came to light. Weapons theft, espionage, Jude finding out one of the bosses had done it, then his being framed, his mind swept. Liam knew the rest.

"You're telling me Jude is some secret agent for this SHADO group? An assassin?" He shook his head.

"Yes. When you think back on everything, I'm sure you'll see the pieces fall into place. The trips, how he'd come home in knots afterwards."

"Why didn't he ever tell me? I thought he trusted me," he said in a hurt voice. "I never would've said a word."

"Oh, sweetie, he didn't want to see you hurt. If you didn't know about his other life, you had less chance of being used against him. Now that you do know, he's going to worry."

"He might send me away." His chin quivered.

"No, I don't think that will ever happen. Even if you make up with Dev and Geneva, he's not going to let you go far. He and Dev will protect you."

"You think so?"

"I'm positive. We just have to focus on getting him better right now."

Liam swallowed. "What if these SHADO people decide I'm some sort of threat because I know about them? They could ice me and no one outside your agency would know."

"You watch too much spy stuff. It doesn't work that way—the agents at SHADO are the good guys, in spite of how this all looks to you at the moment. It's like working anywhere else; we have our problem employees. In Dietz's case, a bad one slipped through, and he convinced a few to follow him. But he's the exception."

"So you protect citizens?"

"Yes. We wipe out terrorist threats long before the media ever gets wind of them. We stop the bad guys short of their goal, or we die trying. Sounds a bit corny, but it's what we do."

"It doesn't sound corny at all."

"Liam, I don't expect you to ever forgive me, but I want you to know how terribly sorry I am that I didn't question Dietz's orders sooner. We're trained to follow orders, period, but that doesn't erase the fact that I was wrong. You were hurt, and so was Jude."

"I know you did what you had to do," he said carefully. "You're not a bad person." He didn't say he forgave her. Didn't embrace her.

The pain was almost unbearable. "I'm a cold person. I'm hard, and have been for a long time. It was easier not to feel, and I don't know how to change."

"Funny, you weren't hard and cold at all when you were with us," he said quietly. "You were warm, and you seemed to care for us. I don't think anyone could fake the passion we all shared in bed, either. I thought you were falling for Jude, too. I wonder who the real Lily is."

The question cut deep.

The answer was, she had no idea.

Sixteen

I love you. Please forgive me.

Jude didn't awaken so much as he ascended from the depths of hell. His teeth chattered. So cold. He hurt so bad, his internal organs giving up the ghost. It was like he could feel his system winding down, like the lights in a house being turned off one by one.

Death would be a blessing.

After all these years of living on the edge, expecting a bullet in the head, to go out like this, in a sneak attack, was a rich irony. He'd lived hard and played harder, and he'd die with barely a whimper.

Focusing on his surroundings, he listened. He could have sworn Lily was talking to him. Saying she loved him and asking for his forgiveness.

Was it as simple as that? Could two people fight past something like this? Could he trust her?

Did it matter?

Seeking some relief from the pain, he rolled to his side. As he did, footsteps approached on a hard surface and Lily spoke softly.

"You're awake. I won't ask how you feel."

"Where are we?"

"Tennessee, at the safe house."

He digested this.

"How many men have you eliminated with the poison?" He hadn't intended to ask, but some perverse part of him wanted to know. "I'm not accusing you. I know it's your job, but I'm just curious."

"That's macabre."

"Humor me."

"Two."

"So few?" He was surprised.

"Well, you know as well as I that it's not wise to use the same method too often. Unlike you, perched atop a building somewhere with a scope, I go in close. People remember."

"Who were they?"

"You know I can't tell you that. But they were working with terrorists. They were a threat to all Americans."

"So I was in good company, then."

The legs of a chair scraped and she leaned close, caressing his face. "No. I thought so at first. I have to believe in a target's guilt to my bones, but with you . . . looking back, I know I never really believed. I didn't want to. I tried to tell myself I was going soft, letting my attraction to you cloud my thinking, responsibility to the job. But my heart was telling me that you couldn't have done what Dietz said."

"Lily . . ."

I love you.

But he couldn't say that now. The timing wasn't right.

"I forgive you." He knew she needed the words. Her scent

enveloped him as her arms came around him, a kiss brushing against his lips. "Thank you. You can't know how much that means to me."

"I know how I would feel if I learned I'd killed an innocent target," he said. The idea sickened him.

"That's always a possibility in our work."

"With great power comes great responsibility."

"So true. Who wrote that?"

"Spider-Man, I think."

"Seriously."

"I *am* ser—" A spasm of pain shook his limbs and he knew he had to get out his request before he lost his nerve. "Lily, if our doctors can't help me—"

"No!" she blurted, voice hitching.

"Listen—"

"I already know what you're going to ask, and forget it."

"You'd want me to suffer? I can't live like this, if there's no end to this agony. Say you'll help me," he entreated.

"Jude—"

"For me. To bring me peace."

She didn't answer for a long moment. When she did, he knew she was crying. "For you. But only if there's no hope at all, which is unlikely. You're going to recover."

Reaching out, he skimmed her shoulder to her neck, then up to her face. Searched for the damned tears, wiping them with his thumb. "It means everything that you'd take care of me."

Pop had cared for him, too. Had loved Jude enough to protect him from the human monsters of the world. He'd have done the same thing Lily had just agreed to do if he were still around for Jude to ask.

He'd flip open the cap on the old Zippo, cup his hands around his cigarette, and light up. Then flip the lid closed, put the lighter back in his pocket. He'd pin Jude with his piercing stare and say, "Whatever is best for you, boy. That's all that ever mattered to me."

Jude almost smiled at the image of Pop and that old lighter.

His thoughts ground to a halt.

The lighter . . .

Jude ran a hand down his body to find he was still dressed in the same clothes he'd been wearing in Los Cabos. A check of his pocket revealed his grandfather's beloved lighter resting there, as always.

And just like that, the rest of the puzzle fell into place.

"My God," he said. He dug into his pocket. Pulled out the Zippo and rubbed the worn surface, smooth and shiny with age.

"What?"

Unbelievable. Maybe he was smarter than he'd thought. "What would you give for proof of Dietz's theft of the weapon and his dealings with our enemies?"

"Anything. But—"

Smiling, Jude said, "Give me your hand."

"Okay." She sounded interested, but unsure.

He pressed the lighter into her palm, curled her fingers around it. "A gift from me. Keep it in case anything happens to me."

"An old Zippo lighter?"

"Flip open the lid and look underneath, very closely." He waited.

"I don't see . . . wait. Is that—shit! Is that what I think it is?" she asked, excited.

"A microchip. With the sixth file on it."

"How?" she asked in wonder.

"The chip is basically a wireless hard drive, not unlike what you'd find in a BlackBerry. It served the purpose in a tight fix."

"I know. I mean, how did Dietz miss this?"

"I can only guess that when one of his men gathered my things in the motel room where they caught me, he glanced at the lighter, maybe even checked to see if it really worked, then discarded it as unimportant. He never looked under the lid, just tossed it into my bag, where it stayed."

"Yes!" She launched herself, caught him in a fierce hug. "You're wonderful, Agent St. Laurent."

Tension thrummed between them, and his mouth found hers. In spite of the ghastly pain, he wanted a kiss. Even if he couldn't do anything about finishing what they started right now.

She rubbed against him, taking the kiss deeper—

Suddenly, gunfire outside shattered the near silence and he jerked away from her, heart in his throat. "Where's Liam? Do you have a gun?"

"In the kitchen, and yes. Stay here!"

"No fucking way."

But she was already gone, footsteps receding rapidly. Ignoring the agony, and the fact that he didn't know his surroundings, he pushed out of bed and staggered after her.

. . .

Lily ran through the house, SIG at the ready, shouting at the top of her lungs.

"Liam!"

When she made it to the open living area, she saw him standing in the kitchen near the fridge, a can of soda suspended halfway to his lips, gray eyes wide.

"Get to the back bedroom with Jude! Go!"

But the front door burst open, slamming against the opposite wall. She barely had time to register Liam ducking behind the bar when a man she'd never seen before rushed inside, Dietz on his heels. She had a split second to wonder what they'd done to Agent Kelly when the first man swung his weapon toward her and opened fire.

Wood splintered near her face and she ducked, using a stuffed chair as a poor shield. Bracing herself, she took aim and returned fire, putting a hole in his forehead. He crumpled into a heap.

But there was no time to savor her victory. Dietz fired several shots, the bullets piercing the chair and going all the way through to hit the wall behind her. No way could she hold out for long. If he improved his aim, she was dead.

She popped out from behind her cover, fired two quick shots, and was rewarded by the sound of his weapon clattering on the floor.

Lily rose to finish him off and realized he'd faked her out. Or he carried a backup. His weapon was trained on the doorway behind her, and her heart sank. She glanced around to see Jude standing there, his face murderous.

"You'll want to drop your weapon before I blow a hole in your lover's head, Lily dear."

"Fuck," she spat, letting the gun fall from her fingers.

He almost sounded pleasant. "I was going to kill you first, but I've waited too long for this moment." With that, he focused on Jude.

Slowly, she inched from behind the chair. She needed a clear path.

"You want me? I'm right here, you son of a bitch," Jude said. "This is between us."

Now. With Dietz's attention on Jude, she lunged forward and delivered a kick, knocking the gun from the man's hand. Shouting in pain and anger, he tackled her. Took her to the floor and grabbed a handful of her hair. Slammed the back of her head into the floor, hard, as she cried out.

Her vision burst and her brain swam as she tried to fight him off. But in hand-to-hand combat, she was no match for his greater weight and bulk.

Snarling, Jude hurled himself at them and succeeded in knocking Dietz off her. The men clashed together, the impact sending them crashing over furniture, knocking over a lamp. They rolled, each struggling for the upper hand.

Jude's rage was palpable, his need to pummel the man who'd taken so much from him an unstoppable force. Lily scooped up her gun and kept it trained on Dietz as best as she could, fear for Jude fueling her adrenaline. She couldn't fire without hitting the man she loved, and the knowledge made her crazy. She wanted to end this quickly, but the two men intent on killing each other prevented it.

Jude got on top of Dietz and planted his fist in the man's face. However, his second punch glanced off the man's shoulder and Dietz turned the tables. No doubt Jude was a good fighter, but fighting blind put him at a serious disadvantage.

The noise of an approaching helicopter, perhaps more than one, droned outside. *Michael, hurry.*

Dietz rolled with Jude, putting him on his back, and delivered several blows to his face. During his struggles, Jude kept rising upward, swinging his fists, putting himself in Lily's line of fire.

Her finger itched to pull the trigger.

Hold steady. Not yet.

Then the unthinkable happened. Somehow, Dietz got Jude turned, pinned on his stomach. Dietz fumbled with something and before Lily could react, he brought his clenched fist down on the back of Jude's neck.

"Gotcha."

Dietz released his grip and Lily saw it. The needle sticking out from Jude's neck. Jude went limp, unmoving.

All of this in the space of five seconds, and she heard herself scream, the gun bucking in her hand.

Dietz jerked and went down just as Michael Ross and a team of several men rushed in, converging on the fallen traitor, dragging him away from Jude.

Jude. The gun slipped from her fingers. She ran to him and dropped to her knees as Michael and one of SHADO's doctors, Taylor McKay, yanked the needle from his neck and gently turned him over.

Jude's eyes were closed. He was unresponsive. Too still. McKay placed two fingers on his neck and shook his head.

"Oh, no, please," she whispered.

"Jude?" Liam appeared, kneeling beside her and grasping her arm with his shaking hand.

"He's alive, but just," McKay informed them, voice full of remorse. "I'll give him the largest dose of the antitoxin I've got, but it's a crapshoot at best."

Lily brushed her fingers through Jude's hair. "Hang on, handsome. I love you."

"He won't die," Liam said with a choked sob. "He won't."

"He's strong, so we'll see." McKay slid a black bag closer to him, pulled out a vial and a syringe. Quickly, he drew the medicine and injected the fluid into Jude's neck. Done, he placed the used needle in a hazard-proof plastic container.

"What now?" Liam asked, fighting back tears. Letting go of Lily, he took Jude's limp hand.

"We get him out of here and fly him back to the compound

as fast as we can get there," Michael said, standing. To a couple of his men, he barked, "Get a stretcher for Agent St. Laurent and get him loaded in the medical chopper. How is Dietz?"

"Hanging in, sir," one replied, bent over the man in question. "Was plugged a good one in his shoulder, but he'll live."

"Make sure he does. I'm going to take great pleasure in making sure he survives to face his punishment. Take him back to the compound as well and keep him under guard while he heals. After I review the evidence, if there is any, I'll decide what to do with him."

"Yes, sir."

"There *is* evidence," Lily said, pulling the lighter from her pocket and handing it to Michael. "It's the last file, hidden in a microchip under the lid. Jude gave it to me right before Dietz arrived."

Was that only minutes ago? It seemed like a lifetime.

Finally, Michael smiled. "Son of a gun. I knew he'd have one last trick up his sleeve."

"We're ready to transport," McKay said. "We're moving Agent Kelly as well. He took two bullets. His flak jacket stopped the one to his chest, but I'm worried about the one that grazed his head. Gotta fly. Meet you all in New York."

Lily watched helplessly as McKay and a couple of agents hustled Jude out to the waiting chopper. A part of her soul went with him, willing him to live.

She did not want to keep her promise to him. Didn't know if she could, if it came to that.

"Can't we go with him?" Liam begged.

"Not enough room, sweetie." Lily hugged him close. "McKay will take good care of him."

"He'd better." Liam pulled back, glaring at Michael. "I'm

going with you guys to this compound whether you like it or not, just so you know. I'm not leaving Jude until he's better."

"You'll ride with us, and you're welcome to stay until he's well," Michael reassured him.

Liam's defiance deflated. "Oh. Thanks, I appreciate it."

"No problem." Frowning, he glanced around. "Carter, you and two others stay back and clean up this mess. I'll send transport back for you when you're finished."

"Yes, sir!"

"Let's get the hell out of here."

Lily didn't have to be told twice and neither did Liam. They followed Michael and the rest of his men to the waiting copter and climbed in. By the time they did, the medical chopper was a speck on the horizon.

When they climbed into the air, Lily let go of the terror and grief she'd been holding inside for hours. Just lost it, without a care for the silent men witnessing an agent's meltdown.

Comforting arms slid around her.

"He'll be okay," Liam whispered. "He has to."

She prayed he was right.

And that their luck would hold out. Just one more time.

• • •

He'd thought he'd known hell.

He'd been wrong.

His floating consciousness registered nothing but unrelenting agony. He was formless, nothing but a mass of blackness, registering words and phrases. Disembodied voices, strangers.

Hemorrhaging. Morphine. Increase. Losing him.

Some voices were familiar.

Come back.

Love you.

Promise.

The pain was too much. He tried to let go, but whatever cord bound him to this place refused to be severed.

So he relished the return of oblivion when he could, hoping each time he slipped away that it was the last.

. . .

He came closer to the surface, became aware of a hand holding his. Fingers stroking.

"Get well, please," Lily. said "Liam is driving everyone insane—he's so afraid for you. Come back, Jude. Don't make me keep my promise."

Promise? Oh. He remembered.

Did he want her to keep it? All he had to do was find the strength to utter the words, and she'd honor his wishes.

And now he found he didn't want to leave. Did he feel stronger? Some, yes.

But, God, he was tired. He ached.

Not as bad as before, though. He could do this.

He wanted to tell her to have faith, to wait for him, but sleep claimed him once more.

. . .

Eight days. Excruciating days watching Jude hover near death, and waiting for her world to end. Watching sweet Liam lose his mind, shadows in his eyes. Despair.

And then, this morning, Jude had awakened briefly. Before going under again, he'd whispered, "Want to live."

More wonderful words had never been spoken. She and Liam had rejoiced, told Michael, the doctors and nurses, his fellow agents. Everyone who'd listen. A new flurry of activity ensued and a campaign began to get him back on his feet. Everyone came to visit, talking to him endlessly, trying to spark something in him. Blaze Kelly came, recovered from the gunshot wound he'd sustained when he'd been ambushed by Dietz. Michael told him about finally cracking the file, and how he was making Dietz wait in anticipation of his punishment.

Jude was in and out of consciousness, but he seemed buoyed by this news and their visits. He didn't talk much, and some of it didn't make a lot of sense, but it was beautiful music all the same.

While Lily was overjoyed to see him making progress, the one dark spot on her happiness was her role in all of this. No matter what he said, the guilt was suffocating.

Liam had yet to say he forgave her. He didn't speak to her about anything except Jude, and he hadn't touched her since they'd arrived at the compound.

When after two weeks the doctors said Jude was out of the woods, Lily packed her meager belongings and went to Michael's office.

When she walked in, he knew.

He shook his head, spreading his hands on his desk. "Don't leave. Not now. Stick this out and see how he feels."

"I can't, Michael," she said, dying inside. "It's killing me, knowing what I've done. If I'd questioned Dietz sooner, none of this would've happened."

"You did question him," Michael insisted. "You phoned my estate several times trying to speak with me about your assignment, and I was so wrapped up in my grief over Maggie's death that I put you off. I assumed my top man would take care of things, and boy, did he. If I had listened to you, none of this would've happened. How do you think that makes me feel?"

"I hear you. I do. But I have to go, sort some things out in my head. I hope you understand."

"I understand, but I'd hoped you would do your sorting here." He sat back in his chair. "All I ask is that you don't resign without talking to me face-to-face."

"Deal. But I'll tell you now, my days as an assassin are over," she said firmly. "My stomach is gone for that type of work."

"You and I agree, then. I never would have put you back into that situation, not now. Think it over, give it some time. When you decide what you'd like to do at SHADO, let me know. Or if you want to move on to something else, I'll be glad to put in a good word for you—off the record, of course."

That earned a small smile. Michael had to keep a low profile and keep SHADO under the radar, always. "I will."

"Give me your contact info when you get settled. I won't be happy if I have to go to the trouble of finding you. And I would find you anyway, so save me the effort."

"I'll call you." Reaching out, she offered her hand and it was immediately swallowed in the big man's grip. "Thanks, for everything."

"Just come back, Lily. That's all I ask."

"You don't ask much."

His eyes crinkled at the corners. "Never."

Turning, she left his office, went to her room, and shouldered her bag, not even knowing where she was headed.

She didn't find Liam and say good-bye. She couldn't look into those gray eyes and see sadness, or, worse, relief to see her gone. So she took the coward's way out.

Lily walked out and didn't look back.

. . .

Jude paced his room in the compound, going out of his frigging mind. He was pissed. And hurt.

One month. A goddamned month of counterdrugs, vitamins, muscle therapy, a careful diet. No sex.

And no Lily.

He was fucking sick of these four walls and if McKay didn't release him pronto, he'd walk.

From his chair, Liam piped up. "Calm down, man. He'll be here soon."

"You're damned right, he will. Even if I have to hold him at gunpoint to make him sign my papers."

"We'll go get her soon. Just hang in there." He paused. "I miss her as much as you do. I'm afraid I wasn't very thoughtful of her when she was here, but I was so afraid for you, I wasn't thinking of anything but getting you well. I think she might've gotten the wrong idea, that I was mad at her."

"Well, she'll get a big clue before long." Groaning, he pushed on his zipper, adjusting his neglected cock.

"You planning to save some of that for me?" He heard the grin in his friend's voice.

Jude glared in his direction. "It's your fault I'm so hard I'm cross-eyed," he hissed. "You're the one who won't even spring for a quickie."

"Hey, McKay said strenuous activity might set you back," he said, defending himself. "My first concern was for your health, not getting off."

"Sorry." He shot his friend a contrite look. "I'm just—"

"Here we go," McKay said cheerfully, striding into the room crackling a sheaf of papers. "Congratulations, St. Laurent. You get to walk. You're a medical miracle."

"So I've heard."

"Sign where I place your hand. Just make a scribble, best as you can do."

Jude took the papers and a pen, and he was a free man. Damn, that felt good.

McKay took the papers back. "Michael wants to see you before you guys take off. Says it's important."

"I'd planned on it anyway, but thanks. And thank you for saving my ass." He offered his hand and the other pumped it with enthusiasm.

"Anytime . . . but not anytime soon, okay?"

"No worries. I'm taking a leave of absence, starting now."

"Good man."

After he'd gone, Jude and Liam walked to Michael's office. Liam helped guide him while he tapped with his new cane. He'd lost track of the old one somewhere in the chaos.

The door was open, the man inside. Jude knocked and stepped in, Liam behind him.

The big man sounded as though he was smiling, something he rarely did. "God, you're a sight for sore eyes. A little thin, but vastly improved from a couple of weeks ago."

"I feel almost as good as new. Lost twenty-three pounds, but I'll gain it back. Wasn't a bad trade-off."

"Hear that. So. I assume you're here to demand the location of a certain agent who also happens to be on leave?"

"Now will you tell me?" During their last three conversations, Michael had refused, holding the information as a way to get Jude to work even harder at his recovery before he spilled. It worked.

"Now that you have your release papers from McKay in hand? You bet. Though I bet you could figure it out on your own, given a day or two."

"Michael."

"Okay, I give. She called yesterday and said she'd decided to head back to Los Cabos—"

"Hot damn!" Jude laughed. "Michael, I love ya, man, but don't call me for at least a month."

"Yeah, I sort of figured. I'll tell you what I told Lily. Give me a ring when you decide what you want to do here. I'll accommodate you any way I can."

"I appreciate it."

"Now get out of here. I think you have a woman to rescue."

He didn't wait around to hear more.

Seventeen

Lily sat in her lounger on the beach, watching the ocean lap gently at the shore. Despite the warmth, she felt desolate inside.

She'd spoken with Michael several times over the past few weeks, and he'd insisted Jude was going out of his mind demanding to know her whereabouts. But that could mean anything. He might only want to have his say, and bring things to a close between them.

So she sat here or wandered the resort, fending off advances from sexy would-be playmates. Without Jude, the thought of sex with strangers no longer held any appeal, more than on a base level.

And that was no longer enough. It was the connection, the sharing, between them that made their adventures so special. Without the ones she loved forming her anchor in life, the act held no joy.

"Sparing any thoughts for me, baby?"

Oh. *Oh, please.*

Pushing out of her lounger, she turned and saw him. Jude,

holding a new cane, looking thinner but healthy, auburn hair on fire in the sunlight. He was dressed for the beach, in swim trunks, and nothing else. Obviously he'd checked in, and her pulse leaped at the implication.

With a happy cry, she closed the distance between them and launched herself into his arms. His body pressed into her, warm and safe, surrounding her. He smelled so good, felt so right.

He was hers, and had come to reclaim what was his.

She lifted her face and her mouth was claimed in a kiss that melted the ice in her chest. Set her ablaze. Their tongues danced, stroked, affirming their reunion. Reestablishing the bond that hadn't been broken after all.

They went down on the sand together, unwilling to be parted, touching every available inch of skin. Jude loosened her bikini top, then yanked at her bottoms. In seconds, she was naked, reaching for Jude's trunks, pulling them down. He was hard and leaking, cock standing at attention.

"Spread your towel on the sand, baby," Jude murmured in her ear. "I want you."

Oh, yes! She spread it quickly and pulled him down with her. "I missed you so much," she whispered.

"I missed you, too, sweetheart. Let me show you how much . . . and how much I love you," Jude added, swooping in for another kiss.

"Oh, God," she whimpered. "I love you, too. So much it hurts. I wasn't sure you'd really forgive me."

"Do you doubt me now?" He turned and lay on his back, stroking his erection.

"No," she said, laughing. She'd never been so happy.

Lily crawled over Jude and straddled his hips. Impaled herself slowly, relishing the connection, his hot cock spearing her. He grabbed her hips and moaned, gazing up at her with those pretty eyes. So clear she could almost believe he saw her.

In his own way, he did.

"God, yes," he said. "Missed this. So crazy about you."

She opened her mouth, but words fled as he began to move inside her, thrusting upward.

"Hang on, baby, and let me give you a ride you won't forget. Make sure you never want to run away again."

"I wasn't running. I was waiting."

With that, they began to move together. Whirls of fire torched her clit, her sex. Never had she experienced anything as wonderful as riding Jude in broad daylight. Him filling her completely, making love by the sea.

Mind-blowing, the sensation of them connected by their hearts as well as their bodies. She gasped as he pumped faster, her hands splayed on his chest. Braced herself as they found just the right rhythm, building the pressure, increasing the tension threatening to explode.

He pounded into her and they slapped noisily, the delicious buzz starting in her womb, ready . . . right there. . . .

"Oh, God! God, yes, yes!"

She went over the edge, came in a fiery burst. He followed, hoarse shouts carrying in the air, cum bathing her in a heated rush.

Completing her.

As they came down, a contentment she'd never known stole over her, soothed her weary heart.

Lily sighed and went limp draped across Jude's chest. He cupped the back of her head and brought her down for a slow, sexy kiss, exploring. Sealing his claim on her once and for all.

When the kiss ended, Lily slid off and snuggled into him, lost in thoughts of all that had happened in the past few weeks. Jude stretched out beside her on the towel.

"Has Michael decided on Dietz's sentence?"

"Imprisonment, for now," Jude said. "Dietz knows where the stolen weapon is, and who the enemy plans to use it on. For now, he's not talking and it's the only thing keeping him alive."

Another mission for a different set of agents. She and Jude were out of doing the dangerous undercover field work. Thank God.

There was only one thing more that would complete her happiness.

"Has Liam forgiven me?"

Jude nuzzled her hair. "You can ask him later. He wants to make amends in person."

"He's here?"

"With Dev and Geneva."

"Does this mean they've reconciled?" she asked.

"They have. In fact, Liam's moving in with them." He gave a wistful smile. "I'll miss him living at the house, not to mention missing his cooking, but it's great he's so damned happy."

"They've told him they love him?"

"Yeah. They've made it clear the three of them come as a package deal from now on."

Lily was thrilled for Liam. But she needed to know *her* place in Jude's home, his life. Without any doubts.

"I can cook, too," she said quietly. Voice filled with hope.

His arms tightened around her. "Can you?"

"I'm no chef, but I'm not bad."

"Can you love a retired assassin? In sickness and in health?"

Her throat clogged with joy. "I believe I can handle that, too. If you can love a retired assassin who nearly—"

"No more of that. Ever. Let's enjoy our vacation with our friends and after that . . . come home, Lily. Please."

"I thought you'd never ask."

Jude rolled her underneath him and her blood fired as he began to love her again.

The sexiest man in the world had brought color to her cold, joyless existence. Healed her weary soul.

She could think of nowhere she'd rather be than in Jude's arms. In his bed.

For the rest of her life.

About the Author

Jo Davis spent sixteen years in the public school trenches before she left teaching to pursue her dream of becoming a full-time writer. An active member of Romance Writers of America, she's been a finalist for the Colorado Romance Writers Award of Excellence and has one book optioned for a major motion picture. She lives in Texas with her husband and two children. Visit her Web site at www.JoDavis.net.